PAPER ARROWS

Susan Slater

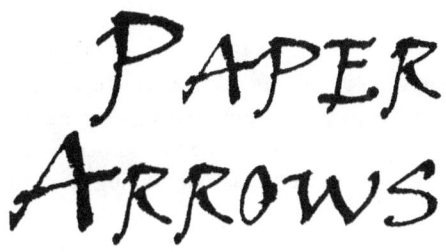

PAPER ARROWS

Ben Pecos Mysteries, Book 8

Susan Slater

Secret Staircase Books

Paper Arrows
Published by Secret Staircase Books, an imprint of
Columbine Publishing Group LLC
PO Box 416, Angel Fire, NM 87710

Book layout and design by Secret Staircase Books
Image of Pine Ridge Reservation flag c Chelovek

First trade paperback edition: September, 2021
First e-book editions: September, 2021

Publisher's Cataloging-in-Publication Data

Slater, Susan
Paper Arrows / by Susan Slater
p. cm.
ISBN 978-1649140661 (paperback)
ISBN 978-1649140678 (e-book)

1. Pecos, Ben (Fictitious character)—Fiction. 2. Native
American—Fiction. 3. Lakota people—Fiction. I. Title

Ben Pecos Mystery Series : Book 8
Slater, Susan, Ben Pecos mysteries.

BISAC : FICTION / Mystery & Detective.
813/.54

Acknowledgement

Of all my years of teaching, my time in the Towa (Jemez) Pueblo will remain special. I taught 6th, 7th and 8th grades at the Mission School. One of the older boys really stood out for his problem-solving skills, his originality, and ability to think beyond his years. However, his ability with the mechanics of the English language was almost non-existent. If your own language is not written, it's very difficult to master a second language fraught with rules. I always double-graded his papers—an A for content and a low grade for presentation.

One Monday morning he handed in several pages of make-up work and I almost fell off my chair. It was perfect—content and mechanics. I complimented him and was amazed at the amount of work he had put in to learn the rules. But I was really curious to know who had been able to get him to do this. I had certainly failed to encourage him to achieve this level of work. He said, "My grandmother told me I had to do better. She says we can no longer fight the white man like in the old days. Today, we must fight him in court with paper arrows."

Forty years ago I knew that someday there would be a book, *Paper Arrows*.

Chapter 1

Spearfish, South Dakota, population 11,801

Alone in the office, Sheriff Mac Sterling answered the call and said he'd investigate. He was heading out anyway—over to the closest strapping metropolis of Rapid City, a town of almost twenty thousand people.

The phone call had been a short one—an inert body beside the road noticed by two people out for a jog. This wasn't his normal duty; he had deputies for the scut work of rousing passed-out drunks. Well, *a* deputy, for now, but Sally Haines had answered a 911 domestic disturbance call earlier and had gone to take a look—get out of the office and at least give the impression of law enforcement at work. She might be out a couple hours. And there was no one else to send.

The pandemic had cut his force to two instead of the usual four—himself and one other. Sally was here three days a week to warm a desk chair, answer phones, and maybe do odd jobs in the field when asked. She didn't have the same constraints nor the same set of skills as his trained deputies had, but it meant something to know she was there when he needed her.

So, Mac didn't really mind taking this call. A body anywhere in that part of the country was nothing new, probably someone just sleeping it off. But the caller said the person looked dead. Seems like 'looking dead' could take on several poses but that was the summation of the information other than the body was male. But age, condition—clothed, unclothed—the caller didn't elaborate and, of course, didn't investigate. He'd mentioned that he thought he should leave that up to the experts.

Yeah, Mac was an expert all right. Born, raised, and staying in South Dakota. Spearfish barely qualified as a 'wide spot in the road'—God, he hated that saying, true though it might be. Population still hadn't broken twelve thousand individuals, with the average high school graduating class less than a hundred, something that hadn't changed in at least forty years. Many left and came back, and even four years in the Air Force hadn't discouraged Mac from coming home.

Home. No matter how big or how little or where it was located, it always had a pull on a person that was difficult to break.

He checked his notes. From the directions given, it

appeared that the body had been found just outside the reservation, off of I-90, which would put him on Rex Udahl's land. *Judge* Udahl, who just happened to own the largest ranch in the area. Not that he'd lifted a finger to acquire it. No, Mama Udahl had inherited the land and passed it on to her only child. Had the original acquisition been on the up and up? Or had the Udahl family cheated the neighboring Sioux? There were stories about government surveyors being bribed and paid off to fudge a boundary here and there. But these were old stories now, a couple centuries old. Born more out of sour grapes than statistically proven research, Mac thought. Indians and whites weren't always bosom buds. In lots of ways that hadn't improved.

He sighed. He didn't relish having to involve the judge in a death. He was not a man to cross. There would be the customary questions and more cleanup and maybe something to ignore, not illegal, just look the other way, that was *if* Mac wanted another hefty contribution to his election fund by locals.

But like it or not, he needed to get in gear. He'd taken the morning off so he was on personal time. Now, there was work to be done before he could leave for Rapid City, and he wasn't solving any problems sitting in the office; he better get on it. He'd take his Jeep just in case it was a false alarm and he could take off on his personal business from there.

But it was the real thing. In fact, the body had been easy to find. And, yes, it was a body—fresh, but still dead. The directions were exact—right-hand side of County Road 5, approximately one-half mile beyond the Bur Oak, that monument to life out in nowhere that kept on keeping on. No one was alive anymore who remembered it as a sapling. Some arboreal society had raised money within the county to have a plaque made. That seemed to make it an official landmark.

He pulled the Jeep over but left it a hundred feet from the scene, back on the road. He didn't want to contaminate possible evidence. Due diligence demanded a careful study of the surrounds. Had the body been dragged? Were there skid marks—long rows of parallel prints made in the hard sand and clay surface by locked brakes of a vehicle trying to miss someone standing or walking in the road? Secure the scene. *Don't form an opinion until you've let the visual form first.* Best, most useful thing he ever learned in two years of criminal law at the community college. Stand in one place and survey the scene. Sometimes keeping an open mind was a challenge; it was always too easy to jump to a conclusion.

He looked in all directions but knew he was alone— unless you counted the jackrabbit some thirty yards to his right who had stopped before reversing direction and bounding back the way it came. It was easy to be alone out here. No buildings, fences, stock pens, or vegetation to obstruct one's view—not even when turning in a three-sixty-degree circle. A person had to love the scenery, have some sort of affinity with barrenness to feel at home. Mac didn't even wonder any more about why he stayed. Home was his only explanation. Wasn't that enough? He'd buried parents and one wife, divorced another. He spoke to an only daughter over in Pierre on her birthday and visited at Christmas, whether he needed to or not. He had a good job, owned his home, and had invested for retirement. There were a lot of people who didn't have half what he had.

He walked toward the body, scouring the road and surrounding ditch for something he might have missed. What, he didn't know; he just knew he'd recognize it when he saw it. Maybe a broken headlight, or piece of chrome from a car or truck that might have struck the guy. But this man hadn't been hit by anything moving. At least there was no evidence of it.

Sheriff Mac stood looking down at the body lying in the ditch almost completely on its side with an arm thrown across a bare chest. The man was young, a Native, dark hair matted but reaching his shoulders. A cheap, fake beaded belt, some touristy trinket already fraying at the corners, cinched a pair of too big, too stiff jeans with rolled cuffs, which proved the fact that their original owner was several inches taller. Looked like thrift store castoffs but probably had been this young man's Sunday best. Poverty wasn't just a word; it was a way of life out here.

He pulled a pair of latex gloves out of his jacket pocket and, to be extra safe, slipped the mask that was around his neck back up to cover his nose and mouth. Better to be careful, take nothing for granted; being vaccinated wasn't a one hundred percent guarantee of anything. He leaned slightly forward and hooked the pointed toe of his boot under the crooked elbow and flipped the arm that was lying across the man's chest to the side.

"Damn it."

Eight hundred seventy-five dollar Tony Lama full quill ostrich boots and the right toe now had some sort of viscous glob of blood and guts that oozed from the dead man's chest full of wounds. Didn't Mac know better than to dress up for this type of investigation? Wear his go-to-town best? Even if he was on his way to Rapid City, he could have worn his Ropers. They'd seen more than one horse and another blemish wouldn't even be noticed. Maybe the Tony Lamas could be dyed. The guy who owned the shoe repair in Spearfish owed him one—this might be a good time to collect.

But Mac knew himself well enough to know that he was just procrastinating, centering his attention on his boots and putting off looking closely at the wounds on the body in front of him. If it was what he thought it was, then this was the second such death in a month—exactly like this one.

He squatted down, slipped his iPhone from a front shirt pocket and snapped several close-ups. On the man's chest—left and right sides both—the pointed ends of short, thin, splintered bone shafts still hung barely connected to the man's torso by torn flesh. The man had been a Sun Dancer. There must have been a ceremony last night and a few days before that. Usually unannounced unless you were a member of the tribe and chose to secretly attend, this was just one more facet of the mystique of the indigenous people who made up the majority in this area.

To an Anglo, few ceremonies could be more heinous than the one that attached ropes to pieces of bone or other material sharpened and stuck through the skin of a participant's chest or back—literally piercing the skin like large, clumsy needles. Sometimes participants would swing by these connections. At the very least the man would drag skulls behind him tethered by the ropes attached to his chest and spend four to five days without food or any sustenance, seeking clarity of vision.

Many years ago these ceremonies had been outlawed by government decree only to be reinstated by the American Indian Religious Freedom Act in 1978—preserving the traditional religious rights extended to not only American Indians but Native Alaskans, Aleuts, and Native Hawaiians. Living in South Dakota necessitated knowledge of obscure laws not even heard of elsewhere. As barbaric as it might seem to him, there was no crime ... or was there?

Finding someone dying in this fashion in October was odd, wrong according to the calendar of known ceremonies. Spring, mid-summer—these were common times for the Sun Dance. Mac could only explain October being chosen because of the pandemic—a ceremony representing life and rebirth would be important in the midst of disaster. Still, something told him he should investigate. But how? He had no access to tribal ways and very limited access to the reservation. He may have lived here all his life but he was still an outsider—made even more suspect because he wore a badge. It crossed his mind that if the body in front of him was the result of foul play, someone may have found the perfect murder weapon.

One thing he had to do was alert the tribe. A man named Red Bull was his counterpart on the nearest reservation—the closest thing to the law or at least what was interpreted as such. The fact that he had the same name as a famous power drink only seemed to give the man a little extra swagger. He'd even affixed an empty can of the stuff to the hood of his truck—bolted the blue and silver container with red lettering prominently front and center for all to view. At least the scruffy white pickup couldn't be mistaken as belonging to someone else. And in its own way, it was a good Indian joke—a barely veiled laugh at the white man's expense.

Mac opened the contact list in his phone. One would think he'd have the coroner's phone number memorized by now. Same office, same number, same old codger who'd retired as a surgeon some ten years back to run for public office. Mac wasn't sure there were a lot, if any, true perks that went with the office. The poor guy didn't even have a hearse, had to use his own F-150 with shelving built into the bed of the truck under a camper top to transport bodies to the morgue, a lab which was another afterthought. Set up at the back of the county's maintenance building, it shared space with what was supposedly the best collection of spare parts for snow plows in the state. Sort of gave new definition to 'living in the sticks'. Another saying he detested.

He had no idea what had made the day so popular but no one answered his phone. He left messages explaining why he was calling for both the tribal rep and the coroner. And then he took a few more pictures and went back to his truck to wait. Someone would answer his call, and he might as well sit out here and wait as go back to the office. He'd tossed the idea of going into town about a half hour ago. Work always had a way of insinuating itself into personal time—especially since he'd become a one-man show.

He knew it wouldn't take long to get answers to his messages. In under a half an hour, Mac saw the white truck with the unmistakable hood ornament come barreling down the road toward him. Application of brakes gave way to a sashaying stop that remarkably did not put the man's truck in the ditch. Mac couldn't help but shake his head. Someday he'd get a call about Red Bull—an upside-down pickup, maybe one that had rolled a few times—he didn't know where or when, but it was inevitable.

"You're going to put that thing in the ditch one of these days." Mac said it with a smile while walking toward the driver.

"Naw, I got him trained. No ditches."

Red Bull had slipped to the ground and pushed the truck's door shut behind him. His long, past-the-shoulder black hair was pulled back into a low ponytail caught by a beaded leather tube at the neck. A blue chambray, western cut shirt with rolled up sleeves sported tiny pearl buttons down the front and on the pocket flaps. The jeans were too tight from Mac's point of view and the guy was slightly built, maybe five foot ten and a hundred and fifty pounds. That was skinny. Mac outweighed him by fifty and was six inches taller.

"Not one of ours." Red Bull stood looking down at the body. "Don't want this to come as a surprise but not everyone with long dark hair and brown skin belongs to the Rez. How long have you lived around here?"

Sarcastic little shit, Mac thought to himself. An honest mistake, easy for him to make. He didn't know everyone on the reservation. He chose to ignore Red Bull's jab. "Ever see him around here before?"

"Nope. And he didn't take part in no Sun Dance."

"But, it looks …"

"Looks, nothing. Somebody fixed him up this way. You got yourself a killing." Red Bull turned and walked to his truck, calling back over his shoulder, "Get on it, lawman. This ought to keep you busy for awhile."

Mac wanted to knock that grin off his face. Instead, he took a deep breath. He didn't have time for this shit. Some play-pretend way to cover up something sinister. Not when so much else was going on in the county. He turned so as not to get a face full of dust when Red Bull floorboarded his truck and spun out.

This was the first day he hadn't been called out to Highway 90 and the sometimes not so peaceful demonstration by protesters verbalizing their contempt of a sovereign power, stopping traffic, and not letting people travel on what was considered a state road—just because those living under that sovereign power wanted to stay safe and keep contagion from invading their homes.

Couple that with the always-boiling-under-the-surface, deep anger and mistrust of a national government that would think nothing of pillaging land for money, ruining sacred sites for the sake of a pipeline; anyone would agree that Mac had his hands full. Every time his phone rang, he mentally crossed his fingers that it wasn't someone reporting an armed standoff that had gotten out of hand.

They'd had more than one of those out here over the last few years. The public hadn't forgotten the second Wounded Knee Occupation back in the early seventies. Treaties could be sore spots. About two hundred Oglala Sioux, some being American Indian Movement or AIM followers, occupied the town of Wounded Knee on the Pine Ridge Reservation. The intent was to renegotiate or at least reopen treaty discussions to attain more equitable treatment of indigenous peoples. The standoff turned bloody and the press gave it front page play for days.

Other than gaining public sympathy, and calling attention to long-standing civil rights missteps, it had been a nightmare for law enforcement—on and off the Rez. Mac didn't need yet another such situation.

And rumor had it that the tribe was preparing to go to court again, another possibly pointless argument in front of the bench, trying to convince an Anglo that land could be sacred, magical, and of religious importance. Actually, the tribe had won one recently. Maybe it had come down to currying favor—wasn't there an election coming up next year? Judge Udahl, never a dummy when seeking votes, had ruled that the tribes had the right to halt travel across Indian land, set up a detour because the tribes needed to be safe, take care of themselves. The pandemic wasn't to be taken lightly. But what would be his stand on the pipeline? A lot of big money was involved. How generous and benevolent would the judge be—especially if he had a stake in the outcome?

Chapter 2

Navajo Reservation, New Mexico

"Expelled? What do you mean, expelled?" Ben got up and closed his office door to keep the phone call private.

"Yeah, Dad, you know, kicked out."

"Zac, back up a minute. Nathan is no longer in school? He's been kicked out?"

"Yeah, that's what I'm trying to tell you. That's what expelled means."

It crossed Ben's mind to say something about the smartass remark, but he chose to ignore it. Zac sounded too upset to know he was pushing a parent/child boundary.

"Tell me what happened." Ben was already starting his own self-talk. Willing himself to stay calm, not think of knives or guns or having put someone's eye out in a fist fight. He needed to hear what Zac had to say and not react, or God forbid, *over* react, until he had the facts.

"Nathan egged an upper classman's car."

Egged? Had Ben heard correctly? He literally had to swallow back a laugh. Wasn't that something a student might be counseled about? But expelled?

"What else did Nathan do?" Surely, he wasn't expelled for egging.

"That's it. One dozen eggs smashed all over. It really messed up the car's rag top. The guy's got a new BMW convertible and his dad's on the board of directors for the school, so Nathan got tossed."

Ben hoped Zac hadn't heard the sigh of relief. Still, he was glad he was sitting down. 'Now what' had begun to loop through his brain. The boys had been in school for less than a month—a month Ben had thought was going well in Bellingham, Washington. A school funded by several Pacific Northwest tribes with boarding opportunities for Natives from other regions, solid in academics, as well as sports. During almost every phone conversation the boys had talked non-stop about soccer, basketball tryouts, even swimming. Nathan was supposedly considering the debate team. What had gone wrong?

"That's not all," Zac interjected.

Ben sighed. "What else do you need to tell me?"

"The whole school's been closed. The soccer coach just got back from England and he's tested positive for Covid. Then five team members did, too. So, this morning the school has been closed until further notice. Who knows when that's going to be?"

"Are you okay? Where are you right now?"

"We both tested negative so we were free to go.

Everyone who tested positive is still at school. Quarantined there. We're in Seattle, at Mom's apartment. Nathan's with me."

"Is your mom there now? I'd like to talk with her."

"Yeah. I'll get her."

Ben sat holding the phone. Fatherhood. Raven's surprise admission a year ago—they had produced a son ten years back—one he knew nothing about, but he was willing to accept and take on the role of father. Well, father to one boy but guardian to the other. It was time for him to step up and step in. But this couldn't have come at a worse time. He and Julie were wrapping things up on the Navajo reservation and expecting to fly down to south Florida the next week.

The only good thing was he still had some time off from Indian Health Service and wasn't scheduled to show up for his next assignment until January 1. But house-hunting had topped the list of things that had to be done and time-wise there were only nine weeks left. And securing a house could be challenging in south Florida—at least one that they could afford. And then there was moving … Julie's job with the Miami Herald was a plum. To be in charge of the paper's leisure section, both online and in print, was a terrific opportunity but only meant that two careers could make things a little dicey when it came to living together. So far, they had been able to be in the same place most of the time. And Indian Health Services had been able to plug him into an opening with the Seminole tribes of Florida so, once again, a separation had been averted.

At the present he was still in western New Mexico on the Navajo reservation. Wrap-up for his old boss Dr. Sandy Black meant completing his program management assignment by making certain that the paper trail would be easy to follow for the person who was coming in to take his place. Once Ben left, it would become a permanent position. Julie had offered to stay and continue to support the administrative side of things, using weekends to establish their next housing venture until she could be replaced too. Life was a little demanding. Now this.

"Ben? Still there?" Raven sounded out of breath. "Sorry to keep you waiting, but we need to talk."

"I agree."

"I don't want to risk pissing you off, but I think it's time you manned up. I don't know how you define 'guardianship' but Nathan needs a male role model. From what you've said before, he hasn't had much of a family—and few men he could look up to. I think a dad stand-in is much needed."

Ben took a breath. No, he wasn't angry. What she said was the truth. But what did a plan look like?

"Any suggestions on what Nathan might be amenable to?"

"He's talked about going home—spending this break in school time to go back to the reservation in New Mexico. You know, with Christmas coming. I don't think he wants to stay down there; I mean he wants to get back to school here. I honestly think he's enjoyed this last month in Bellingham. He's really a natural in sports and has received lots of positive attention. And he and Zac are inseparable."

"Any idea what was behind the egging?"

"Well, according to Zac, the kid with the BMW is Plains Indian and was into bullying Nathan, downplaying his heritage. It was a macho thing."

"But not one that I would expel an almost-teenager for."

"I agree. It's just that his father has some pull."

"Okay, what if I fly out? I'll meet with the school board in person if I have to, but I'm going to try to establish a dialogue from here. I'll even meet with whomever I have to on Zoom and get Nathan reinstated right away if I can. That will free up time in Washington to rent a car, pick out some camping gear and get started on the drive back to NM. It's going to give us lots of quality time to engage. I'm thinking in addition to camping out, maybe some fishing and hiking—October is the best month in that part of the world, not too cold yet."

"Perfect. Seriously, Ben, that sounds great."

"You know Zac is welcome to come, too."

"No you don't. Zac is mine for the holidays. In fact, I'm going to need his help once I can get the dogs back to Moose Flats. I know he wants to start training his puppy. Romo is the perfect age to get started as a sled dog."

"Just a suggestion. I don't want Zac to feel left out, but I think the best combination is for just the two of us—Nathan and I—to be alone, without too many distractions."

Another five minutes with Zac and Ben asked to speak with Nathan. Nathan was apologetic but said the older kid was an asshole—which didn't sound too forgiving. Nathan brought up coming back to New Mexico and Ben offered to fly up and drive him back. Nathan was lukewarm at first, but perked up when Ben mentioned camping out and fishing and maybe even hiking if the weather stayed warm. Ben didn't rule out a side trip. Maybe they could get some skiing in—Colorado wasn't too far off the path home.

He'd send Nathan his itinerary once he'd booked his flight and then the two of them could map out their return trip. It would be fun, a history lesson combined with some together time. Ben felt a blip of excitement. He was only sorry that Zac and Julie couldn't join them.

* * *

"I think you've hit on the perfect solution. A car trip will allow for lots of discussion. I mean, where else could you set up a captive audience scenario? I can easily see that Nathan needs some one-on-one adult discussion time. He's a good kid. I hope you can talk some sense into the school board." Julie paused. "He seemed to be doing so well."

"I'm not sure—because a contract and money are involved, signed and paid for by both me and the Navajo Nation—that an expulsion of a minor can happen if I'm not notified first. Actually, I would have expected his tribe to be notified also. He needed, at the very least, to have been turned over to a parent or, in this case, a guardian. He won't be thirteen for another month. I'm thinking I have some leverage here. Legal leverage. I doubt the school wants any bad publicity or, God forbid, have their government funds reduced or even revoked for mishandling the situation. I've left a message for the Navajo Nation lawyer to give me a call. I want to make certain I'll be saying the right thing—I don't want to appear threatening and really screw up Nathan's chances of getting back in."

"I only hope that he'll want to go back if you get him reinstated."

"I think being with Zac is pretty important—that and sports. Nathan's been introduced to a whole new world—one that I think he likes, sees the opportunities. He's pretty together for his age."

"When will you leave?"

"I can get a flight out Friday. That gives me three days

to get ready to go. I'll call around Seattle and rent an SUV—
something that will carry all the camping gear we'll need.
I just hope I'll be able to get a response from the school."

"You know, the trip is going to be fun."

"I believe that. I wish you and Zac could come along."

* * *

The Navajo lawyer suggested that he overnight a letter
to the school with an attachment that outlined the monetary
agreement signed by the tribe. Nathan was a ward of the
Navajo Nation with Ben having been granted guardianship.
Copies of his letter would go to tribal representatives of
the National Indian Policy Center in Washington, D.C., as
well as the Washington State Board of Education—funding
and policy issues would be covered simultaneously. The
lawyer assured Ben that there would be no veiled threat of
withheld funds or loss of accreditation. The letter would
simply point out that an underage child being released
from the care of a Native educational institution that
offered boarding without proper notification of parents or
guardians or securing safe travel to his home was not only
a breach of contract with that individual but also with the
tribe that he represented. It invited sanctions being levied
upon the school itself. That sounded pretty threatening to
Ben.

But what it got him was an immediate apology both
in writing and by phone. There was a lot of bowing and
scraping and excuses about a situation being overblown,
a board member taking matters into his own hands,
overreacting because the event involved a member of his
family. Out of pique the man had acted irrationally without

the knowledge or support of other school board members and had overridden school policies and had not informed the school's superintendent before acting. Supposedly. But Ben had no reason to not believe them. He was assured the board member had been reprimanded and placed on one year's probation. Nathan was welcome back once the quarantine situation was over and there would be written documentation to attest to that fact. Ben sighed, that was fast. But what a relief.

Chapter 3

Sea-Tac Airport, Seattle

"You're welcome to spend the night on the couch. I need to be out of the apartment by the fifteenth so pretty much everything's in boxes." Raven, Zac, and Nathan had met Ben at the airport. He was fortunate to have reserved a one-way car rental on short notice, so spending the night in Seattle wasn't necessary.

"Nathan and I talked about getting a head start this afternoon. I need to pick up the SUV from Enterprise, get all our supplies at REI sporting goods, and then we can take off—drive 'til we get tired."

"Okay, if you're sure."

"But thanks for the offer."

"I wish I was going with you." Zac obviously felt left out.

"Not with that dog of yours needing to be trained."
Ben playfully added, "I'm sure he's jealous of your being
in school without him as it is." It was already the start of
winter in Moose Flats, Alaska, and Ben was secretly glad he
wasn't going in that direction. Fall in the Dakotas sounded
a lot more inviting. It was meant to be a surprise but Ben
was planning on a hands-on history lesson with a little
detour to the two Dakota states so rich in Indian history.
Nathan needed to be introduced to reservation life beyond
the Navajo Nation.

Ben passed on having lunch in order to pick up the car
and start back. Probably wouldn't be the first McDonald's
that they'd eat over the next ten days. Raven brought her
car to the baggage entrance and Ben saw Nathan's bags
were already in the trunk. He threw in his duffle and they
were off to Enterprise.

The navy-blue Chevy Blazer was gassed up and waiting
for them at the rental agency. He'd completed paperwork
and paid for it online, probably saving an hour's time. Ben
had to admit he was excited to get out on the road. It would
be great to put the pandemic behind them for a while and
get to know each other—no deadlines or other constraints,
just the two of them, their gear, and a road going anywhere
they wanted it to go. Not a bad way to vacation.

They made it across town to REI on Yale without
getting slowed by clogged traffic. Seattle could be a
commuters' nightmare at times. The store advertised as
'Seattle's REI Flagship' was impressive. The "wow" that
escaped from his passenger said it all. The store was awe
inspiring—especially if you'd lived on a reservation all your
life and hadn't traveled.

"I've made two lists. I think if we split up, we'll be on

the road quicker. Here's your list and a copy of the store's
directory. Everything on your list is pretty much in one
department—ice chest—I've listed the dimensions—two
flashlights, extra batteries, Velcro ties … don't be afraid to
ask for help or come find me if you can't locate something.
I'm going to be picking out a tent and some bedding, and
a couple air-mattresses, for starters. Here's a cart. Meet you
back at check-out. Shouldn't take us more than forty-five
minutes, don't you think?"

Ben hoped he wasn't wrong by dividing up duties.
He wanted Nathan to feel like he was on equal footing—
recognized as an adult who could make decisions on his
own. Now was an opportune time to begin building trust.
This trip depended on establishing a solid foundation of
sharing thoughts—positive, as well as negative—maybe
even reaching some conclusions on what the future might
hold.

"Hey, what's this?" Almost exactly forty-five minutes
later Nathan had pulled his cart in behind Ben's at the front
of the store. "I don't remember putting a snowboard on
the list." Ben was laughing. "We can always rent skis, but
I'm not sure about renting a board. Good thinking."

Ben would be throwing a couple thousand dollars on a
card, but there wasn't a thing that wouldn't be used again—
especially if the boys visited them in Florida. The fishing
gear might be overkill; he had no idea whether Nathan liked
to fish, but it was worth a shot. Well, maybe the snowboard
was a one-time thing, but Ben had promised the possibility
of a stop in Colorado. And it might be something that
Nathan would want to take back to school. Washington
state had snow.

Loaded down, the Blazer had ample room for all their

gear. Nathan stepped up to ride shotgun and with a mutual thumbs-up, Ben pulled out of the REI parking lot. A couple of Big Macs later and they were on the road, leaving the city behind.

* * *

He couldn't have wished for better weather—high sixties during the day and forties at night. Definitely jacket weather in the evenings but no snow or bitter cold. Ben had purchased a couple of twin-sized down comforters but he doubted they would need them; the flannel sheets might be warm enough. He'd probably tire of the moose motif in a red and black block pattern, but it was woodsy and just seemed right for a camping trip. He had to admit this was fun. How long had it been since he'd had this kind of unencumbered time to do what he wanted? No calls, no deadlines ... how many years was it 'til retirement? Yeah, right. He didn't even want to put a number on his working years. It'd be a while.

Their first stop for the night would be Denny Creek Campground off of I-90. They wouldn't be that far out of Seattle but there would still be light enough to set up camp before nightfall and check out their equipment. The photos online looked fantastic—electricity, showers and restrooms, nice separation of wooded camp slots for tenting, a nearby creek and some super great trails for hiking. If truth were known, Ben was the one who wanted to get in a little fishing. He hoped he'd have an eager companion. But easy access to water wasn't the site's only attraction. The fact that the campground was only fifteen minutes away from pizza and groceries sealed the deal.

"This place is dope." Nathan had hopped out of the truck and was standing on the cement pad meant for RVs and turning three hundred sixty degrees, taking in the towering pines, the metal grill with a stack of wood beside it, and lastly pointing at the creek that bordered the back of their assigned space. "Can we go take a look?"

"Sure. You know, when I was your age, I would have said this place was 'rad'."

"What's 'rad' mean?"

"Dope—about thirty years ago." When he was really young, everything was 'cool' but that made him feel old to even mention it. Still, he wasn't sure he could refer to something he liked as 'dope'. Every generation had its own slang.

"Can we have pizza? I saw a restaurant close to here."

"Sure. Sounds good. Let's get set up here first. They advertise 24-hour security so I think everything will be safe."

The pop-up tent was easy to assemble. Before they left, two air-mattresses with sheets in place were snugged up against the back of the tent and a Coleman lantern hung from a hook in the center. It looked inviting, Ben thought, and realized he was tired after a day of travel. Oh well, pizza would revive him.

* * *

The Mom-and-Pop restaurant, affectionately called Joe's after the owner, was worth the thirty-minute wait for an outside table. Of course, the complimentary garlic bread and dip helped the time pass. Specialty of the house was a mozzarella cheese, cubed tomato, and local herbs with a choice of meat on either thin crust or a stuffed crust. Ben let Nathan choose, and sausage and a stuffed crust turned out to be a great choice. The super-large pie was big enough for leftovers—a slice apiece for breakfast. A quick stop at the next-door grocery for ice and milk and juice also followed the Styrofoam take-out carton of pizza into the cold chest back at the campground.

"Can we stay here an extra day?" Nathan had kicked off his jeans but left on the hooded sweatshirt before crawling into bed.

"Only if you agree to go fishing with me in the morning." Ben got the nod and grin he'd hoped for. After a call to Julie and a quick conversation with his better half, he turned down the lantern, stretched out on what was a pretty comfy air-mattress and let the sounds of the rushing creek lull him to sleep.

Chapter 4

Coroner's office, Spearfish, South Dakota

"Got anything for me?" Mac got as close to the examining table as his nose would let him.

"Hold your horses. This one ain't gonna be easy. See here? And here? This fellow's been strung up and left to hang for a while." Doc Tully was pointing to four sizeable holes across the man's chest sticking out of bluish, scarred, puckered skin. "My guess is that he was already dead when he was strung up."

"So, I'm not looking at some part of a ceremony gone wrong?"

"Nope, not to my way of thinking just by looking. I'll know more later. Doesn't help that he's been dead more than twenty-four hours. A lot of what might have been helpful has dried up or been washed away."

"Did he have any identification on him?"

"Not a thing. But these tattoos should be helpful."

"Tats?"

"Here. I took some pictures." Coroner Tully moved to a computer suspended just above the end of the examining table. "Pretty unique, no?"

Mac moved closer for a better look. "Anyone I should know?" The inked head and chest of a man in a sombrero, bushy mustache and crisscrossed ammunition belts on his chest was a fairly good likeness of Pancho Villa if he had to guess. "Pancho Villa?"

"That's my take. The art is pretty good." Doc Tully zoomed in on initials bordering the lower right side of the tattoo. "These might be helpful. This was expensive. Must have taken hours and multiple sittings."

Mac didn't know that much about ink art but the portrait started between the shoulder blades and continued downward to below the beltline. In other words, it covered the man's entire back.

"The guy's Hispanic." This time Mac made it sound like a statement.

"I heard you tried to pawn him off on Red Bull."

News traveled fast. "Yeah, my error. Didn't win me any points."

Doc Tully chuckled, "No, it wouldn't. But it surprises me that Red Bull didn't, at least, know him. Someone copied a ritual to make a killing look like an accident. Sort of smacks of someone having more than a little knowledge of indigenous ways. At least what goes on around here locally."

"I know I haven't seen him before but with all the

protesters taking up residence out here, it's tough to keep up with new faces." Mac had wracked his memory to make a match but this guy was an unknown.

"I know you've done the counting but isn't this the second or third such death in as many months?"

"Yeah, one belonged to Red Bull, part of a ceremony so I don't count that as possible foul play. And the other body—the result of a drunken bet that an Anglo couldn't stand the pain—was claimed by relatives before it became our problem. Again, unfortunate, but understandable. Macho posturing gone wrong. Postmortem attributed that death to a rip-roaring infection not caught in time. Family was there every step of the way. Something tells me we're not going to have that kind of luck this time." Mac slipped a pair of readers from his shirt pocket along with a 3X5 inch spiral notepad. "Let me borrow your pen and I'll take down the initials of the artist. And forward those pics to me if you don't mind. I should have enough to go on and come up with a name soon enough."

But it wasn't that simple. He spent a couple hours online back at the office, trying to run down the artwork and initials, with no luck. Then Mac crossed off four hours on his daily calendar for the following day and, in the morning, took off for the state capital—Pierre. He knew of a tat artist who'd set up shop there five years ago. Mac wasn't sure he was still around, but he kept an up-to-date web page. He wouldn't even know about the guy if his daughter hadn't started dating him for some short-lived fling that was ill-suited from the start. But it had gotten her to move out of Wyoming and finish a degree in education closer to home—even staying in South Dakota after graduation. To be fair, the guy was nice enough, but didn't have one inch of skin that hadn't been used as a canvas. That had taken some getting used to, and Mac wasn't sure he had, in retrospect.

Still a trip up-state was a nice diversion. A city of a bit over twenty thousand had some hustle and bustle to it—something he missed—bigger, but not too big. It probably didn't qualify as a 'city'; most people would just call it a town. Yet, the state capitol building was impressive, with a dome that could be seen for a mile or two, lighted as it usually was at night.

Parking on the main street was diagonal—pull into the curb at an angle. No parallel challenges. And, people still knew one another, even cared for each other. Well, that might be pushing it. He'd found out the hard way that the gossip was accurate. His former wife became 'former' because of stories that turned out to be true. Her next husband was also a lawman. Funny how many women married the badge and not the man. And, if gossip was correct, that marriage was a goner, too. But that was all water under the whatever. He'd moved on. Not with someone new, but with new conviction that not everyone was meant to pair up and live happily ever after.

As he pulled into town, it crossed his mind to touch base with Michelle, the daughter who'd given up on sowing wild oats in another state and settled down to become a half-way decent kindergarten teacher in Hughes County—or so her mother reported. He didn't see her often enough, he knew that. It was easy to let life slip on by. She had her own life; he hated to interfere. But if truth were known, their politics were different. As a teenager she'd loaded up all the guns in the house and dumped them in the town's landfill. He was damned lucky they were uncovered by a friend and not someone who wanted to hock them and get a few bucks. His daddy's musket-loader was in the bunch along with the first Colt revolver ever made. It took him a while to get over what amounted to theft—at least that was how he saw it. And even though it'd crossed his mind, there was no prosecuting your own child. His threatening to prosecute probably put the nail in the coffin as far as his marriage to her mother was concerned.

There were no grandchildren. Maybe that was a blessing. At least, not yet, or should he say that he knew of. He told himself, probably erroneously, that that would make him keep in touch—a grandson to go hunting with. Guess it would have to be fishing unless his mother was against killing those too. No, he doubted children would make a difference; a loner was always one. Wide-open spaces and a sparse population fit him to a T. He might grouse about getting stuck in South Dakota, but he knew when he was ten that he'd never leave the state—at least, not for long.

He pulled right onto the side street, then left into an alleyway that ran behind a three-story hotel. The tat parlor was halfway down and hidden from view, but easily accessible with ample parking—unless it was garbage day and then spaces were limited. Today he parked in front of the entrance. He'd been there once before and the place hadn't changed. The one large window facing him still had iron burglar bars across it and the front door was metal. Was there any place of business that didn't need to protect itself from break-ins? Even in a town of only twenty some thousand?

He pulled his mask snugly over his nose, opened the door, but hadn't stepped over the threshold before the man in the last booth called out. "Sheriff Sterling, what can I do you for? If we weren't in a pandemic, I'd say you'd joined the perps with that mask on."

It wasn't even funny. He'd heard his share of mask jokes. Mac shut the door behind him before walking toward the man with a broom. At least he wouldn't be interrupting the guy's time with a client.

"Good to see you, too, Jeffery. Gotta couple of questions for you. I think you can help me out." He'd printed out two of the best shots of Pancho Villa and one of the victim's face—not pretty but the angle kept the bruising to a minimum. "Need to know if you recognize the artwork."

He held out the prints but before Jeffery could take them, the door opened. Mac turned just as his daughter stepped into the shop. "Michelle, I'd hoped to see you today."

"Micki, Dad, my name is legally Micki now. No more Michelle, please."

"I have a feeling I'm behind."

"Really? And here I am wondering why you're in Pierre if it's not Christmas. You've got a couple more months to go before the obligatory family visit." Tight jeans, a tighter tank top, hoops at her ears, blond hair slicked back into a shoulder-length ponytail—she was beginning to remind him of her mother, and the sarcasm wasn't lost on him but he decided to ignore it.

"I'm surprised you're not in class. Didn't your mom tell me you were hanging out with kindergartners now?"

"Yeah, but not on weekends. This is Saturday, Dad. A little confused, aren't you?"

Damn it. Saturday. Of course. But the days seemed to

just run together anymore. It wasn't like he had weekends off, not since Covid depleted his workforce by half. Or any set time—he took off when he could or worked seven straight when needed. But this made him sound like a candidate for assisted living.

He tried to laugh it off but knew his chuckle fell flat. "Too much work to do. Weekdays? Weekends? All the same to me."

"So, why are you here?"

"To get some help. I thought Jeffery might recognize Pancho Villa here." He handed his daughter a picture.

He wasn't sure what happened next. He heard a strangled cry as Micki dropped the photo, backed away from him, turned and ran for the front door, letting it bang behind her as she disappeared down the alley.

"What the hell?"

"Let me see that." Jeffery picked up the photo Micki had dropped. "Oh my God, you crazy old fool. If you cared enough to come around more often, you'd know that's Micki's ex-husband."

Chapter 5

Denny Creek Campground, Washington

Sunday morning and Ben felt rested, honest to goodness relaxed with not an ache or a pain from having slept on an air-mattress in a tent in the woods. Saturday had been all about the outdoors—three hours of catch and release, wading along the creek, a hike in the surrounding hills, cold pizza for lunch eaten by the side of the trail, skinny dipping in a holding pond and come dusk, a bonfire topped off with as many s'mores as each of them could consume. But the joy of the day was realizing how much he enjoyed spending time with Nathan. The young man was smart and quick to catch on to whatever was presented. Ben swore the kid was better at casting than he was. For someone who had never fished before, Nathan learned lightning fast, and seemed to enjoy it.

Getting an early start turned into after nine before the SUV was packed and ready for the road. Ben had to remind himself that they weren't on a schedule. It was as if he was having to teach himself how to relax and stay that way. He did a cursory trip around the campsite to make certain they weren't leaving anything, and after double-bagging their garbage and dropping it into the galvanized container up by the road, he secured the lid by turning it to the right. The lock acted as much needed extra bear-proofing. Another reminder that they were in the wilds. Finally, they were ready to leave.

Breakfast was McDonald's at the first town they came to—two egg McMuffins each, one orange juice, and one extra-large coffee, extra cream for Ben. They ate inside before getting back in the SUV and settling in for a day's driving. He put Nathan in charge of maps. He'd thought ahead and picked up state maps of Washington, Idaho, Wyoming, and South Dakota. He planned a scenic tour, not exactly in a straight line like the proverbial crow flies, but meandering, with stops along the way including visiting Mt. Rushmore.

That American treasure only reminded Natives of illegal occupation, the theft and desecration of an age-old religious site. The kind of things not found in school texts. And Ben believed it was important for Nathan to be exposed to this history. In fact, the trip in its entirety put home-schooling in a whole new light. Learning by seeing and living the moment gave lessons a depth and scope not offered by just working on a computer. It gave this trip meaning in addition to bonding.

They had around twenty hours of driving to get to

South Dakota's capital if they went from Walla Walla, Washington to Boise, Idaho; Boise to Casper, Wyoming and finally Casper to Spearfish, South Dakota, which would put them about seventy-two miles from Mt. Rushmore. They weren't in a hurry. If they managed four or five hours of driving a day, that would allow ample time for stops along the way. If they found campsites half as nice as the one they just left, it'd be a great trip.

"I've been meaning to say I like your hair that way." And that wasn't a lie. Nathan's Mohawk was now two inches wide by two inches tall starting from the hairline at his forehead to below the occipital ridge in back. But on the shaved sides of his head were two arrows deftly cut into the shortened hair—one on the right and one on the left, each an inch above his ears and pointing slightly upwards but in opposite directions.

"Yeah, I want to keep it. The guy who did it lives in Seattle. He's a friend of Zac's mom."

"He did a good job." It wasn't lost on Ben how important it was for an almost teenager to be an individual, start affecting his own look but not stray too far from his age group. A hoodie over torn jeans seemed to be a staple.

"Do you think egging the car was wrong?" Nathan turned to look at him.

Ben kept his eyes on the road and didn't overreact. This was the opening to the conversation that he wanted to have and he didn't want to muff it.

"I try not to be judgmental. There are always two sides to every story. And, I think there are degrees of wrong. You had time to give some thought to what you did—you bought the eggs, sought out the target and made the decision to deface property and not harm the individual himself. But we have laws for a reason. Everyone wants to feel safe and know that his property is safe, too. It's not acceptable to—as they say—take the law into your own hands. But I don't know what provoked the situation. Was it something that should have been reported? Something authorities needed to deal with?"

"I'm not going to be a snitch."

"And I respect that. Can you tell me what this person did?" For a minute Ben thought Nathan wasn't going to answer but only continue to stare out the passenger-side window.

Finally, "He disrespected the Navajo. He called us pussies, farmers not warriors. He said I didn't have balls."

"Did you suggest he Google the Code Talkers? Or look up the Navajo men's contribution to WWII?" A sideways glance caught the barely discernible negative shake of Nathan's head.

"Yeah, but Crazy Horse, or Geronimo, or Sitting Bull weren't Navajo. Those guys were bad-ass."

"Navajo men were known as fierce Marines. United States Marines. Somewhere around four hundred enlisted during WWII and fought for this country on the world stage. That's one hell of a contribution. Meaningful for all Americans. Many were highly decorated."

"Pueblo Indians didn't fight. Your tribe are farmers. Are you still proud of them?"

Did Ben detect a note of disdain? "My mother had a showing of her pottery in the Smithsonian just after I was born. She was a well-known Native artist. I value that. I value contributions to our ways of life that aren't forged in bloodshed. What tribe does this kid with the BMW belong to?"

"Crow. His name is Alex Crowfoot. He's an upper classman, a junior."

"We're going to be driving through his ancestral land—Montana and Wyoming."

"It pissed him off that I was better in soccer."

"You can learn a lot in sports but competition is best saved for the opposition on a playing field."

"I offered to pay."

"For the rag-top? How were you going to do that?"

"I talked to the guy who runs the cafeteria. He said I could come in after school and help clean tables. But then I got kicked out."

"So, you apologized?"

"Not really. I just said I wouldn't do it again."

Ben nodded. "I like the way you took responsibility. I don't like the fact that the school looked the other way when Alex's father took it upon himself to discipline you by expulsion. There needed to be hearings, counseling—we got an apology from the administration and an offer to look at both sides. They want to talk to you and to Alex. Are you comfortable going back to school when it opens and taking part?"

"I want to go back. Nothing against Miss Otter in New Mexico, but I like the sports and the field trips—we got to see killer whales in the Puget Sound. I miss Zac; he's a good friend."

Ben drove a few minutes in silence. He was feeling optimistic. This was a chance for Nathan to excel, whether in sports or academics, or both; Ben wanted him to make the most of the opportunity.

"You'll be entering high school next year. Have you thought about what you want to do after high school?"

"Go to college. I have to become a lawyer."

"Have to?" Ben was at a loss.

"I promised my grandmother. She said it was the most important job that I could have."

"Do you know why she thought that?"

"She said the Indian people could no longer fight the white man the way they used to. Today the Indian must fight the white man in court, with paper arrows."

"She has a point. It's a much-needed occupation; indigenous people need representation. I'm glad you have a plan."

Chapter 6

Spearfish, South Dakota, Sheriff's Office

Mac sat leaning forward, elbows on the desk, chin on his clasped hands. It couldn't be worse. He'd had to call his ex-wife to get the particulars. He'd thought of just calling Micki, but Debbie was the lesser of two evils. Then he could have kicked himself. He really had to stop thinking of his family that way.

Evil? No, they deserved better treatment if for no other reason than that they *were* his family. Past tense, but like it or not, hindsight wasn't going to change anything. He'd been left out of the loop, but no surprise, it wasn't the first time. Debbie wasn't thrilled to get a call but filled him in. His daughter had married in March—it was done in secret, no one was invited, just a quick meeting at the courthouse in Sioux Falls. The choice of a large city was meant to cover anyone reading the announcement of a marriage license being issued in the local paper in Pierre. It didn't take much to set the Pierre gossips into action. Even Micki's mother had been in the dark. Now, there was a temptation to gloat, but he passed up the opportunity and felt better for it.

More information meant a call to Jeffery at the tat parlor. Supposedly, in Jeff's lingo, the marriage was snakebit from the start. Diego—David to his friends—Gonzales was a professional protester. That was surprising. Did they make such a thing? Of course, they did; but out here? Mac knew the Lakota people were involved in opposing the currently proposed government pipeline project, and he wanted to think the Anglos supporting the pipeline, for example, were at least residents of the state and had an honest personal stake in the outcome—saw it as offering better jobs or fiscally enriching their state in general. And the indigenous tribes, weren't they exercising their God given rights, thanks to the constitution, to voice opposition to something deemed injurious to their way of life? Threats to their land raised strong reactions out here. He always liked to think of Red Bull and his people as the first environmentalists.

But outsiders? He'd really had the blinders on. Mac guessed that like lobbyists, someone would organize and pay people to cause trouble, maybe block action on a key issue like the one faced by locals now. He was Pollyanna enough to want to believe that those people who made his life miserable by blocking a major highway through his state and demonstrating at least did it from conviction—some heartfelt, 'I'd give my life for this cause', kind of conviction.

But he guessed not. Politics and money did strange things to people. The local Natives had a reason to protest what was happening to their land. But a David Gonzales? Where did he fit in?

Where did he come from? Who paid him? How did he and Micki meet? Her mother wasn't any help with that. Other than saying summer before last, Micki had met him in summer school at the state university. Micki was starting a Masters in Special Education and this David guy was in charge of field trips in the geology department. But according to Jeffery, he wasn't a citizen. He'd come to the States from Mexico, and Micki came to believe that she was just a way to get a green card, change his illegal alien status to something more permanent; and she didn't like being used.

Come to find out, this was a major hurdle with Micki's mother, Debbie, too. Always the religious conservative, Debbie drew a line when it came to offering a home to those who had their hand out. Or, at least, that's the way she saw it. You didn't give up on your country and try to move to another when times got tough. Mac shook his head. Debbie, fervent but dumb. Well, he could amend that to read not exactly worldly-wise which was kinda cute in high school but wore thin later. It used to be funny to know she was a natural blond. He'd used it as an explanation more than once, like the time she'd blown up her car engine because she thought the check engine light was cute as a decoration, and perfectly okay to ignore.

Micki was the spitting image of her mother—same height, blond ponytail, butt-hugging Levi's ... But Micki didn't share her mother's narrow view of the world—evangelical and bigoted. He liked to think Micki's acceptance of people regardless of color or ethnicity

came from him. It amused him that Micki had married a
Mexican. He could only imagine the arguments over that.
And it wouldn't surprise him to find out that leaving after
less than a year's duration of marital strife was probably
more than encouraged by her mother.

He pushed back from the desk and stood up. All this
musing wasn't getting him any closer to finding the guy's
family, notifying them of his death so arrangements could
be made for his body to be released. But wasn't that going
to be difficult if the guy was from Mexico? Surely, he had
family in the States. He dreaded it but he needed to talk to
Micki. Or maybe the Pancho Villa tat would be of help.
Jeffery would know if the artwork had been done stateside.
If so, that might give him a home base for David Gonzales.

The phone on his deputy's desk rang. There was one line
coming into the office for official business, not personal.
But because of its location, he knew the number had been
given out to friends and was treated like an extension of
her cell. The last time he'd answered Sally Haines's phone
when she wasn't there, it had been some half-drunk, half
hungover, horny one-night stand from the day before. That
had been embarrassing. He didn't want to think his slightly
plump, double-D cup sidekick had another life—at least
not one that blurted out his enthusiasm for some Olympic-
worthy gymnastic maneuver in the bedroom that he was
looking forward to doing again. Mac never did tell Sally
what the guy had told him. Better to leave some things
unsaid.

But this call promised to be worse. The call was just
a "heads-up" according to the guy on the other end of
the line, from the Federal Marshal's headquarters out of
Virginia. He had info that needed to be shared and he

assured Mac that a unit would be on standby, ready to support whatever he needed. The Special Operations Group or SOG, a specially trained, highly disciplined tactical unit known to be able to respond to any problem, anywhere, had information of a possibly dangerous mob planning to convene in his part of the country. Their purpose: to vocally and in all probability violently threaten any opposition to the proposed local pipeline. The group with known ties to Progress America, a radical, gun-toting gang of white supremacists, was prepped to kill or, at the very least, take hostages.

He did share that the suspected group was traveling his way incognito, disguised as vacationers—some even with children. Campgrounds were beginning to fill up. The officer suggested that he contact law enforcement in surrounding counties and share what he knew. All this was being monitored by the Feds. When they had more intel he'd pass it along. After the perfunctory thank you and command to stay safe, Mac hung up.

South Dakota was a fisherman's paradise and had the lakes and accompanying campgrounds to go with it. Patrol the area? Not well, unless he had a hundred men at his disposal. Did the guy in Virginia just not know the Badlands? Sprawling, few people, little commerce ... a challenge to oversee and that was an understatement. He leaned back in the chair and gave into a little 'why me, God?' questioning before picking up the phone to start a canvass of surrounding counties. He'd need a commitment of force on standby.

Chapter 7

On the Road, Day Six

Ben never said things like, "it doesn't get any better than this," but once a day on this trip the saying would pop into his head. And he had to admit, he was having a great time. Yes, he missed Julie and talked with her daily. He also wished that Zac could be with them, but the freedom of the open road, sleeping under a star-studded sky, getting reacquainted with the vastness and the beauty of this land and being able to share it with a young man he'd truly grown to care deeply about—well, maybe it really didn't get any better. The moniker Big Sky Country was fitting. It was liberating to be mask-free and not mix with others unless they had to.

They'd been lucky weather-wise, with only a persistent

drizzle one evening outside Casper that eventually just petered out. At least it proved the tent was waterproof. This would be their sixth night on the road and they were crossing into South Dakota. By far the best campground had been their first in Washington, but Ben was looking forward to South Dakota's vast network of waterways. Ninety-eight percent of the state's waters were open for fishing. And there were fifty-six state parks.

Nathan had even asked if they'd be able to get some fishing in before they visited Mt. Rushmore and what they hoped to catch. Ben threw out a few possibilities like bluegill, largemouth bass, walleye, crappie and bullhead. Nathan nodded but Ben knew he'd probably never heard of those fish before. It was just a matter of finding the right spot and supper would be waiting. Ben promised to ask the locals where to go the next time they stopped for gas. And they didn't have to wait long. The next stop was just five miles up the road.

Gas was an afterthought at Sadie's Bait and Tackle. Two pumps out front of a fisherman's haven of anything and everything that would appeal to a fish. Or as Sadie said, "Everything in this store is designed to make a fish just sit up and say 'Howdy'."

Owner, proprietor, resident from a family ensconced in the county for some five generations—at least according to the sign on the door, the fifth generation of fishermen. Expertise and knowledge appeared to be free for the asking. Sadie would know every square inch of her family's home base and be able to steer them toward some good fishing.

"Come on in, folks. Where you from?"

"Coming from Seattle but taking our time to enjoy the countryside and do some fishing. I'd like to catch some largemouth but stay away from live bait if I could. I think we have some worms left from a few days ago but minnow buckets or any carrier with water sloshing around could put our camping gear in jeopardy. The SUV's packed pretty tight." Ben was admiring a wall of brightly colored lures. "What would you recommend?" Ben gestured to include the collection behind him.

"Can't go wrong with a spinner for bass. You familiar with Nichols Lures? The Pulsator Willow Spinnerbait?"

"Can't say that I am." Fishing was a fun hobby, something to do when he had the time, not something he'd researched or even practiced suggested techniques or new equipment.

"Take a look at the ones in the case over there. Normally, live minnows would be my choice in that you'd have a variety of fish to catch, but I understand the problem of transport. Oh, I can also fix you up with a state license—gotta have one if you're sixteen or older. Will that be two licenses, or just one?"

"That leaves me out." Nathan looked dejected, then slyly smiled, "My uncle here is over sixteen."

Ben smiled. So now he was Nathan's uncle. That was probably better than having to explain the term guardian. "I remember being sixteen if that counts."

"Me, too," Sadie sighed. "And you, young man, hang on to being young as long as you can—sixteen will get here in no time. I remember being your age thinking I'd never be of legal age—that meant buying a beer without someone calling my dad. Now look at me." She followed up with a laugh. "I promise, age won't pass you by."

"Would you recommend any place close that we could try out these spinners after setting up camp for the night?

Maybe even finish off that carton of worms on some trout. Some place not too far off the beaten path, if that's possible."

"You're heading right toward the best fishing in the whole state, Spearfish Creek Canyon. It's right off of ninety, with great amenities. You get tired of fishing there's plenty of places just a hike away. Take a camera; it's pretty up there." Sadie pulled a copy of a hand-drawn map out from under the register and spread it on the counter, pointing out which turnoffs he needed to take, marking a couple with red X's. "Beautiful and safe. I send a lot of people there."

Spinners, a copy of the hand-drawn map to Spearfish Creek, a license, soft drinks, fresh bag of ice, and they were off. Sadie followed them to the front door, watching them load their purchases in the back of the SUV before backing out of the parking lot and pulling forward onto highway ninety. She waited until they were obscured by the first turn in the road before pulling her cell out of her jean's pocket, dialing, and holding it to her ear.

"Sheriff Sterling? Gotta minute? Sadie here."

"What's up?"

"You know that Amber Alert that went out last night?"

"Sure do. I'm keeping an eye out as we speak."

"Well, I think I might have something for you. You've always said to call if anything odd came my way. Well, I may have the hot tip of the day. Had a guy stop in just now pretending to be a fisherman but had to ask how to best catch largemouth bass. Didn't seem to have a clue about spinners. The odd thing was, he had an Indian kid with him and I don't think the man's a Native. Maybe a mix of something, a big drink of water—he's over six feet and probably in his thirties. Wasn't that alert for a pre-teen Indian kid? Out of Seattle, maybe traveling in the Pacific Northwest with someone in his thirties posing to be his uncle? Well, this kid said his traveling companion was his uncle. But I'd bet the farm on they're not being related. They admitted up front to being from Seattle."

"Yeah, sounds like you're on to something. You able to get a plate?"

"No, I'm sure it was a rental—California tags. But it was a dark blue SUV just like in the alert. And they were acting funny—you know what I mean? The guy just stood and stared at that wall full of lures—like he'd never seen anything like that before. He ain't a fisherman—that's just a cover."

"They heading out on ninety?"

"Yeah, I sent them to Spearfish Creek."

"You know, I gotta hire you one of these days. Be careful, now. I don't want my non-deputized deputy getting hurt. And, Sadie? Thanks, I appreciate the help."

Mac slipped his cell back into his shirt pocket. Why did trouble always come in bunches? He had enough to worry about with rabble-rousers heading his way, now this. Abduction across state lines was a federal offense. Maybe he could report what Sadie had passed on and skip out on getting involved. But things in law enforcement didn't work that way. You followed up on any lead whether it was your problem or not, especially if it was in your territory. He pulled a U-turn and headed west on 90. He was about an hour away but it didn't sound like the guy suspected anything. Mac was only half kidding when he mentioned Sadie working for him. She was good.

First of all, he needed to cover his ass. If Sadie had

encountered the subjects of the Amber Alert, he needed to be prepared—at least be legal and have a warrant in hand if he caught up with them and needed to haul them in. And he had a feeling that this was the real thing, too much added up—the guy's age, being called uncle, the kid's age and the two of them being from Seattle driving in a dark blue SUV. That was right-on evidence, not coincidence. He got out his phone again, dialed the office and put the cell in the phone holder on the console. Someday he'd get the electronics fixed on the cruiser but it was difficult to be without wheels for the day or so it needed to be in the shop.

"Sally? Glad I caught you, need your help. Sadie Edmond just called in a tip on that Amber Alert. Seems the perp and the underage kid were in her shop. I'm on my way to intervene but I'm still an hour out heading toward Spearfish Creek Campground. I need to cross my T's on this one, make sure I'm legal in detaining them so I'm going to need a warrant. Call over to Deadwood, Lawrence County court, and have them send you an e-warrant. Make sure the magistrate has signed it. Call Sadie for their names—at least the adult will have probably paid for his fishing gear with a credit card and that should have a name. Not that it's his legal name, and I doubt that it's the James Parker that's on the flyer; but it's the one we'll put on the warrant. Then I want you to bring it on out to the campground. Time is of the essence or however that goes. I just need you to break a few speed limits. See you in an hour."

Chapter 8

Spearfish Creek Canyon, South Dakota

Ben turned off at the first red X marked on the map. The going was a little rough for a quarter mile but then the road smoothed out as it followed a trail along Spearfish Creek. Beautiful. Just drop dead beautiful. Even Nathan seemed mesmerized by the sun on the rushing water cascading between and around various sized boulders sticking up out of the water and glowing a tannish-pink in the late afternoon light.

The first campsite held three RVs and four tents, each occupying a pad designed to accommodate vacationers by providing a metal post with electricity, garbage containers, a butane powered grill, and a water spigot. All the comforts. Ben mentally promised himself that this wouldn't be a quick overnighter. This was a place that they could spend a couple days.

He pulled in beside a cabin with a big information/office sign above the entrance. According to the posted listing of open sites, one with electricity, a gas grill, and "a canopy of protective vegetation"—whatever that was—would cost him forty-five dollars a night. There were two that appeared to be available. Only two left out of what looked like upwards of forty spots that catered to different camping needs from RVs to tents. Seemed odd to find an almost full campground in October, but most people had been cooped up for months. Fresh air, wide-open spaces definitely had an allure. Ben filled out a registration card and paid the clerk inside for two nights, got two keys to the showers and another to the laundry facility, then waited while Nathan used the office restroom.

The clerk had shown him their assigned campsite on a four-foot by four-foot map of the area inside a glassed-in case hanging on the wall behind the counter. The area was heavily wooded, covering a couple hundred acres of land punctuated by streams and feeder creeks. Touted as a 'fisherman's paradise' on several posters, the photos would put Colorado to shame. And from what he'd seen so far, the posters weren't embellishing the truth. This was paradise. Ben realized how much he was looking forward to a couple days of solitude in the wilds.

Nathan pressed the button to lower his window and then leaned out to first look behind them, and then to the front, as Ben followed a gravel road along a creek.

"Wow. New Mexico isn't this green."

"In some places, it is. For example, in the mountains. But remember New Mexico is basically a desert."

"Are we going to be by ourselves?"

"I don't think we're close to any other campers. Is that okay?"

"I like that." Nathan sat back and closed his window. "Can we fish this evening?"

"Sure. Dawn and dusk are usually the best times." Ben noted a number twenty-one attached to a post to the right of an area leveled for a tent. "Here we are." He pulled the SUV off the road next to a picnic table and garbage container. "I don't know if they have security but I think everything will be safe. Unless a bear might want that snowboard." Nathan smiled but shook his head at the lame joke.

They were actually getting good at pitching the tent and setting things up for the night. It was half past four and with fishing poles and tackle box in hand, they were headed for the creek.

"Let's use up the worms. I bet there's some trout along here. I wouldn't mind catching tomorrow's dinner."

"I'm hungry now."

Ben laughed. "Me, too. I wasn't thinking; we could have brought food with us here. I stuck a couple sodas in the ice chest and we still have a lot of stuff for sandwiches—ham, cheese, even some peanut butter—chips are on top of the console in the front seat. I'll watch our poles if you want to go back and put dinner together. This is a great place for a picnic."

Ben watched Nathan retrace his steps back along the creek's edge. So far, he'd have to say that the trip was a success. He really didn't think he'd change anything about it. Nathan had turned into a great traveling companion.

* * *

Nathan stopped at the creek's edge to pick up a couple patterned rocks—one pinkish with gray matrix, the other a shiny black. Both had spent a long time in the water, long enough for their rough edges to become entirely smooth. He stuck them in his pocket. He'd left his collection of rocks in New Mexico, so maybe he'd start a new one. He always wished he would find an arrowhead.

His grandfather had had a box full that Nathan had played with when he was small. He'd match the sharp, pointed artifacts as to color and size, even mounting two larger ones to finely hewn oak branches to make spears with the help of his grandfather. Before he became ill, his grandfather shared his knowledge, stories that had been passed down for centuries and encouraged Nathan to become a leader of his tribe. College first, then he'd see.

The trees and underbrush thinned just before he reached the road and the creek sharply turned to the right. Their camp was between the creek and the road. It was sheltered from the gravel path that doubled as a road—at least it was big enough for cars to travel single file. Its edges were defined by brush labeled with signs that pointed to buckthorn and chokecherry alongside dogwood and sumac. Some were losing their leaves and others formed a stark, but bright patch of contrasting color—reds and yellows against the dark greens. Nathan loved the foliage.

Suddenly, he stopped. That was weird. There was a man in uniform—a cop judging from the Sheriff's SUV parked behind him—just coming out of their tent. Just because he had a badge, did that make it okay walking inside someone's property? He guessed it did.

"Hey, you're just the guy I'm looking for." The sheriff stepped away from the tent. "Great campsite you got here—I like being by the water, too. Your uncle around?"

"I don't have an uncle."

"Now don't fib to me. The lady up at the bait and tackle store said you were traveling with a man you called your uncle. Did he make you call him that?"

"That was a joke. Why would he make me call him uncle?"

"So people wouldn't suspect any wrongdoing. If he's real, he's going to be your mom's brother or your dad's—which is it, son? Or is he only a make-believe uncle?"

Nathan wasn't making sense out of anything the man was saying—badge, or no badge.

"I don't have a mother or a father or uncles or aunts or a grandfather and grandmother."

"Maybe not around here, but someplace else? How could I get ahold of your mother?"

"I don't know 'cause she's dead." The guy was pissing him off. What was with him anyway?

"You don't need to be afraid. I'll keep you safe. You can talk to me. Where are you from, son?"

"I go to school in Bellingham."

"So, let me guess, you're Quinault?" Nathan shook his head. "How 'bout Swinimish?" Again, no. "Okay, then, I bet you're Nooksak. Maybe, Haida?"

"Why are you asking me all these questions?"

"It's okay to be scared. I understand. The man you're with has probably threatened you."

"Ben's son is my best friend. I lived with them for awhile. Why are you saying crazy stuff? Are you a real sheriff?"

"Take it easy son, I'm here to help. A lot of people are worried about your safety. Look here." Mac unfolded a flyer that prominently displayed the picture of a young Indian boy underneath a plea for information of his whereabouts. "How old were you in this picture? Seven? Eight?"

"That's not me."

"You're telling me you're not Ethan Standingbear?"

"My name is Nathan Yazzi."

"What kind of name is that?"

"Navajo."

"You're a long way from home. Why aren't you in school?"

"It's closed. There's a virus." Nathan looked perplexed. Where was this guy from? He didn't seem to know anything.

"And this man that you're with, what's his name and where are the two of you headed?"

"Ben Pecos and he's my guardian. We're going to New Mexico."

"Hate to break it to you but you're going in the wrong direction."

Ben stepped into the clearing in time to hear this last part of the conversation. "Hello. How can I help you?" Mac had moved his hand to his hip and unsnapped the buckle on the strap that kept his gun in place. The move wasn't lost on Ben as a warning to be careful. Whatever the reason was for the sheriff to be there, it involved something against the law.

"I need to have you put your driver's license and car registration on the table here."

"The car's a rental and the papers should be in the glove compartment." Ben pointed to the SUV before carefully removing his billfold from a back pocket and opening it to show his license through a plastic window.

"Take it out, please, put your billfold and your license on the table. I'm not going to ask you again."

"Can you tell me what this is all about?"

"He thinks my name is Ethan Standingbear and you're my uncle." Nathan took a step toward Ben.

"Stay right where you are, son." The lawman handed the flyer to Ben. "This mean anything to you? Says the two of you are traveling in a dark blue Blazer. Probably like that one behind me."

Ben studied the flyer. "I can see why you'd confuse us. I'm Nathan's guardian. I flew up to Seattle to pick him up when the pandemic closed his school. I thought I'd give him a hands-on lesson or two in geography by driving back—taking in some Indian country, areas he's never been to before."

"That's a good story. I hope for your sake it's true. I'm going to have to take you back to the office to get this all straightened out."

The siren drowned out any further conversation. Another SUV with law enforcement decals and signage roared up the road and skidded to a stop. A female deputy hopped out from behind the steering wheel and already had her gun drawn.

"Got here as quickly as I could, Mac."

"Put the gun away, Sally. We got a kid here. Get the warrant?"

"Right here in my pocket." She patted the folded paper sticking out of her jacket's breast pocket but with her other hand kept her gun aimed in their direction.

"Great, hand it here. And, seriously, holster your gun. That's an order."

"Okay, will do, but I wouldn't trust a pedophile as far as I could toss him. I'd feel safer if I had an advantage here." She handed the warrant to Mac after holstering her gun.

Nathan turned to Ben and whispered, "What's a ped … ped-o …? Can you shoot them?"

Ben held back a laugh. In actuality there was nothing funny about the spot they were in. Indian kid of approximately the right age with an older man driving a car that matched the one being sought—it honestly didn't look good. He could only hope that the female deputy wasn't trigger-happy and she left her gun in its holster.

Mac turned to Nathan. "What about you kid? You got papers?"

Nathan looked confused. "Toilet paper?"

"Don't need a smart mouth. I'm here to save your bacon."

Ben quickly put a finger to his lips. He could tell Nathan had no idea what the saying meant, especially when he leaned toward Ben again and whispered, "We don't have any bacon. Was somebody's stolen?"

"Gonna have to take these two back to the office and get things sorted. Sally, you take the young man in your car. I'll cuff the mister and put him in mine."

"Not going to look good if we're really not who you think we are and all our gear gets stolen. You going to give us time to get it all back into our vehicle? I'd feel a lot better if I can leave our stuff locked up in the SUV." Ben crossed his fingers that the sheriff would be understanding—there was a possibility that they were telling the truth. And this kind of error wouldn't make his office look good.

"You got lines in the water?"

"About a quarter mile up the creek."

"Sally, why don't you and the young man gather up the tackle. He's not going anywhere without his *uncle*. I'll lend a hand here getting their stuff back in their car. I'll let the campsite office know what's going on. And I'll put *Mr. Pecos* here in the back seat of my car—need to keep him where I can see him while I pack up this tent."

* * *

An hour later Ben and Nathan were sitting on hastily set up folding chairs in the sheriff's office. Sheriff Sterling had snapped their pictures, scanned them into the computer used only for official law enforcement business, left a couple voicemail messages, and now it was time to wait. The handcuffs had been removed but Ben felt the deputy watching his every move. He still needed to be careful.

"Shouldn't take 'em too long in Pierre. These cases take priority once an Alert goes out. Anybody thirsty?"

"You got a Coke?" Nathan asked.

"Pepsi work?"

"No, that's okay."

Hurriedly Ben chimed in, "I'll take the Pepsi. Kid doesn't know what he's missing." He ducked his head and winked at Nathan. There were times a person should tell the truth, then there was a time when a little white lie was necessary. But how did you teach that?

"It's almost seven already. I'm going to guess that office personnel have gone home over in Pierre. We might not get an answer tonight. I want to alert our instate office before involving the Feds. Just in case you are who you say you are. No need to embarrass anybody. Our cells here aren't luxurious but we can dig up some soap and towels and make up a couple cots. We should have word in the morning."

"I'm hungry." Ben didn't doubt Nathan; they hadn't eaten since noon.

"We were getting ready to make some sandwiches when you came. Any chance we could order in? We'd be glad to treat you. There's money in my billfold."

"Keep your money. Don't worry about feeding these two—I'm taking them off your hands." No one had heard Red Bull come in the back door. "I'm appointing myself your representative. A little sliver of that campground encroaches on the Pine Ridge Rez. Strictly following rules, you were apprehended on Indian land. Sally Haines called, thinking you might need to touch base with Native law enforcement. The minute she gave me your name, I knew there was an error."

"Robert?" Ben couldn't believe he was seeing clearly. Robert Red Bull was a trusted leader when he wasn't making trouble over boundaries and causing headaches for government environmentalists. Ben had met him at a pow wow in Albuquerque some five years back. "I was hoping you were still in South Dakota—you were on my list to look up right after a visit to a couple national monuments."

Red Bull laughed. "I'm still here—can't hold a candle to the statue of Crazy Horse though; you'll need to see it. Tribe twisted my arm and got me into law enforcement. Means I have to work with the likes of him every once in awhile." It was said with a grin and the sheriff didn't seem to take offense.

"So, you two know each other?" Mac wasn't sure he liked this turn of events. How far would Red Bull go to protect a brother? Would he lie? But this Ben guy seemed to know Red Bull, called him Robert …

"Sheriff Sterling, this is Dr. Benson Pecos. A star in Indian Health Service's posse of up and coming, bright, knowledgeable, medical personnel. A shrink by trade, he's a Pueblo man from New Mexico. Not sure about his sidekick's name." Red Bull turned to Nathan. "Two-arrows, it's your turn."

Nathan smiled, obviously pleased at the call-out to his hair design. "I'm Nathan Yazzi. Ben is my guardian and I go to school with his son in Bellingham. I'm going home to New Mexico to wait for school to reopen. We're camping out and I'm learning how to fish."

"And there you have it. I'd bet there's a little problem of mistaken identity here. Am I right?" Red Bull leaned over the corner of the Sheriff's desk and picked up the flyer showing the young Indian boy, the object of the Amber Alert.

Reluctantly, Mac nodded. "Might be."

Red Bull put the paper back on Mac's desk. "'Fraid you're gonna have to keep looking. And since I was about ready to get something to eat, I'll take these two along for company. They'll be with me on the Rez if you need them. Come on, boys, this is Saturday. Chicken livers tonight at Grandy's with mashed potatoes and a side of deep-fried gizzards and brown gravy."

Ben stifled a laugh as he saw the look of disbelief on Nathan's face. Had someone just mentioned poison?

Chapter 9

Sheriff's Office, Town of Spearfish

Mac guessed he should feel relieved to have one problem taken off his hands. They'd still have to go over to the county seat and have the court dismiss the warrant; but with tomorrow being Sunday, he had another twenty-four hours before that could happen—which left him with a couple other problems that needed his attention—including identifying the killer of one dead supposed Sun Dancer and preparing for the demonstrators that were on their way, coming his direction. Thank the Lord, things were quiet for the time being. Calm before the storm? Yeah, that saying fit his situation real well. But he welcomed the quiet. He did his best work at the office after seven in the evening.

Some would say he just didn't have anyone to go home to; even his former wife had tried to give him a dog. It was true he didn't really want a dependent—two legged or four. He loved his job, found it exciting and challenging; he didn't mind letting it take over his life.

Which reminded him that he was only putting off finding the family of the Hispanic man who was found dead by the side of the road. Probably, it was time to 'fess up. He wasn't being lazy or trying to duck his duty; he was just putting off talking with Micki. As a former wife, she was the logical place to start—it just wasn't going to be pleasant.

Besides, this wasn't a good time. He doubted that she was going to be sitting home on a Saturday night. The kid used to like to party. She had never lacked friends in high school—a cheerleader, her popularity hinged on cute and perky, not academics. But maybe he wasn't being fair; she'd gotten a teaching degree. That took some smarts and discipline.

He reached for his cell. What did he have to lose? He could always leave a voicemail and try again tomorrow. He punched in the last number he'd had for her and got a voice message saying she was out but would call back. Yeah, sure. He doubted that. If he hadn't gotten her with a surprise first try, maybe they'd talk eventually but probably not. She wasn't going to call him, and leaving a message was probably futile. He slipped the phone back in his shirt pocket only to have it ring a second later.

"Hello, Dad."

That was promising; he was still in her contacts list. And she still recognized his parentage. But the number coming up on his phone's screen wasn't the one he'd called.

"Hi, Micki. This is a different phone number than the one I just called. Should I make a note of this one?"

"No, I'm borrowing a friend's phone. Mine is acting squirrelly—it goes to voicemail whether I answer or not."

"I appreciate you getting back. I want to ask you—"

"Before you say anything, listen to me. This is important, maybe life and death. And I'm not being melodramatic— this is for real. Do not try to find any family for David if that's why you're calling. It's dangerous. I don't know what happens to unclaimed dead people from another country, but let someone else figure things out. In fact, I don't think you have to worry; I think David will be taken care of."

"How do you know that?"

"No questions. Trust me on this. You don't want to know more, just ignore. And the less that's said about my having been married to him, the better. I'm telling Jeff the same thing. I'm sure he'll be questioned."

"Who's going to be doing the questioning?"

"Dad, please. I've said more than I should have now."

He didn't even get his mouth open to respond before the call was dropped. What the hell was going on? He didn't stop to think; he dialed Debbie. If he had given it some thought, he would have found it odd that she answered on the first ring.

"Dammit, Mac, can't you follow directions?"

"Well, hello to you, too, Debbie. I take it you're with our daughter?"

"Good to know you're acknowledging the relationship."

He bit his tongue and swallowed the smart remark he'd almost made. "I'm a little in the dark here. Who's in danger if I'm just trying to do my job?"

"Can't you just trust Micki? If she says cease and desist,

just do it—job be damned."

"That job is still paying you a chunk of money every month and probably bought Micki a college degree. Not that I'm complaining. I want to see you both successful."

"And I don't want to see you dead."

Once again, Mac was left with a disconnected call. This time the phone stayed in his pocket. What could be so threatening? More like who? The dead body of an illegal alien killed a long way from his home with no emergency contacts and no one stepping forward, inquiring about his whereabouts. To some extent it was as if he didn't exist. Mac wished that he wasn't consumed by curiosity. He'd always been like that—tell him not to do something and sure enough he couldn't rest until he had. He'd always thought looking at the 'left eye of the camel' made him a good lawman.

Chapter 10

Near Pine Ridge Indian Reservation,
Oglala Lakota Sioux—3,468.85 square miles,
estimated resident population: 28,787

After a quick trip to Spearfish Creek Camp to pick up the loaded SUV, Ben followed Red Bull to Grandy's at the edge of the reservation. The outdoor picnic tables looked like a new addition and were set the obligatory ten feet apart. It was an hour from closing and getting dark but they had the outside area all to themselves. When Nathan asked if they had hot dogs, Red Bull told him they made them with ground chicken gizzards. The look on Nathan's face was priceless. He ended up ordering a chicken sandwich and fries—and didn't share their laughter.

"Mac Sterling means well. If I have to have a sheriff

close by, I could do worse. He's a little tone-deaf or should I say color-blind when it comes to Natives but that's a common white man's problem. He tried to pawn some dead Mexican off on me a couple days ago. Swore that even if he wasn't a member of the tribe, I should still know him. Just because the guy was sporting bone needles in his chest like a Sun Dancer."

"What's a Sun Dancer?" A blob of mayo oozed out of Nathan's chicken sandwich.

Red Bull didn't answer but unbuttoned his shirt and exposed a bare chest scarred with puckered bumps of skin six inches apart that formed a kind of ladder pattern on his upper chest involving the pectoral muscles. "There's more here." This time Red Bull exposed the skin on his back. On each shoulder blade the skin was gathered in bunches, knobs of wadded flesh positioned as if measured exactly an equal distance apart.

"Did it hurt?" Nathan's sandwich now lay in its foil wrapper, forgotten.

"That's not an easy question to answer—either something hurts or it doesn't, I know what you're thinking. But the ceremony is performed to pay tribute to the Great Spirit. We fast—no food, not even water for four days. You sacrifice and give of yourself to be worthy, to make certain your prayer is worthy. I guess I would say that the pain is welcome, expected, and worn with honor."

"Wow. Your tribe does this?" Red Bull had Nathan's complete attention now.

"Yes. The Sun Dance represents centuries of sacred knowledge of a people as old as the earth they inhabit. My people. It's a way of life, not to be questioned, just accepted. It takes place on sacred ground and the ceremony itself is held in a round structure sometimes referred to as a lodge. To symbolize creation, there is a tree of life in the center. Lakota people also construct an arbor of twenty-eight trees; fourteen trees are lined up with another fourteen trees so that their branches reach from left to right. These represent the ribs of the buffalo but the number twenty-eight pays homage to White Buffalo Calf Woman and the days of a woman's cycle that ensures fertility, procreation and birth. It is this cyclical rotation of life that gives us meaning and infuses us with the stamina and knowledge to continue living by incorporating the history of our tribe into our daily lives."

"Can anyone go to the ceremony? I mean someone like me?"

Ben worried that Nathan's supper was completely cold right down to the congealed blob of oil puddled under his fries. But this was information that he would never have gotten in a classroom. And Red Bull was proving to be a well-informed and patient teacher.

"Only one requirement; you have to be Native. I think you've got that one. You might have to wait awhile. I don't know of another ceremony being planned. They are usually done in the summer, during the solstice. But because of the contagion, families are feeling the need to ask for guidance and sacrifice for healing the community. Will you be in the area for awhile?" Red Bull turned to Ben.

"We still have a few monuments to take a look at."

"Good, because I want to twist your arm into offering your expertise to our village planners. It's no secret that alcoholism is a tremendous problem for us. We always make some newspaper's front page by having the lowest income per capita or the most deaths from alcoholism in the US. It's a constant struggle to save lives and change lives. We've got some programs that are still on paper, with no ideas as to how to implement them. Your help would be invaluable. And I'm not asking for a freebie—there's money for professional help."

"I'd be glad to help. Nathan? Think we could stop here—maybe three or four weeks?"

"Yeah, that'd be great."

"It's a deal then. I'll talk to the elders and let IHS know that we're putting you to work."

Ben nodded but was trying hard not to think of what Julie's reaction would be. This hadn't been in the plan. He was already thinking of shipping their gear when the time came and flying back to Albuquerque. He could make up a week's time that could be used here. If he wanted to rationalize, he'd only be adding an extra week. That didn't sound half bad.

"I could save you some travel time and a little money. My sister is in Rapid City. She's a nurse and got called in to help out at the hospital there. I know she'd be glad to have someone looking after her place while she's gone."

"Sounds great. I accept your offer."

"With our schools shut down because of the pandemic, we've started up a kid's camp—fishing, hiking, hunting, that sort of thing for the boys. We have a teepee town south of the village center. Participants sleep outdoors, cook on campfires, wash their clothes in the creek. The elders enjoy getting involved with our youth. They'll be the guides. I guess you could call them counselors. The camp is kind of the last outdoor hurrah before the snows begin and a pretty good antidote to the pandemic. Fresh air and lots of individual activities will keep everybody safe.

Nathan? Can I get you enrolled?"

"Yeah. I'd like that."

* * *

Red Bull's sister's house was a modest, two-bedroom bungalow about a block from the tribal offices. It was one house on the main road flanked by identical bungalows stretching in both directions with more on a street immediately behind. Without carefully counting, Ben thought there might be thirty in all. They were cookie-cutter-stamp-out identical, so much so that Ben suspected FEMA had a hand in their erection. But Ben would be able to walk to work, and get groceries close by, otherwise he would have had a thirty-five mile, one-way trip every day. The minute they walked in the door, Nathan immediately checked for WIFI and was thrilled he wouldn't have to give up his computer games. Maybe this wasn't exactly how Ben had thought of this trip but helping others was always a priority. He was anxious to lend his expertise. But first thing Monday morning he had to show up at Sheriff Sterling's office and clear his name. In the meantime, he had another hurdle to jump. He dialed Julie's number.

Chapter 11

Lawrence County, South Dakota—County Seat for Cities of Deadwood, Spearfish, Whitewood and St. Onge

Erasing the warrant wasn't going to be easy. It required meeting with the county judge.

"You know, I'm going to have to go with you. I'm still standing in for the arresting officer, Sheriff Sterling. I need to show that until your identity has been cleared, you've been monitored and detained by reputable law enforcement personnel. Can't appear to be lax with the rules around here." Red Bull was smiling but Ben knew it was the truth.

He was still under a cloud of suspicion and still the subject of a current warrant. With luck Sheriff Sterling had contacted IHS or the Navajo Nation legal offices and had received proof of who Ben was and why he was in South Dakota with an underage young man.

Proof of guardianship was important but Red Bull didn't see a reason for Nathan to have to go with them. A copy of the paperwork legalizing Ben's authority should be all that would be needed and that had probably already been emailed to the sheriff. Nathan actually asked if he could stay on the reservation. He'd offered to help break horses that day with a bunch of teenage boys that he'd met at the store, and Ben could tell he was excited to work with animals again.

"I just got off the phone with the sheriff and he's suggesting we meet him in Deadwood—that's the county seat. We'll be able to appear before the judge—you're lucky this is his day of rotation and he'll be in Deadwood. Our circuit court judge is Rex Udahl; he's more or less a local; has a big ranch over east. He handles all family and juvenile cases and would be the one to check the evidence and dismiss the charges of child trafficking. Because a warrant was issued before your arrest and proof of innocence was not conclusive at the scene, this is on your record until a judge erases it. But it won't go any further; the Feds won't be notified. Sorry. I know this is something you hadn't planned on."

"Let's just get it done." Ben was getting tired of red tape.

* * *

Red Bull's truck had seen better days. The upholstery looked like it had been chewed. Judging from the dog hair, it probably had. Ben didn't have a suit with him but had a clean off-white shirt and a navy jacket and, luckily, a pair of unwrinkled khakis. Not exactly business attire but presentable. Running shoes were just going to have to be overlooked. And, hey, wasn't the no-sock look in?

It took them under an hour to reach Deadwood, a frontier town that looked like it had materialized straight out of someone's old west coffee table book of photos—a main street from the 1800s, a couple hitching posts still preserved on one corner, a brick courthouse with freshly painted white trim—signs directing the tourists to where Wild Bill Hickok had been shot. Posters depicting the "dead man's hand," a pair of black aces and pair of black eights. Signage pointing to the original saloon, Nuttels and Mann's, but a note that it burned to the ground in 1879. Interesting. Ben noted that the site was currently another bar.

"Whole town's a piece of history. Calamity Jane lived around here, too." Red Bull didn't seem too enthused. And frankly, Ben wasn't sure Nathan would be that interested in a slice of the white man's legacy, but they'd have to visit.

Red Bull drove by a main street of canvas awnings rolled out over shop windows along wide sidewalks. Two grand hotels, the Franklin and the Fairmont, had offered lodging to "guests of distinction" over the last century according to a state historical plaque. Ben honestly felt like he was taking a step back, maybe a couple centuries—time-travel, for sure.

"Well, we've arrived—80 Sherman Street." Red Bull pointed through the windshield at a buff-colored stone, three-story building with a clock tower. "I'll park around in the back. Looks like Sheriff Sterling beat us here." He pointed to the sheriff's SUV parked at the curb. The sheriff was waiting for them just inside the heavy double doors that opened onto a large lobby area. The building reeked of old charm, and that aura had followed them inside. Marble, old wood, and arched doorways added to yesteryear's opulence. Ben had to admit that the town itself made the old west come alive. A young woman sitting at a desk in the rotunda asked them to wait while she buzzed the judge's chambers.

"Judge Udahl will see you now. His office is the third door on your left—just continue straight down this hallway." She pointed to a corridor that stretched behind her. The men thanked her, walked to the third door, and stepped inside.

"Come in, welcome. I'm Nancy. Let me know if you need anything—a soda or coffee?" Ben shook his head. He wasn't here for a social hour. Red Bull also declined the hospitality, only the sheriff inquired if she had a ginger ale. "Well, I'll take a look. Just a moment then, please. In the meantime, I'll tell the judge you're here."

The sixtyish woman smiled, pushing back from her desk, and walked to the door at the end of the room. First knocking lightly, she opened the door a crack and nodded to someone inside, then immediately turned toward them. "Right this way, gentlemen."

The room was cavernous, so big it dwarfed the heavy leather couch and side chairs, not to mention the enormous ornate desk—four feet by six feet of solid wood. The judge stood and offered his hand.

"I've got sanitizer if you trust shaking hands?" He pointed to a good-sized container with a pump dispenser sitting on the corner of his desk.

"I'm good with that." Ben stepped forward with his

hand out.

The judge was exactly Ben's height, mid-fifties probably, and solid. Ben would guess he worked out or maybe did a little hands-on work at his ranch. A head full of dark hair was parted on the side and a thick lock fell over the right side of his face, obscuring half of his eyebrow. He wore a light blue, possibly cashmere, sweater under a tailored black dress jacket but the slacks were Levi's, and the footwear, boots.

A smart move to dress like the locals, Ben thought. But he marveled at the feeling of no-nonsense that the judge exuded. This was someone used to calling the shots—not someone who waited for things to happen. Ben couldn't place where they'd met before, but the judge looked vaguely familiar.

"Sheriff Sterling, Officer Red Bull, I'm going to ask you to wait outside while I talk with Dr. Pecos here. Nancy has the paperwork you need at her desk. Everything's in order; the warrant has been dismissed. But I want to thank you, Sheriff Sterling, for your quick action on what could have been the thwarting of an unfortunate situation and possibly the saving of a life."

Ben stood while the judge waited until the men left, watching Red Bull pull the office door closed before he spoke. "Drag that chair closer to the desk. I have some things I want to share with you. I admit this is awkward— something I never imagined I'd be doing. But bear with me."

Ben pulled one of the overstuffed armchairs closer to the desk and sat down. This was all odd. Why a private audience? Was there other wrongdoing that Ben might be suspected of?

The judge sat behind his desk and opened a folder, rifled through some papers before pushing it aside, and then just sat looking at Ben, elbows on the desk, while steepling his index fingers, touching his chin. Deep in thought? Mentally practicing how to begin to say something? What could be so important to get this kind of silent scrutiny?

Ben willed himself not to squirm. He was an adult but this was worse than the principal's office in grade school that time he'd kicked a soccer ball through the auditorium window. It had caught his attention that the degree in a frame behind the desk was a *Juris Doctor* from University of New Mexico. Did that play a part in all this? Had he met this man before?

"Are you comfortable? Did Nancy offer a soft drink or coffee? Maybe water?"

"Yes, she did, but I'm fine, thank you."

Suddenly the judge sat back in his chair. "Do you believe in coincidence?"

Weird. Where was this going? "Probably not. I think things happen for a reason."

"Absolutely. I'd agree with you. In fact, it's been proved to me a number of times in my lifetime. I believe this might be another example."

"Are there more questions as to my background and reasons for being in South Dakota?"

"No, no, nothing like that. I know you are who you say you are. I was in contact with Pueblo tribal authorities in New Mexico and IHS earlier. Identity is not the issue here." The judge leaned forward again but didn't break eye contact. "There's not a good place to start. And I'm going to start at the end and not the beginning for good reason. We can discuss the beginning later."

The judge took a deep breath. "I lost my mother twenty-eight days ago. Covid. She had been a smoker and her lungs were compromised. It was sudden. She was seventy-six and couldn't fight the virus off. Still, it was unexpected. We thought we had taken every precaution—quarantining, total isolation, even curtailing visits from me because I'm exposed to the public. She was sick for five days and then passed after only ten more in the hospital.

"I'm the last of my line, Dr. Pecos. My father was killed in a car accident when I was thirteen. I'm an only child of an only child who married a child with only one brother—in short, there are few of us left, some distant third or fourth cousins but that's about it. My mother was overprotective—what do they call it? A micromanager? She oversaw everything about my life. And yes, I'm unmarried. How could I find a suitable mate who would be acceptable to my mother? I know what that makes me sound like—I had my fun behind her back and never brought a date home. It was easier that way, sidestep her wrath but stay in her good graces." The judge paused to slightly shake his head.

"I live just west of town on a fifty thousand plus acre ranch. My mother inherited it from her father and, now, of course, it's come to me. Have I bored you yet with the litany of my life? Trust me. I'm telling you all this for a reason." The judge opened the folder in front of him.

"After mother passed, I saw to the paperwork—notifications, reading of the will, changing names on deeds of trust—everything that involves the living, in addition to services and graves and markers. And there can be surprises. Trust me, in my business I've seen more than one family torn apart by the indiscretions of a parent or grandparent. Sometimes in death people become someone you'd never suspect them of being. In mother's case there was a safe-deposit box at the bank that I never knew she had. The key was in an envelope with her will. The box was empty but for two letters and two Polaroid photos." The judge slid an envelope across his desk toward Ben, then placed two photos beside it.

Ben leaned forward but he didn't need to get closer. He knew the child in the photos; he recognized the church in the background—he recognized the handwriting addressing the letter. He looked questioningly at the judge.

"Just read. When you finish the letter you have in your hand, I'll give you this one."

Ben made himself take a deep breath before carefully slipping the pages out of their envelope. It was a single sheet of writing and the second sheet was an address and phone number, both belonging to an art gallery in Taos. The letter was addressed to a Mrs. Frances Udahl, Spearfish, South Dakota. The letter was signed Nia Pecos. Ben's mother.

Ben stalled, unfolding the letter by picking up and examining each of the photos. He was five when they were taken, wearing an oversized red knit muffler wound three times around his neck and almost obscuring his face. The cap with fake-fur flaps had leather straps that tied under his chin. It was winter in the Pueblo and if he looked frozen, it was because he felt frozen. He still had the red muffler— one of the last gifts his mother made for him.

The Pueblo church in the background was outlined in snow. Two inches mounded on the crosses, marking graves in front of the church. His mother had borrowed the camera and he remembered her saying, "Now, I have a photo so you'll always be with me." Yeah, sure. She had died six months later.

He smoothed the letter until it lay flattened against the desk. It was handwritten on a page of lined, Big Chief writing tablet paper. The judge had pushed away from his desk and was standing by the only window in the room, his back to Ben. It was an attempt at giving him privacy, Ben thought, and he appreciated the effort. With a deep breath, he started to read.

Mrs. Udahl, I honestly never meant to write this letter. Sometimes things are done that cannot be undone but leave us with consequences that must be addressed. I will simply come right out and say it, you have a grandson. His name is Benson after my father and I gave him my family name of Pecos. I dated your son, Rex, while we were both students at the University of New Mexico. I was forced to drop out of school when my mother became ill and my relationship with Rex suffered when I moved back home to the Pueblo. It was simply too difficult with our respective responsibilities to maintain a relationship. When I realized that I was pregnant, I kept it a secret. Your son was not in a position to take on the challenges of a family. I respected that. I am only writing now because I need your help. I'm asking for assurance that your grandson will be taken care of if anything should happen to me. He's five years old and deserves the kind of life that your son could help him have. I know you would be proud of him— he's bright and creative and mature for his age.

Again, please accept my apologies for the shocking content of my letter. I've let things go far too long. I'm relying on your goodness to help me make the situation right.

With respect,

Nia Pecos

Ben folded the letter and slipped it back into its envelope, putting the two pictures with it. The judge had moved to stand behind his desk with a second letter in his hand.

"I'm not proud of this one. It isn't easy to understand my mother's blind devotion to me. Blind to the point of not stepping outside her own emotions and narrow view of the world to consider the needs of another—in this instance a child. And, yes, there are bigoted overtones. I won't make excuses for her. It was the way she was brought up and taught to believe." He handed a second envelope to Ben.

This time the paper was quality with a matching pink-hued envelope. Ben had a feeling that at one time the two smelled of roses. He knew this letter would be even harder to accept but he opened it and sat back.

My darling son—as the cliché goes, if you're reading this then I have passed from your life. I've chosen to write now because the virus must be viewed as a real threat and we both know that I'm certainly vulnerable. I'm also writing now because I want you to hear these things from me and not be blindsided by strangers. I know your view of the world is different from mine but I believe that you realize how hard I've worked to make you successful and to love you unconditionally. Let me add that no one could have asked for a more loving and supportive son in return. With this said, I ask that you understand why I did not share the letter from Miss Pecos with you. Yes, I have kept a secret for some thirty years. You were destined to be successful, learned in your field, an example of a high achiever meant to lead others. Your career would not have been possible with a marriage to an Indian woman. I know young men must sow their wild oats but choosing this young woman was not very smart of you. Did she try to trick you by becoming pregnant? Force you into doing something that quite frankly might have ruined your chances to be successful?

I actually think not. I really believe that you knew nothing of the pregnancy. I'm afraid her letter and this one are a shock you had no way to expect. Yes, I took action on your behalf and I feel your life has been better for it. What you do now is your own choice but I would hope you pursue your dream of leading our great state. Bear in mind, a governor would not have a woman of color for a wife and a half-breed for a son. Nor would he allow someone to demand money or land that is not his, that he hasn't worked for, by threatening blackmail, for example.

I have feared the worst might happen. I cannot tell you how for years I have flinched at every knock on the door, at every ring of the telephone fearing that a stranger was going to demand what your grandfather left to us—left for us to protect and prosper by. Be careful of threats and someone trying to besmirch your legacy. Politics can be brutal. Every inch of your life will be under a microscope. You must make certain there is nothing for them to find. At this late stage in life, let bygones be bygones. I can think of nothing you would gain by confronting this individual who, I'm assuming, has no idea that you exist. Be smart and careful.

With all my love,

Mother

Ben took his time folding the letter and placing it back in its envelope. It had been a long time since he'd been referred to as a half-breed. Playground taunts from a long time ago still carried the sting of rebuke. He didn't glance at the judge or give him any sign of acknowledgement. The judge's mother, Ben's grandmother, was a bigot. Did he wish that he'd never found out that information? Yeah, probably.

Funny that the judge had asked him if he believed in coincidence because the irony was his own son had been born into the same kind of situation—a pregnancy that was never shared with the father until the child was ten years old. But in that instance Ben was turning a wrong into a right.

"Was she correct in assuming you're still interested in running for governor?"

"My team is in place. This next year is going to be a challenge. I'm stepping away from the bench the last half of the year to dedicate myself fulltime to campaigning."

"And your reaction to 'let bygones be bygones'?"

Ben watched as a muscle twitched along the judge's cheekbone. He was not comfortable with all this, but he was making eye contact. "I'm going to ask you to forget what you've read." He pulled the chair out from behind his desk and sat down, picking up both letters and dropping them in a top drawer.

"Then why did you share the letters?"

"Ego, curiosity—call it whatever you want. You have the right to know what's behind half of the genes contributing to your genetic makeup. And, I wanted to see what that combination looked like. I must say you've done very well. My congratulations on a Ph.D. and your work with Indian Health Service. But you can imagine my shock when just three weeks after discovering the letters, a warrant for your arrest crossed my desk. I don't know how you believe, but the universe sometimes has its own peculiar reasons and ways of doing things."

"Before you shut the door on me, do you want to know that you have a grandson?"

A derisive snort of a laugh and a shake of the head. "Difficult to believe that this could get more complicated— but it just did, didn't it?"

"It doesn't have to be complicated."

"No, it doesn't. All this can be forgotten. We can just go on as before—pretend the letters never came to light."

"Is that truly what you want?"

"I think it would be best for all involved. People are strange. For one thing, they can be unforgiving. Even a whiff of my ignoring a son for over thirty years—whether I knew about you or not—is pages of fodder for the newspapers. The opposing political party would consider finding out this information a coup. And I wouldn't come out looking like a champion. This is a state of seven indigenous tribes; I need their vote. I don't need them knowing that I abandoned one of their own. Trust me, lack of knowledge would not be an acceptable excuse to them. Please do not share this information—not with anyone. I believe that would be best for both of us."

"Then you have my word." Ben got up and turned toward the door.

"Dr. Pecos? Thank you. I appreciate your honoring my request. I sincerely believe that this is the best path for both of us."

Ben nodded but didn't turn back around. He opened the office door and walked to the foyer. So far, the anger he felt was under wraps but he didn't trust it for long. Red Bull didn't look happy about being kept waiting. Sheriff Sterling had taken off earlier, leaving his reservation counterpart to twiddle his thumbs.

"That must have been some questioning. I take it you passed?"

"Yeah. He just wanted to make sure I am who I say I am. And then he had to tell me about an upcoming run for governor."

"Well, the important thing is the warrant's been erased.

I was afraid he'd changed his mind. He isn't exactly known as the red man's friend. There's been more than one land dispute over the years. Let's get going."

Chapter 12

The ride back to the Rez was a quiet one. Red Bull was a good driver but pushed the speed limit and tailgated. Ben wasn't a back-seat driver and kept his opinions to himself. Besides, he welcomed the time to replay what had happened in the judge's office and sort through his feelings. Had he ever thought he'd find his father? Had he ever looked? No, and no.

Frankly he wasn't sure how he felt. Or even how he was supposed to feel. Maybe it would be best to just pretend the letters had never existed. He was glad his mother didn't know the rest of the story. She had counted on help that never materialized. She had known when she wrote to the judge's mother that her health was in jeopardy. The slight to his own mother, the callousness of the judge's mother … these were tough things to get past.

Red Bull slowed finally, stopping in front of his sister's house, now Ben's temporary living quarters. "Any chance I could run by after work and share our community plans for the new adult programs? We're enlarging the community center to include some classrooms and a lecture hall. I'd like your input. We'll break ground after the first of the year—if our proposal gets funded, I should add."

"Come on by. Bring a copy of the proposal and a projected budget, if you have one."

Red Bull grinned. "You see, that's where you come in. We need the help of someone who's done this sort of thing before—someone who can help us write one."

"I'm your man. And thanks for the ride to Deadwood. Believe me, I'm glad the afternoon was successful."

A quick handshake and Ben got out of the pickup, watching Red Bull pull a U-turn and head back toward the reservation offices.

Nathan had left a note reminding Ben that he would be having dinner at the boys' camp and would also be spending the night at the teepee village. Ben was pleased and wished that Zac could have had the same opportunity.

He was still mulling over what the judge had shared with him. Would he tell anyone? Only Julie. He didn't believe in keeping secrets from her. And this was a big one. There was also a part of him that wanted to suggest a DNA test. Just to be certain. And maybe as time allowed, the judge could give him family information. It was just such an odd feeling to have someone want to sweep his very existence under the rug.

There were other questions that Ben had always

wondered about—was the judge little more than a one-night stand for his mother? Or were there real feelings between them? At one time had his mother expected the judge to marry her? As a teenager, he'd queried his grandmother but always thought maybe she had embellished the story of his parents to make being an orphan more acceptable. What little his grandmother had told him about his father when he questioned her, supported the judge's story—a fellow student, a serious romance that probably wasn't going to go anywhere, doomed by a mixing of cultures. Ben picked up his phone.

"Got some time?" Julie sounded out of breath.

"Perfect timing. I just left work."

He filled her in on the case of mistaken identity and having to meet at the judge's office to erase the warrant.

"You're lucky that the judge acted so quickly. He must have immediately realized that there had been an error."

"That wasn't all he realized. Julie, what if I told you that I found my father?"

"What are you saying? The judge knows your biological father?"

"Yeah, because it's him." The stunned silence gave Ben a moment to take a breath. "He had proof." Ben shared as much of the two letters as he could remember verbatim.

"Inexcusable. What his mother did was criminal even. I'm so glad your mother never knew the callousness, the racism of that woman. But don't you need proof? I mean more than two letters, one written over thirty years ago? And it isn't just for you anymore, there's Zac and the children we plan to have. There has to be a DNA test."

"I agree. That would be conclusive proof but I trust my instincts. I believe the man is my father. I'm not even sure what I'll do with the information. I gave my word that I wouldn't say anything. So, asking him to take a test is out of the question. I know he suspects I'll try to lay claim to some of his fortune. You know, the wronged son wanting restitution. Did I mention that he's running for governor? He has good reason to want me to stay quiet."

"Then we'll just have to be sneaky. You know, you could just take something from his office that had his DNA on it. I mean he wouldn't have to know."

"Not sure I want to drive back over to Deadwood just to rummage through the trash hoping to find an empty Coke can. And steal something from his office? Hey, I just got my freedom back. I don't want to jeopardize it again. Plus, I'd need some reason to show up there."

"Turn it into a history lesson for Nathan. And 'borrow' a pen or pencil—do it legitimately."

"You may be on to something. I'll give it some thought. Are you sure you're in the right business? Maybe I should be watching you more carefully." He got the laugh he expected. The banter felt good. He missed the comfortable camaraderie they had. She was the helpmate he wanted—needed actually. She'd probably never realize how much he hated being separated.

The call stretched to over two hours. Ben spent the rest of their time on the phone by outlining what materials he'd like her to send. There was no reason to reinvent the wheel when setting up alcohol outreach programs. He had plans that had already been given a stamp of approval by IHS. And he could share a budget that had already been blessed by the tribal biggies. He was pleased that he could be of help and if all went well, he'd start interviewing personnel in the upcoming week and try to find a permanent base of operations that could be used until the new construction was finished.

He requested that Julie send a copy of the budget first. It had been approved for the Navajo reservation when setting up community outreach programs, and Ben spent the next couple hours tailoring it to Pine Ridge. It was always incidentals that killed proposals or left them underfunded. Things like rent, if they needed to use facilities not owned by the tribe, unanticipated utility bills, travel expenses, classroom materials to include laptops and software—these were often overlooked.

It was a little tedious working on his phone but he'd stop by the tribal offices in the morning and see if he could borrow a computer before having copies printed out. He couldn't believe that he hadn't brought his laptop, but then he really had thought that the trip would be a vacation.

He had just finished a PB&J washed down with milk when there was a knock at the door. It was six-thirty already and Red Bull was on the doorstep.

"Come in."

"I can't stay. I'm going to leave some papers with you— sort of where the tribal committee is stuck on putting a proposal together. Maybe you could take a look and we could meet in the next day or so?"

"Sounds good. My wife forwarded the budget from the Navajo project. I think there's a lot that will be helpful to Pine Ridge. Seriously, it doesn't make sense to start from scratch. I'm glad I came along when I did."

"Me, too." Red Bull seemed about to say something else and continued to stand just inside the door.

"Do you have time for coffee? I just put a fresh pot on."

"Yeah, that sounds good."

"Grab a chair. I'll be just a couple minutes."

Ben pointed to the small dining room table just outside the kitchenette. Seven hundred square feet total living space would cramp a family but for one it was almost luxurious—small, but comfortable. It was preferable to living in their tent for the next three weeks. He poured two mugs of coffee, set them on the table and returned with a carton of half and half.

"Sugar?"

"No, this is fine. I know you're going to wonder why I'm including you in what I'm about to share, but I have a conscience. I take responsibility for your being here and I feel I need to give you a heads-up because I truthfully don't know what to expect. We're supposedly in the path of a group of demonstrators—maybe more like a mob of protesters—who see the tribes in the Dakotas and neighboring Minnesota as standing in the way of progress. We've successfully shut down the proposed pipeline from Canada across this region citing the disruption to sacred tribal lands once. Now the current administration has started it up again. It hasn't made us popular. Thanks to the pandemic, jobs have been lost everywhere. But because of the size of the industry that this affects, we're seen as the bad guys. Taking jobs, killing the white man's chances to be successful … you get the picture." Red Bull took a moment to doctor his coffee. "I wouldn't mention this—wouldn't even think it was worth mentioning if I didn't know that this mob will be armed."

"Armed? Are you certain?"

"Yeah. Someone has paid the big bucks to not only organize the protest but to also provide firearms and probably pay the protesters. Oil is big money. I'm not pointing a finger at the industry but at this point I'd say they are a prime suspect. They certainly have the most to gain."

"I hope you're wrong. I hope the group is peaceful."

"Here's the proof that I'm not. Last week the body of a young Hispanic man was found dead on a back road at the edge of reservation land not too far from here. Someone made his death look like the result of participation in a Sun Dance."

"Why?"

"Not sure I have an answer, other than the death was supposed to look like a Native was the perpetrator. I've been told that the man was a gunrunner. The arms I mentioned are being provided for the group by being smuggled in from Mexico. The man murdered was high up in a cartel headquartered just across the border—at least, that's the scuttlebutt. I'm not sure I trust it, but I'm not going to overlook it. Either way that could be dangerous."

"Sounds well organized. Are you working with Sheriff Sterling?"

"That's where my problem lies."

"How so?"

Red Bull stirred his coffee and added more cream. "I'm dating his daughter and the man killed is her former husband. You can guess who my informant is. And I'm asking for you to keep all this just between us. I don't want to put Micki in any more danger than she already is. The guy was stalking her, scaring her to death, and then he shows up dead with the remnants of bone needles in his chest like a dancer. It wouldn't take much for people to jump to the conclusion that I was involved, if you get what I'm trying to say."

"Yeah, puts you in a bad spot."

"So, the less her old man knows, the better. Mac's divorced from Micki's mother and the family isn't close—Mac didn't even know that Micki had been married. It was short-lived—under a year. Micki felt used by the guy, thought he was angling for a green card. I think he was trying to establish some kind of base in this part of the state. Other than her being here, it's not clear why he'd chosen Spearfish. But that begs the question of who would want him out of the way, and why."

"Tricky."

"Yeah, and dangerous all the way around. I don't want a modern-day Wounded Knee reenactment. By the way, do you carry?"

"You're the second person this past year who thinks I should. But, no, I don't have a permit."

"I think I'd like to remedy that. I'll loan you my boot gun. I don't carry it anymore."

"I'm not sure I'm comfortable with having a gun around Nathan. He's a great kid but even the good ones can do things they shouldn't. It would just give me something to worry about."

"Good point. Give it some thought. If you change your mind, let me know."

"By the way, he loves camp. Thanks for getting him in. I'm glad I don't have to worry about where he is or what he's doing."

"He impressed a couple elders with his horse knowledge. He has talent with animals. I sense his life hasn't been easy. I'm glad he's with you. I believe we'd have far less drug use if young men had successful Native models to look up to."

"I think you're right, and thanks for the compliment."

Chapter 13

Mac leaned back in his office chair—mostly wood, swivel base, arms worn smooth, vintage 1940-something. Nobody ever threw anything out in this burg. Sometimes he felt he was just one step away from being replaced by a mannequin so that his office could be part of the yearly Old West Tour.

At least the place was quiet. He needed to reflect on what exactly had happened earlier that afternoon with the Indian kid who hadn't been kidnapped. For one thing, Mac had dodged a bullet. At least he hadn't embarrassed himself by jumping to conclusions, not following rules and locking up a Native—one who held a pretty prominent position, it seemed, wherever he was from. At least he had federal connections. Damned if you don't, but more often damned if you do out here—no matter what the situation might be. It had been close. Sometimes it was like walking on a field of eggshells.

The reservation had its set of rules and he had his. Who would have thought that a child, an adult, and a blue SUV could match an Alert so exactly and yet be completely innocent? Luckily for him it had been easy to prove their innocence and hopefully his careful but diligent research had gotten the respect of Judge Udahl. Doing things by the book was the only thing he demanded of law enforcement in his county.

So, one mystery solved. He now had to address the rest of what was on his plate. And that was a lot of unknowns. Were the paid demonstrators still on their way? Who had organized them and who was paying them? Where were they headed? One thing he did know was that he better be prepared. Waiting to see the numbers would be too late. He needed to add about four good men to his crew for starters. And maybe have a couple more on standby.

He pushed aside the thought that the demonstrators might be armed. Who would they intimidate? Or worse yet, harm? That seemed just too far-fetched. Maybe there'd be a group sit-in, or a demonstrator or two who decided to block the highway by stretching out across the median, but that would be easily remedied.

What was puzzling was the fact that the body of the Hispanic man found last week had been claimed, released from the county morgue. A woman showed up with what proved to be correct paperwork to ship the body to Mexico. Purporting to be his sister, the costly transfer was apparently paid for by family.

There had been too much going on for Mac to spend the necessary time on the case. If the body had been released, foul play must have been ruled out. He hadn't even gotten a copy of the toxicology report. He had some checking up to do.

He quickly penciled in a reminder on his desk pad to call the coroner's office in the morning. Good old pencil and paper. He didn't care if it did date him. He knew where information was and he wouldn't run the risk of losing it.

He'd given Sally the afternoon off with a warning to keep her phone with her. He hadn't shared information about the demonstrators. If he could find a way not to use her as part of the manpower buildup he was organizing, he'd take advantage of it. He was thinking of putting her in charge of the office and leaving her behind if he got called to intervene in any action. He had a hard time putting women on the front lines of battle—armed or not.

And if he wanted to be honest, he didn't trust her with a gun. She was just a little too eager, too 'shoot first, ask questions later,' kind of oriented. And, simply, she would be a distraction if allowed to be part of the police power that might be needed. At least for him.

He was about ready to give it up for the day. He'd left messages on the voicemail of the four men who often helped out as deputies, asking that they give him a call in the morning and he'd fill them in on particulars. He wasn't going to leave lengthy phone messages and have to repeat himself four times. This was the dinner hour; he suspected each of the men might be in transit home from their day jobs or they'd already picked up family and had gone out to eat. Before he could get out the door, Sally walked in.

"Forgot my eyeliner. Be back in a minute." She walked

past him down a short hallway.

At least they had a private bathroom. It appeared to be an afterthought, squeezed as it was into the corner next to their conference area and breakroom. A sink and a toilet, no shower. He'd been promised an update to the arrangement. More than once he'd had to keep someone overnight who needed a good scrub-down with soap and water. A couple of them had challenged a half bottle of Febreze and still left an odor of unwashed body behind when they bonded out.

But he'd given up on getting a shower. Too expensive and he didn't want to appear demanding in an election year. Plus, at this point it was more Sally's room than his. He never said anything about the array of cosmetics strewn across the back of the sink and littered across the toilet's tank. He just looked the other way.

"Boy, do I have some juicy gossip for you." Coming back into the room, she paused at his desk.

"You know me, I'm not much on believing whatever's going around. Some people don't have anything better to do with their time."

"Oh, you'll want to hear this. And I know it's true."

"Okay, give." It didn't hurt to humor her a little.

"Your daughter is dating Officer Red Bull."

"That's bullshit. I'd suggest you don't repeat what you know is a lie." Micki and Red Bull? No way. That shrimp? Micki was tiny, maybe five foot one, he might seem tall to her, but still ... a man's man needed to be six feet to command attention and respect. No, his Micki wouldn't be interested in some sawed off—

"So, I suppose seeing 'em kissing doesn't count? Just good friends smooching the hell out of one another like all good friends do."

He didn't like the sarcasm in her voice. "For one thing, he's ..." Mac paused.

"An Indian? That's a little racist, isn't it?"

"I was going to say forty or better in age. That's a little old for Micki, don't you think?" He ignored the racist comment; she knew better.

"Mac, your daughter is thirty-four. Some relationship experts would say that's a perfect age spread. Anyway, I've got to get going. Have a good evening. Glad I could bring you current with recent community activity." A forced laugh. "You know you'd be stuck in the dark forever if you didn't have me."

Mac bit his lip but only waved as she waltzed out the door. Superiority complexes in dumb people pushed his buttons big time. But what was he going to do, fire her? That wasn't even an option in a town this size. It pissed him off that no one had told him; that it was Miss Know-It-All who broke the news about his own daughter. Debbie had ample chances—even Micki could have clued him in. Oh well, he knew now. And he wasn't sure it'd change anything. Best he didn't dwell on it and just get on with business.

He put a sticky note on the phone to call the coroner in the morning. Notes in two places should keep him from forgetting. He needed a sense of closure in the case and it already felt as though he had been overlooked. But, it was getting too late in the afternoon to catch the man in his office.

Mac just had to trust that there wouldn't be questions. No Feds coming in late in the game, for whatever reason, to demand answers. He probably had nothing to worry about. Jake Tully played things by the book; he wouldn't release a body if murder was suspected. Still, he would have expected the man to give him a call either way. He stretched and yawned. It was time to get take-home and watch some football. Who cared if fans weren't in the stands, he didn't miss the bodies as long as the noise was amplified.

* * *

Morning kept coming quicker and quicker. Sun was already peeking in the east window of his townhouse. Eleven hundred square feet, all his, and Mac called it home. It was in a new subdivision at the south end of town, about a block from the old high school. It wasn't anything special and he wasn't sure that its appeal didn't rest solely on its being new and clean. Could he help it if he liked fresh paint and new tile with clean grout?

He tossed a Jimmy Dean sausage and cheese breakfast biscuit in the microwave, poured a glass of juice, and turned on the coffee maker. Seven-thirty. A full hour past his usual up-an'-at-'em wake-up time. He hated a change in routine—planned or unplanned. He was just a creature of habit and fought off terms like stodgy and stick-in-the-mud—even if they vaguely fit. Last night's game had been good and had gone into overtime so an hour's extra shut-eye should be allowed.

He called Jake Tully from home and caught him on a coffee break. Barely eight-thirty and the man was on break already? He must spend the night in the morgue.

"You were on my list to call. The virus has managed, unfortunately, to keep me busy. But here's what I got.

Report came back that death was insulin induced."

"Insulin? Sounds like health issues and not murder."

"Yeah, and it would seem to support his being part of an actual Sun Dance. Four to five days without food or water and then a shot of insulin? I'd expect the same consequences. His sister verified that he had health issues, but my Spanish isn't the best. There wasn't any way to detain releasing the body. Hey, look at it this way, you're not involved in some drawn-out, probably dead end, investigation."

Mac had to agree with that. It was a far cleaner ending than he'd anticipated. But if the man had been involved in a Sun Dance why hadn't Red Bull fessed up? There was no way that a ceremony could be held on his reservation and he not know about it. More questions. Maybe they should just be ignored. He needed to know when to simplify his life and leave well enough alone. It wasn't as if Debbie hadn't yammered on and on about boundaries and how people used him. Just another reason they weren't together. He thanked the coroner and hung up.

Chapter 14

Pine Ridge Reservation

Ben couldn't say no. Not to an invitation for a supper in the teepee village, along with an afternoon of exhibits and events to showcase Lakota life as it used to be—presented by fifteen pre-teen and barely teenage boys with their mentors. Apparently, once a month the camp issued invitations to family members and friends to join them in a feast day celebration. Nathan was demonstrating riding techniques with two other boys his age and he had shot one of the rabbits that was part of the main course's stew, with a bow and arrow.

Ben was impressed and thrilled that Nathan was making the most of this unique opportunity. Rules were simple—no cell phones, no cars within one mile of camp, no recording devices and/or cameras, no food or drink other than what was provided, and no animals domestic or otherwise unless it was your only means of transportation to and from the site. Once again, outdoor activities left mask-wearing up to the individuals but weren't encouraged in the fresh air. Stabling for horses was provided on a first come, first served basis but involved some work. The horse's owner would be given a schedule to help in feeding his, as well as any other mount, and contribute time to mucking out the stable area in addition to pasturing animals during the day, retrieving and bedding them down at night. It was a good lesson in responsibility, Ben thought.

He had promised to meet Nathan at the outskirts of the camp promptly at one that afternoon. A mile wasn't that far to walk and Ben had to admit he was enjoying the fresh air. He needed to do this more often. The day was so clear he could see the eight teepees in the distance for most of the walk.

If he remembered his Native history, teepee was a Lakota word meaning 'they live there.' Thanks to the horse, teepees became the first mobile homes. And they were a lot bigger than most people thought. When he last talked with Nathan, six other boys shared one teepee. Even with a fire pit in the center, there seemed to be ample room. Women were usually the ones in charge of dismantling, moving, and setting up the conical houses. Thirty minutes to dismantle and thirty minutes to reconstruct—Ben found those times hard to believe but they seemed well-documented. Buffalo hides scraped smooth and various sized saplings were the staples and could be added to a travois for travel. It made a nice contrast to the Hogans and Pueblo apartment-style houses that he and Nathan were familiar with.

"Ben, over here." Nathan's voice carried in the still air.

Ben waved and cut across a grassy ditch to join Nathan on a sandy rise. "Great day for a celebration."

"I think you're going to like the stuff we've planned. Come on, we're going to go this way."

There were already several families gathered in the center circle formed by the teepees—members of each family were together but distanced from the others. Wooden benches had been placed theater-style, a semi-circle that took up seventy-five percent of the center space.

"Any place in particular I should sit?"

"No, you're tall enough, maybe toward the back?"

"Good thinking."

"There's going to be a bunch of little kids but they'll mostly sit on the ground in front. I've gotta go now but I'll come get you and we'll eat there." Nathan pointed at the third teepee to the left of the open area. "That's where I stay."

Nathan walked to the teepee that was squarely facing the semi-circle of benches and disappeared inside but not before giving Ben a wave and a big smile.

Even Red Bull was there, walking the perimeter of the circle with three other men—each wearing a khaki shirt with tribal insignia on the sleeve, and each seemingly lost in thought. Ben wondered why they were here. There were certainly no cars to maneuver into parking spots and he'd bet money on there not being any brawls to break up. Families watching their sons, nephews, and cousins present tribal history made up a benign event, one to be applauded and appreciated, not disrupted with rude or inappropriate behavior. Ben had barely finished that thought when he heard his name ring out.

"Pecos." Red Bull was motioning to him to join the small group of law enforcers at the end of the last row, opposite to where he sat.

Ben excused himself as he worked his way to the end of his row of seated spectators and walked up the center aisle to the back. "Hope you're here to enjoy the show and this is not official business." Ben shook Red Bull's hand, then introduced himself and bumped elbows with the three men standing beside Red Bull. What a weird gesture of greeting.

"Me, too. But intel has it that we might be in for a little trouble sooner than I thought—if not today then in a day or so, the stuff I mentioned last night."

"Here? *On* the reservation? I guess I was expecting demonstrations to be out on the state roads—blocking interstate travel, maybe picketing the capitol, whatever it would take to raise awareness."

"Someone posted flyers around several towns in the area yesterday. Stopping *progress* seemed to be a rallying cry. Just more finger-pointing at the Natives. But progress? Why would indigenous people want months of strangers trampling across the reservation—maybe years, if you add in the upkeep of a pipeline. We're taking a stand for a centuries-old way of life, a fragile way of life, and no one's listening. I think Natives are wearing a bullseye on their backs."

Red Bull paused to direct the three deputies to patrol a half-mile radius beyond the teepees. "In fact, I'm pleased this camp will keep some of our youth busy. I don't need heroes. I have a healthy appreciation of what guns can do—especially in the hands of hot-heads."

"I agree."

"Anyway, please remember, if you see or hear anything that doesn't exactly ring true, call me. Here's my cell number." Red Bull handed Ben a card. "And I have a handgun for you. I left it at the office. If you change your mind about carrying, stop by in the morning and ask the secretary to get the package with your name on it off my desk. Consider it a loaner; I'd feel better if you had it."

A call to take their seats put a stop to any further conversation, and Ben walked back to his after assuring Red Bull he'd keep an eye out. It was more than just a little worrisome, and yet hard to believe that danger was so close by in this idyllic setting. Suddenly the audience quieted. A man approached the center of the semi-circle. He stopped about ten feet in front of the rows of benches, now filled with people, and began in his native Lakota Sioux language.

"*Hau*." Ben guessed the man had just said 'welcome.' The audience answered almost as one with two words that probably meant 'thank you.' Ben found himself relieved that the speaker then continued in English. As on other reservations, the native language was not a known entity for everyone—especially not the young.

There were no programs, but the outline of performances as explained by the narrator covered five storytelling events. Then there would be a break with refreshments, served behind the second teepee, and finally demonstrations of prowess with a bow and arrow, horseback riding, and what was billed as 'a window into the old ways.' This last was to include preparation of hides, cooking native dishes, and the making of weaponry.

Ben glanced at the audience and saw that it was made up mostly of children. What a learning opportunity. Two individuals wore badges identifying themselves as State

Historical Society members. When the narrator had finished introducing the program, the flap of the center teepee was pushed aside and five young men carrying stools moved to sit at the back of the semi-circle. One set his stool in a row with the others but moved to stand in the center. Nathan sat on a stool closest to the speaker.

"*Wowacintanka*." Ben noticed some in the audience solemnly nodded. But not to leave out those guests who did not speak the Lakota language, the young man translated. "To persist, to strive in spite of difficulties. That is our camp slogan. We are learning to bring honor to our people—to solve problems, not make them."

Then he paused after this introduction to hand out printed sheets to those sitting at the ends of the rows of benches. "Please, take one and pass the others to those sitting next to you. Thank you for your assistance. You'll see the presentations listed by topic and directions as to where they are being held. It will help you choose what is of most interest to you."

Ben glanced at the one-page program. The opening part would cover Lakota history—flesh and blood leaders who had a permanent place in the history of America. Then there would be several tales from the spiritual world. Calf Woman and the tribe's beginning, spirits to be embraced and those to be feared. Interesting that Nathan appeared to offer a comparison of deities from the Navajo and present a common ground. He would follow a discussion of the Lakota flute-maker and compare him to Kokopelli, perhaps the most well-known Southwest Kachina and another flute-player. Ben was impressed. It wasn't easy joining a new group and offering to take a leadership role. Nathan was mature for almost thirteen. His grandmother was right; he should go on to study law.

The young man who spoke first did so with reverence. The leaders he introduced were almost household names: Sitting Bull, Crazy Horse, Geronimo, Cochise, Chief Joseph, Red Cloud, Pontiac ... the list was lengthy and all Lakota Natives. The speaker then gave a very modern twist to his presentation. He introduced the ongoing story of the world's largest monument—a long-haired rider sitting on horseback carved completely out of granite—which, to date, has the distinction of being the slowest in the world to complete. Located in the Black Hills, it was begun in 1948 and estimated at the time to be completed in thirty years. That had somehow stretched to over seventy and it was still far from finished. Ben marveled at any art that was designed to be 563 feet high and 641 feet long.

"The unfinished statue has sparked controversy." The young presenter then referred to his notes before continuing. "Natives say the emphasis has been on the troubles surrounding the sculpture, not on its very reason for being, which is to honor the man it represents. Crazy Horse was a leader in the Battle of Little Bighorn, a great victory against the US Army. Yet he never sought praise or celebration for his deeds. He never flaunted his accomplishments. He was entitled to wear the emblems of success in battle, eagle feathers, but he seldom did. He dressed plainly; he was truly a man of humility. Would he have wanted a gigantic replica carved out of a mountain in his name? Many people think not. Will our children and grandchildren see Thunderhead Mountain or the shadowy unrecognizable face of a forefather roughly shaped by dynamite and bulldozers?"

The young man concluded with, "We have so many

things to be proud of. We must never let those from the outside diminish our great deeds or great leaders. We are Lakota."

The audience clapped and called out in support. Ben looked around as over half of those seated were now standing, continuing to show their support and praise. What a rousing way to start.

The next speaker calmed the group down by literally lighting a small campfire near the center of the packed dirt, make-believe stage. "My stories are best enjoyed as my ancestors have shared them for hundreds of years—in the open, around a campfire. That is where I first learned how everything in my world has a spirit. A winter storm, the wind, a sapling, a blade of grass—all live through their spirits. The stories told me how I was to grow up, what was important, how I would become a man to be listened to, where I would find strength and where I would not. And I didn't have to try to learn everything at once, pack my memory with detail because I could hear these stories, listen to my favorites many times throughout my life. I've chosen one of those favorites to share with you today."

The young man moved his stool closer to the campfire. It was so quiet—as if the audience were breathing together, a soft breath in/breath out punctuated only by the occasional crackling of the resin from pine branches as they caught fire and sparked upward, exploding in a dozen pinpoints of light. Before he began, the presenter opened the book in his lap and carefully and slowly turned a few pages before inserting a slip of paper as a bookmark.

"I want to tell you the story of how our tribe came to possess music—music made by a flute. Then my friend Nathan Yazzi from New Mexico will share the Southwest's story of Kokopelli—the humpbacked flute player of his tribe, the Navajo, and Pueblo tribes in the area."

The young man looked out over the audience and smiled shyly. "These stories date back a thousand years or more and have been kept alive by their being told again and again. Stories are explanations early people have of what happens in their lives—what makes things happen in their world. Was it a tornado or the Black Giant that roared through a village, killing people and animals, destroying homes and food supplies? We have many deities—spirits that we pay homage to—ones that keep us safe, ones that entertain us. Many tribes believe in tricksters, clowns who usually mean no harm. Coyotes or rabbits who might hide things from us, cause confusion or lead us to embarrass ourselves."

He stopped and reached into a large canvas bag he had set beside his stool and pulled out a wooden flute. "When they were children, Cloud made a promise to Dawn Woman. He would be her husband. But as an adult, Dawn Woman's father accepted the gifts of Hollow Horn and gave his daughter as a bride to this man. Cloud was heartbroken but what was done could not be undone.

"To rid his body of pain, Cloud ran trying to shed the hurt, faster and faster until he had no more breath and fell to the earth collapsing beneath a tree. It was here he heard the mournful sound that seemed like his own heart crying out. It was a voice sent to soothe him. It would grow louder as the wind picked up, then subside as a gust dropped to a light breeze, then it disappeared completely at nightfall. Curious, he climbed up into the cedar tree above him. A branch, riddled by woodpeckers hunting the worms inside, was hollow, long dead, but it was the wind in these holes that had made the sound of his pining heart. The branch broke off easily in his hands and he carried it down the tree to sit with it below. If there was no wind, why not his breath? He experimented by closing some of the holes in the tubular piece of wood with his fingers, and opening others all while he breathed into it. The sound of his mourning heart filled the air. He called it *Hokagapi*, 'to make a voice'."

At this point the young man began to play his flute. The air was suddenly filled with a lilting melody that seemed to drift over the heads of the audience and hang there.

Ben glanced around. The children were enraptured. There was a power in storytelling that never failed to draw people to it. Storytelling was not new. But a modern world no longer relied upon the tradition of oral transmission alone. Using imagination and finally pictures, it was man, centuries later, who wrote them down and even played them on large and small screens to the delight of children and adults throughout the world, telling stories that in the modern day might not otherwise be shared. Ben would bet there wasn't a child in front of him who could not name ten Disney characters. He hoped their memories were as good with tribal stories from the past.

The presenter continued his story. "The story of Cloud and Dawn Woman had a happy ending. Two young people who realized their true love for each other. Dawn Woman professed her love and asked Cloud to bring joy to their union by asking his flute to play happy music in celebration. What resulted was a joyous song of life."

The young storyteller bowed slightly toward his listeners and after one last lilting song, which rose on the air suspended over those gathered in front of him, he acknowledged the cheers of the audience.

He stood, putting his flute back into the bag beside him and introduced the next speaker.

Nathan entered the semicircle carrying a life-sized cardboard cutout of *Kokopelli* painted in desert-bright colors of greens and blues, the feathers on his head bending backward as the figure leaned forward, the end of a flute in his mouth and both hands grasping the instrument as if he were playing a tune. The first speaker stepped forward to stand behind the figure and hold it, facing the audience.

"In the religion of my people, *Kokopelli*, the flute player, is a God of harvest, a God of plenty, even the God of fertility. Some believe that he chases away the winter and brings the spring with his song. My people have told his stories for more than three thousand years. As God of the harvest, some believe that the hump between his shoulders contains seeds, the essence of plants that will prosper and provide for all. He spreads joy with his song, but he is also a trickster. He hides things and sometimes makes beautiful women fall in love with him."

Nathan continued to present stories of *Kokopelli* before ending by joining his helper in a brief flute duet.

Ben was impressed. The two young men did a great job of storytelling and accompanying the stories with actual song. At intermission Ben made certain that both presenters knew how good he thought they were.

"Do you think you could help me later?" Nathan was finishing a Coke and carefully placed the empty plastic bottle in the trash bag beside the food table.

"Sure, what do you need?"

"I guess it depends on whether you can ride a horse."

"This is either a joke or a test of some sort?" Ben

wasn't sure which but Nathan had his attention.

Nathan laughed. "Nope, it's an honest question. I need to bring four horses down from the pasture later. We'll ride up to get them on a couple horses that are kept here. We never leave them in the pasture at night—too many wild animals."

"I'll help."

"Can you ride bareback?"

"Hey, now you're pushing it." Ben was laughing but fingers were crossed that this time Nathan was joking.

"Yeah, thought I might be. I've got a western saddle that'll work. Meet me at the barn over there when this is over."

Nathan was pointing to a corral and dark green barn with a slate roof behind the circle of teepees. "See you in a little while."

Chapter 15

Pine Ridge Reservation, South Dakota

The program had been a resounding success. Ben had a feeling that it would become a staple of the boys' camp if it wasn't already. He was actually looking forward to some time with Nathan, and an excuse to get away and see more of the Pine Ridge landscape was perfect. Tomorrow morning he'd be in the office and might not get another chance to enjoy the environment. He was going to try to not embarrass Nathan but it had been years since he'd been on a horse. Was it like riding a bicycle? Once learned, you never forgot? He could only hope. Nathan had saddled a good-sized buckskin gelding and left him tied beside the barn. It was evident that Ben would be the only one using a saddle.

"Ready?" Nathan walked out of the barn leading a smaller, Appaloosa mare with only a saddle blanket thrown across her back. At least, she was wearing a bridle. "We're going to take the road for a part of the way, then cross a couple fields and follow a stream to the end pasture. It's pretty out here."

Ben nodded; pretty didn't quite capture it. Fall made contrasting colors stand out against the green and gold of grasses and trees. This really had to be the best time to visit the countryside. The buckskin was well mannered and held still while Ben mounted. Nathan jumped on the back of the mare, lying cross-wise before throwing a leg over her back and pulling himself upright, and they were off. The quiet, broken only by the calls of birds, and the scuffling sound of hooves on the sandy road, was almost something he could feel and pull around him like a jacket. Nathan smiled but didn't interrupt as the solitude settled over them. Perfect weather, perfect time of day—Ben hadn't even realized how good it would feel to get away from civilization for a while. Even the horses seemed to enjoy leaving the barn.

For a while they played name that bird; grackles and cowbirds and wrens and small finches were pointed out equally as adeptly by Ben as by Nathan.

"Where did you learn the names of wild birds?" Ben was amazed.

"I thought I'd impress you but to be truthful, we had a workshop on local birds. Some are endangered like the chestnut-collared longspur."

"So, you like it here?"

"Yeah, a lot. Some of the elders and teachers are putting together a ceremony for next week. I'll get to see

Sun Dancing."

"Sure you want to do that?"

"Our whole class is going. You have to be at least twelve."

Ben could see that his thirteenth birthday in three weeks set him apart. "You'll have to let me know what you think. Remember Red Bull's scars from taking part in the ceremony? I'm glad you'll be able to see it. It's an important part of Lakota culture."

Conversation seemed unnecessary. Mostly they simply rode, letting the horses pick their own pace. The grass was often uneven; grazed down in some areas and, due to the lateness in the year, wouldn't be growing back. But the colors of gold and orange, here and there red, outlined the trees and bushes along the trail. The changing of the seasons always affected his mood. Ben thought fall was his favorite time of year. And spring? That time of renewal and promise? He wondered if in all of Florida there were deciduous trees. He was afraid it would take some getting used to, this new home, and reminded himself to call Julie later that evening.

They saw the four horses standing at the far side of the pasture as they crested a grassy rise. Then they saw the backhoe. Like an unwieldly, mechanical, green bug of some sort, maybe a metal praying mantis. The thing looked out of place in the pristine meadow.

"I've never seen that up here before."

"It's not a part of the reservation's road-clearing machinery?"

"They've got some tractors and stuff but most of it's old. Wonder who that guy is?"

Stepping down from the backhoe's cab, a man, shirtless

and bare to the waist with long black hair flowing loose over his shoulders, waved and called out, "*Hola.*"

"*Hola.*" Ben answered.

"Is that guy Mexican?" Nathan waved. "Do you know Spanish?"

"Another five words and we're probably at the end of my vocabulary. Let's ride over and see what he's up to."

As they approached, the man put down the wrench he was carrying and stepped away from the backhoe. He held out his hand. When Ben hesitated to shake hands, the man quickly withdrew his. "Aiiii, *con permiso*, I am forgetting the illness. *Me llamo* Carlos. *Soy de Mexico. Habla Espanol?*"

"*Poquito. No mucho.* English?"

"Si—yes, but no much."

"I'm Ben and this is Nathan. We've come to get the horses." Ben gestured at the four now staring at their new pasture mates.

"*Mucho* wild animals here at night—lion and the *oso* ... bear, no? And wolf, the *lobo?* It is good to take horses home."

"Do you live on the reservation?" Nathan asked.

"No, no, I work for El Jefe, the judge man." Carlos flung out an arm and pointed over his shoulder. "I live at his ranch."

"But this land belongs to the Lakota." Nathan added, "What are you doing with that?" He pointed at the backhoe. Ben was worried that Nathan was sounding a little overprotective but Carlos just shrugged.

"The judge, he is good to the *indios.* He, all the time, helping with food or jobs. Ah, you know how they say, I scratch yours and you scratch mine."

Ben was tempted to jump in and add 'back' but the

word seemed understood. There didn't seem to be any further explanation forthcoming, so Ben added, "May I ask what you are doing today?"

"The mother of El Jefe died last month. He is building a, *como se dice*, memory place?"

"A memorial."

"Si, yes, a memorial. She had many gardens, some flowers, some with things to eat. One had a pond with fishes. I will take new soil to give life to gardens. I will mix with the horse poop. The gardens will honor her."

"I see." He thought he saw Nathan's jaw twitch at 'horse poop' but he held the laughter in. "I'm guessing that the judge has gotten permission for you to take topsoil."

"Si, I think so."

Yet, something was odd. Ben looked at the swath of bare dirt not far from the creek. Ugly. Defacing property at best. Yes, it would probably grow back in the spring and be covered once again by wildflowers and grasses. Runoff would replenish the rich, black earth. But taking a backhoe to sacred ground? Who would okay that? And he was convinced that the land this side of the creek belonged to the Lakota.

"We better get going." Ben turned his horse and motioned for Nathan to follow but Nathan was staring at Carlos. The young Mexican man had turned and was bent over the hitch that secured a flat-bed cart to the backhoe revealing a neck-to-waist tattoo of what looked to be Pancho Villa. The pictorial covered his entire back. Ben was impressed; the tat was exceptionally well done—obviously the work of a professional.

Chapter 16

Back at camp, Ben helped Nathan rub down the horses and give each a flake of hay before putting them in their stalls. The four that returned with them remained in the corral and would be taken back to pasture in the morning.

There was still food left from the earlier celebration and Ben and Nathan sat down to some fry bread and bison jerky before Ben drove back to the bungalow. He had every intention of spending a quiet evening on the community project he was designing, until he saw Red Bull's truck parked in front of the tribal office. He pulled into the parking lot.

Red Bull was walking out the front door when Ben got out of the SUV. As long as it was fresh on his mind, he might as well run the strange encounter they'd had at the pasture by him. Ben was just not easy with the topsoil explanation and the fact that permission had been given to tear up reservation land.

Red Bull listened quietly and, at first, Ben thought he wasn't going to comment. Then, "Would you recognize this Mexican kid if you saw him again?"

"Yeah, if he had his shirt off."

"What do you mean?"

Ben filled him in on the tattoo of a rather accurate Pancho Villa. This time, it wasn't Ben's imagination, Red Bull was pissed. He bit his lip and leaned back against his truck.

After a couple minutes of staring into space, he turned to Ben. "Can I trust you?"

"Of course." Ben was now the one perplexed. What kind of power did a tattooed Mexican kid have to upset a reservation sheriff? Seemed overkill to be that angry over tearing up a six-foot-by-six-foot block of turf. Wouldn't that be an easy problem to handle? Go to the judge and get the straight scoop and act accordingly.

"Remember my telling you about the Hispanic guy that was found dead last week? His death was made to look like part of a Sun Dance ritual? Well, it sounds like your guy in the pasture is a part of the same gang—a vicious, take no prisoners, bunch of thugs. No one who talks gets out alive. They're close-knit, all have done time, and all have run guns with various groups. Every single one of them is wanted—in some country, somewhere—just not ours. They're free to roam ours with the worst offense possibly being illegal entry. They all have tats of Pancho Villa. I wish I knew how many there were. The tattoos seem to indicate a position of authority. They'd stayed out of the US until recently. And now eleven hundred miles from the border, they've decided to congregate up here."

"Any idea of why here?"

"Money talks. My guess is they are getting paid. One of the do-gooder groups organizing protesters to stop the pipeline has probably recruited them. It's the gun-running part of the equation that scares me."

"Do you believe the story about taking topsoil for a memorial to the judge's mother? Supposedly to enrich her gardens."

Red Bull laughed. "I forget you never knew old lady Udahl. Rough old bitch—racist, never met an Indian she liked. Went to court to change the school bus route—didn't want all those red children waiting on her side of the road. And her raising flowers? They'd sooner wilt than bloom for her. Frankly, I was surprised that a virus was able to take her down."

Ben didn't like to hear it, but it wasn't something he hadn't suspected. In more than one way he was glad he'd never had to interact with his grandmother. Wow, even the word made him feel sick. "How's the judge to work with?" There, he might as well know.

"Better. In fact, in comparison, a gem. He tries anyway. Every year he leads the township in raising money for reservation schools or a new clinic—whatever's needed. And we can always count on a ten to twenty-thousand-dollar check from the Udahl Co-op, the group of ranchers in a thirty-mile radius who take being a part of this community seriously. Last year we provided some much-needed laptops and iPads. Listen, if you have the time, I'd like to run back up to the pasture. It's more than an hour before dark and I'd like to see the area that the Mexican guy was tearing up."

"Sure, not a problem."

"Then let's take my truck. We can get close by sticking to the trail but might have to hike a half mile."

* * *

The backhoe and its driver were gone when they got there. The peeled-back swath of earth looked raw, a gaping wound in the otherwise pristine creek bank. Red Bull shooed away a couple crows who were enjoying a late afternoon snack of grubs.

"Don't know who would give someone the okay to do this." He walked closer. "Hey, be careful. Somebody's riddled the ground with holes. Looks like someone went crazy with a posthole digger. What the hell? They're everywhere." He stood in one spot and pointed to at least six that stretched from where he was standing to the creek. "Why would someone do that?"

Ben crouched down and inspected one of the perfectly round indentations about a foot into the ground. Were they almost all done this close to the creek because the land was softer here? And if they were postholes, where were the posts? Was this some kind of pen? But the configuration made no sense as a pen—four holes in a straight line, one foot to three feet apart, and then two more holes behind those.

"Any ideas what the person was making? A trap, maybe?"

Red Bull stood up from inspecting two holes at the end. "Unlike any trap I've ever seen. I can't imagine what he thought he'd catch." He took out his phone and began snapping pictures. "I can't make any sense out of this. And look here. Why bust these apart?" Red Bull pointed to several rocks along the creek's edge. All had been split into pieces as if someone had taken a sledgehammer to them.

"Maybe to outline the garden? Place around the edges of a path?"

Ben picked up several slivers of granite that had been chiseled from a large boulder and stuck them in his pocket. This wasn't some chance swing with a sledgehammer and, oops, hit solid rock. No, there was some plan in action here. The chiseled markings alone seemed to indicate a reason of some sort to take samples from the creek bed. But damned if he could guess why. Ben scooped up a couple tablespoons of soil, rubbed some of it between his fingers. It looked like good, rich dirt to him and if he didn't believe Red Bull, a garden explanation made sense. Then he rolled the specimen into a Kleenex and tucked it into his shirt pocket. He wasn't sure what he would do with the samples but if this area was important to someone, it might be important to him, too.

Red Bull stepped back to survey the blight of scraped ground and random post holes. "This is trespassing and disturbing sacred land. Garden or not, it's illegal. I think we need to visit the judge."

Chapter 17

Judge Udahl's Ranch (adjacent to Pine Ridge Reservation)

Ben wasn't sure what he expected—maybe something out of *Gone With The Wind*. And that wasn't too far from wrong. The house at the end of the curving drive was sort of a South Dakota rendition of Tara. The sprawling ranch house was red brick with a pitched metal roof left natural, a matte-finished tin. Ben guessed the square footage of the house to be at least thirty-five hundred and that wasn't counting a four-car garage with what looked to be a work area along the far side. At a distance, two huge barns stood out behind the house, and Ben could just see the edges of several corrals. He had to remind himself that this was a working spread.

Buffalo lined up to stare at them in half-acre double-fenced pens along the drive. And the pen of buffalo was next to another fenced area holding at least thirty yaks. "The place is impressive." Ben turned to Red Bull. "And worth a lot of money." Now he could understand the Udahls being worried about someone showing up with his hand out. The judge, an only child who would inherit everything—but wait, there was another only child out there, himself. His mother's letter must have scared Mrs. Udahl half to death. Ben almost smiled at that.

"Yeah, more than just a few million. But I'd be the first to say that the judge tries hard to be fair. Of course, doing things for the community means more votes coming his way. We're out in the boonies. Nobody is going to complain and shoot the gift horse."

There were two Range Rovers, both new models, sitting in front of the house where the drive curved to make a half circle before returning to meet the county road. Both were caked with mud that looked fresh. If the cars were any indication, the judge might be home.

But no such luck. The middle-aged woman in a heavily starched white, embroidered apron over a plain green, loose-fitting dress who opened the door, adeptly blocked any clear view of the interior. Whatever she had been doing, it was obvious that she did not appreciate the interruption. A swipe of white flour across her left cheek seemed to indicate baking. Red Bull introduced himself and Ben; then, he asked to see the judge.

"This is the judge's travel day. He's in Pierre, more than likely. I don't keep his calendar. I'm Evangeline Isher, house manager. Is this a matter that I might help with?" She swept gray-streaked curls off her forehead and adjusted the round, metal-framed glasses that perched rather far forward on her nose.

"I have questions about someone from the ranch coming onto the reservation to collect topsoil. I was told it was for the garden memorial."

"Garden memorial?" Her brow wrinkled, "For here at the ranch?"

"Yes, something the judge has planned in memory of his mother."

"Flowers, even edibles?" Ben offered.

"Odd. I'd know of a memorial if there was to be one. I assure you, nothing of the sort has been planned. But let me see if his administrative assistant is available to speak with you. Miss Rose Aguilar has worked for the judge for three years now. She would be the one to ask. One minute, please." Evangeline stepped back and pushed the door closed as she turned to go into the house.

They didn't have long to wait. In under three minutes the door was thrown open and Miss Aguilar was encouraging them to follow her to the study. Ben couldn't help but notice that she was wearing nylons—with a dark seam up the back. It gave the gray tailored suit, nipped in at the waist, and the pastel pink silk blouse a definite '50s look. Who would dress like this at a ranch out in nowhere, South Dakota? Was there a dress code? Could the judge be that strict?

But he had to admit the woman was striking and would be so wearing anything. Dark hair in a bun, perfect ivory skin, brown eyes that were almost black under thick lashes—the woman was a stunner.

She pushed open the study door to reveal overcrowded bookshelves and worn leather furniture, once opulent and expensive. This was a much-used room, Ben thought. Even the scattering of hand-knotted Persian rugs appeared well worn. Aside from its touch of age, the room screamed, 'I'm expensive; if you live here, you're rich.'

Rose let the door close behind them. "Here we go. Much more comfortable. I'm familiar with the name Red Bull and have seen your photo in the local newspaper, but you're a new face." She turned toward Ben as she motioned for him to take a chair next to an overstuffed couch. Her smile was infectious. She perched on the arm of the couch, giving Ben her full attention. "Now, who are you?"

"Ben Pecos. I'm with Indian Health Service, most recently working on a special project on the Navajo reservation in New Mexico. Officer Red Bull and I are planning a community project for Pine Ridge."

"Oh, how exciting. Well, welcome. Now, what is this I hear about a memorial for poor Frannie ... er, Frances Udahl?"

Red Bull ceded the floor to Ben before sitting on the opposite end of the couch. "Ben can give you a first-hand account of what happened."

Ben started with the defacing of property, including the rocks along the creek bank, and ending with a description of the man, Carlos, right down to his broken English and Pancho Villa tattoo.

"This is so strange. I know we don't have a Carlos employed. And a memorial? One hasn't even been discussed. Not to brag, but I would know; I play a small part in keeping the books around here. And quite frankly, Frannie was a no-nonsense type. I personally think she would abhor the fuss over producing any kind of memorial. She was frugal, possibly to the point of being a bit of a miser, in her own way. No, she would have considered an expenditure like that to be a frivolous waste."

"What about the tattoo? Ben says the Pancho Villa image covered the entire back of this individual?" Red Bull asked.

"Oh my gosh. That sounds painful and expensive. No Pancho Villa tats that I've seen around here. A lot of our workers have tattoos, ones commemorating a girlfriend or sports activities—that sort of thing—not historical persons. And to think someone pretending to work for us was defacing—stealing, really from reservation land—I can't tell you how offensive I find that. We've been good neighbors certainly for as long as I've worked here. We respect each other's boundaries. I'm sorry that even for a minute you thought the judge might be involved."

Red Bull nodded slightly but chose not to elaborate on her protestation of innocence. Instead, he asked, "What percentage of your work force is Hispanic? Mexican to be exact?"

That question seemed to slow Rose's otherwise ready responses, Ben thought. Not a question she was anticipating. He noticed the pursing of the lips and a release of breath that sort of popped her lips apart.

"Well, if I can be excused being a little ethnically incorrect ... too many. Yes, yes, I know that goes against my heritage. But some of them are no better than itinerant gypsies. Without going into detail, things disappear when a group comes through. Once, expensive bedding right off the clothesline in back. But often they are fantastic with animals and the judge always feels sorry for them. So, sometimes they end up working for him."

"But none currently?"

"That I don't know for certain. The judge has given

them a plot of land some distance from the house. I haven't gone out that way recently. In times past the judge has provided food—even food for their horses, if there were any. There's a well on the property—in all, they have about two acres with lots of scrub brush and trees. It's certainly primitive but no one complains."

"Here's my card. The number on the back is my cell. Call if you see anything, or remember something that might not have seemed important at the time. And let me leave a note for the judge. May I use that desk?" Red Bull pointed to the large, ornate, walnut desk in the corner.

"Please, help yourself. This is the judge's unwind area. He often spends a couple hours at night reading or catching up on correspondence. I'll tell him you've left a note. You'll find pen and paper in the middle drawer."

Rose offered a tour of the barns but they were running out of daylight. They simply thanked her and put off scoping out the ranch for another day. Ben had a feeling that there'd be another time for that. They each thanked her for her time and walked back out to the cruiser.

Chapter 18

Pine Ridge Reservation, South Dakota

Red Bull was silent driving down the long unpaved driveway to the county road. Ben looked over his shoulder as the house disappeared behind them. Once again, he was struck by the ornamental juniper and colorful, pink-topped grasses that formed a pattern along the road. It really was a showplace and probably took a lot of work by groundskeepers. Yet, other than the two women, there were no other hired hands in sight.

Was that as strange as it seemed? Or was everyone in one of the barns, or the maintenance workshop, fixing things or taking care of animals. Plus, they really hadn't gotten the answers they'd hoped for. Had it been worth the trip over? Yes and no.

It had given Ben a chance to see his history. That was worth something. Impressive and then some. And it fed into a place of anger—anger at a callous, insensitive woman who played God. Deciding to ignore another woman's plea for help and masterminding her own son's life, depriving all concerned of family and the possibility of love and support. It went beyond unfair and tipped the scale toward being criminal. And somewhere down deep a plan was forming to at least have the judge acknowledge Zac—perhaps, set aside the money for a college education. Ben wanted nothing for himself but wasn't it his responsibility to see that Zac was recognized and supported?

"Did you believe the Aguilar woman? Or did you find it interesting that she really disliked Hispanics when it was pretty obvious that she is one? There's a lot of bigotry in this county." Ben was startled out of his reverie. Red Bull as usual had found the accelerator once he'd turned onto the road leading back to the reservation.

"I guess I want to believe her. Even sharing what she did about the Mexicans—her true feelings—seemed honest, believable. If they are in a camp somewhere away from the house, maybe she doesn't know who's there and who isn't."

"Yeah, I guess so. I'm just feeling the need to keep an eye on any comings and goings out there. I just don't know how I can do that without trespassing. But I think there's a large group of protesters gathering somewhere—right now they're off the radar—but that doesn't mean they're off the premises."

"Too much wide-open space out here to do much undercover."

"That's for sure." Suddenly, Red Bull banged the heel

of his hand against the steering wheel. "Damn it. You're not going to believe this. I just stole one of the judge's pens. I can't believe I finished the note and put it in my pocket." He tapped his shirt pocket with his right hand. "Force of habit. I always carry a pen right here."

"Wait a minute, let me help you. The judge invited me to meet with him again to plan a Native rally for his campaign. My time here is limited, so, I should get together with him later this week. I'll return it and offer apologies, of course." A little white lie but worth it; he'd need it for his plan.

"Thanks. Appreciate it. Here, put this somewhere safe. With that hand carved cap, it's got to be something special. What is that cap supposed to be? A chess piece?"

"The Rook, I think." Ben took the pen, careful to only touch its tip, wrapped it in a second Kleenex that was in his own shirt pocket and placed it next to the soil sample. Then, he was tempted to gloat a little—without lifting a finger he'd been able to score the judge's DNA! He'd put money on it. The carved cap with its indentations almost assured him of a good, readable sample. He couldn't wait to tell Julie. And this changed everything—gave Ben the upper hand, at least. He would have irrefutable evidence of the judge's paternity. Being a judge wouldn't protect Rex Udahl from the truth if Ben wanted to share it. At least Ben could suggest a plan to provide four years of college for his grandson. He'd need solid proof to make that happen. The judge had certainly been less than anxious to follow up. Remaining ignorant was his preference. Now, simply forgetting about possible paternity wasn't an option—not any more.

* * *

"You're right; it's perfect. But what changed your mind? I thought you were a little lukewarm about pursuing the family connection." He'd called Julie when he got back to the bungalow.

"I guess the sheer magnitude of the man's wealth. I won't be asking for something he'll miss. A hundred thousand to him is like ten dollars to us. And, I don't rule out a little anger. Even from her grave, I'd like his mother to lose this one. Be held accountable anyway."

"I have to say I agree. And I can't think of any reason that a request to help Zac with college, with nothing for yourself, wouldn't be seen as the kind of care and consideration that a father should show his son. Do you really think the judge will fight the request? Turn you down and make you take legal steps?"

"I fully believe that."

"Then why do you think he showed you your mother's letter?"

"I think he was scared to death that I'd find out somehow on my own. For example, sooner or later someone subscribing to Ancestry.com could have provided a link to the truth. The fact that he'd tried to bury the truth wouldn't be well received in this part of the country."

"I hope you're wrong and when the judge realizes you're only asking for something for his grandson, he'll come around. In the meantime, overnight me a sample of your DNA and the pen. I'll try to get the test done through Indian Health Services. I'm sure there must be a lab in the state that could help us. Dr. Black should be able to pull some strings. With DNA proof the judge will know you're serious, and that you have everything needed to bring a suit if you so decide."

* * *

Ben was the first person through the door of the Spearfish Post Office in the morning. He handed the carefully wrapped package to the postal worker behind the counter and paid the fee to have it in Julie's hands by the next day. He still was finding it hard to realize he was holding definitive proof of his heritage. Rex Udahl's son. Still didn't sound natural. But to be fair, finding out about Zac in the past year had taken some getting used to also. Ben Pecos's son. That had certainly changed the trajectory of his life. Maybe he should cut the judge some slack? Give him a chance to do the right thing. So far, that didn't look promising.

The rest of the morning was taken up with errands— get the SUV washed, do laundry, grocery shop—all the mundane activities he'd rather skip. But as long as he was off the reservation, he'd try to get as much done as he could. He had a one o'clock meeting with the elders back at the tribal offices that would take the better part of the afternoon. Then, just maybe, he'd have some time to get some fishing in.

It wasn't until the third stoplight on Main Street that he realized he was seeing an inordinate number of out-of-state license tags. When the two skinheads in a pickup flying a confederate flag pulled up beside him, he realized that he was seeing evidence of protesters. So far everyone seemed peaceful. A confederate flag didn't automatically put a gun in your hands; it just meant that you had a different ideology. Or so Ben wanted to think. Still, he was glad he didn't have Mac Sterling's job or even Red Bull's. Law enforcement could be a dangerous, thankless occupation.

Chapter 19

The first death occurred at 1:10 in the morning in front of the Moonshine Bar and Grill at the end of Main Street. As Mac Sterling was to learn later, the fight started inside around midnight and with the closing of the bar moved outside to the parking lot. The one who supposedly pulled the trigger first was a nineteen-year-old Indian kid from the reservation who worked at the restaurant, doing everything from general maintenance to washing dishes to acting as a bouncer when needed. Actually, no witnesses saw him pull the trigger but several bystanders swore he had a gun.

He was a fixture at the Moonshine. No one knew his real name but everyone called him Two Shoes because of a story that had followed him since grade school. When he started kindergarten, an evangelical Christian group had given his family shoes for their children, two pairs each—sneakers and dress oxfords. At the age of five he had been so afraid that someone would take his new shoes while he was at school that he wore both pair—one set inside the other and the nickname stuck.

After an hour of questioning, Mac found most onlookers took Two Shoes' side and, to a person, stated he'd been heckled and then hounded and finally shoved face first against the rough brick side of the building. All this because he refused entry to two drunken, rowdy types with shaved heads and had escorted a third man out of the bar. Nobody seemed to know whether Two Shoes carried. Did he shoot the man with his own gun? Both men purported to be from Wyoming but were traveling with a man who later gave his name as Alonzo Martinez from New Mexico.

But the melee didn't stop there. Apparently, the parking lot had filled in record time. Had word gotten out to be on the lookout? Possible demonstration of force at the tavern? In the name of Two Shoes and fairness, guns appeared from back pockets and glove boxes of vehicles. Locals got the brunt of things. The final count was two dead, nine wounded. Mac put in a call to three neighboring towns to send ambulances. He also checked on availability of hospital beds in those towns. Someone gave him a number of twenty-three perpetrators, a crowd from maybe outside the state who had shown up to cause trouble. More than one bystander swore that the Martinez guy was handing out weapons from the tailgate of his Toyota Tundra.

"Everything under control?"

"Doesn't it look like it?" Mac turned toward Red Bull.

He hadn't meant to sound so short, but was the man being snide or was it an honest question? Amazing how quickly he'd gotten to the bar. Maybe, he'd already been in town.

"I'm going to take Two Shoes off your hands. I'll ask Dr. Pecos to help interrogate all those from the reservation. I think we'll get at the truth quicker and it'll free up some of your time. You'll know where to find people if you need them."

Mac just nodded. Red Bull was right; this was turning into an all-nighter.

* * *

It was after three when Red Bull knocked on Ben's front door. "Sorry about the hour but I need your help." Ben motioned to the dining room table.

"Do I have time to put on a pot of coffee? I saw a couple travel cups next to the sink. We can always take the coffee with us."

"Good idea, but I'm hoping that I can put you to work here." Red Bull filled Ben in on what had happened at the Moonshine. "I want you to talk with Two Shoes. I've got him with me in the truck. He sometimes has difficulty standing up for himself. I don't want him bullied; I want the truth. And it would be best if relayed to a neutral person. If he isn't the shooter who started things, I don't want him convicted and prosecuted by word of mouth, if you understand me. Too easy for a reservation kid to take a fall for something he didn't do. I want everyone to know that, as the bar's bouncer, he has rights—he can make decisions about who should be let in. And he can throw someone out if he thinks it's necessary. If you can get his story, have him put his part in writing. I'll go to the station and try to help Sheriff Sterling interrogate the others."

Ben doctored his coffee and put a third cup on the kitchen table—maybe Two Shoes was a coffee drinker. Red Bull took his coffee black, thanked Ben once again and said he'd send Two Shoes in.

If first impressions stuck and colored all else, then the first word that came to mind when Ben saw Two Shoes in the doorway was 'Giant'. The kid filled the opening but there wasn't an ounce of puppy-fat anywhere on his body. This was a young man who'd spent months, maybe years, in a gym. No wonder he'd gotten a job as a bouncer. The sleeves of his t-shirt strained over muscular arms and the body of the jersey material was stretched to its limit over an impressive and massive chest.

"Dr. Pecos, Red Bull said I should tell you what happened tonight at the bar—my side of the story."

"I'm going to take notes, then I want you to read them, sign them if I've gotten things straight—like they happened, and I'll pass them along to Red Bull. How does that sound?"

"Okay."

"This coffee's yours if you want it." Ben pointed to the cup on the table.

"I don't drink coffee, but thanks. I'd like a glass of water if you don't mind. No ice."

"Bottled water okay?" At the affirmative nod, Ben walked to the fridge. He was glad he'd gotten groceries and hadn't forgotten water. Ben had seen a tablet of lined paper in a drawer by the sink. He got that and two ballpoint pens that were next to it, picked up the bottle of water and sat back down at the table. "Let's start with your name, address, age, and then I'll ask you to state where you work, what you do there, and how long you've been employed."

The young man scooted his chair forward and leaned his elbows on the table. "My real name is Tommy Bald Eagle but everyone calls me Two Shoes. I live one row over from this house on the Pine Ridge Reservation, number eleven. I will be twenty years old on the fifteenth of next month. I have worked at the Moonshine Bar and Grill in Spearfish for almost two years—I started as a dish washer when I was eighteen. The owner of the bar is Eric Strand. He also owns the Fitness First gym and has supported me as a junior bodybuilder."

"Paint me a picture of what happened tonight. Think in terms of where, when and why and describe the action."

Two Shoes nodded. "About eleven forty-five, the bartender came to get me—I was restocking the storage room. The night had been pretty slow, just regulars. We'd just gotten a big shipment of liquor and snacks that afternoon. He said two guys were really going at each other in the parking lot, throwing punches, calling each other names. He was able to keep them in the parking lot but was afraid they'd try to come inside. I stopped what I was doing and ran for the front door just as it opened. A big guy, maybe in his twenties, tried to push me back and enter the bar. He was bleeding from his nose and had a bad cut on his forehead. I knew he'd need stitches."

"Was he able to get past you?"

"No way. He was maybe a couple hundred pounds. I bench press over two fifty. I had the advantage and pushed him back outside but yelled for our bartender to call a doc. The guy who was beating on him just sort of disappeared back into the crowd. But the crowd was already riled up.

There was this Mexican guy standing by the tailgate of an old red Tundra. The truck had Chihuahua tags. He was breaking open packing crates and handing out rifles. I grabbed him by the arm and spun him around not realizing that he was holding a Glock. Before he could level it at me, I knocked the gun from his hand and it slid under the pickup. I went after it, pulled it out and stood up just as I heard a shot. The shot didn't come from the gun in my hand, Dr. Pecos. I'm not lying to you. I took the gun and put it in my belt and later left it on the bar."

"Is there surveillance of the parking lot? Cameras?"

"Yes. Every angle of that area is covered. Have to, we've been broken into before."

"What happened to the Mexican guy with the red truck?"

"He took off. Didn't even close the tailgate and a crate of guns fell off. But by then shots were being fired from several directions. Sheriff Sterling's siren was what really broke up the fighting. People just scattered. Most had cars or trucks there and they just took off. That's when those of us who were left saw the bodies. The parking lot looked like some kind of massacre took place. Only two died but lots were injured."

"Were any of these people familiar?"

"That's what's strange, nobody was. Oh, a couple guys from the bar but the ones fighting weren't from around here."

"Any idea where they were from or what they were doing here?"

"People talk. There's supposed to be a demonstration against the pipeline. People on the Rez want it stopped ... now, before any more of it is completed. A lot of wooded area up north has been torn up and sacred lands trashed. People on the Rez are upset. But the pipeline means good jobs—jobs that pay a lot. For Anglos, that is. We're all hoping we can get the thing stopped once and for all."

"Why don't we stop here for now? I want to get your account of what happened back to Red Bull and Sheriff Sterling. I'll give you a ride back to the bar if you need one. Take a look and if everything is like you said, sign at the bottom and date it."

"Uh, Dr. Pecos? One more thing but I don't want this in your notes."

"Okay." Ben put his pen down. Two Shoes certainly had his attention.

"About three weeks ago this guy comes to the gym asking for me. I was in the weight room in back so they called me up front. The guy's name was David, something or other, said he was from Mexico originally. He asked me to step outside—said what he wanted to talk about was private."

"You'd never seen this man before?"

"Never. He said his ex-wife lived in the area—in the state somewhere— but he was here on business."

"What kind of business?"

"Mining. He gave me his card but when I googled the company later, it didn't exist. I tossed the card."

"What did he want from you?"

"Directions. Well, that's what it came down to, but not until he'd laid on a lot of BS about seeing me in the Teen USA bodybuilding competition last year in Denver. Said he'd done some gym work himself and wanted to pick my brain about workouts and whether he could hire me as a trainer."

"But you don't think that's what he really wanted?"

"I know it's not. He said he was an assayer working on a big project that would probably take him months to complete. He was gathering and testing samples of rock and topsoil in runoff areas. He wanted to know how to get to the mouth of Little Spearfish Creek, and would I take him there."

"So, he was really working for the pipeline company?"

"I don't think so. He said he worked for the owner of the mining company—he never mentioned oil—only that there was a big investment being made in this area. He looked me up because I'm a Native and he needed a guide across Indian land. The area he was interested in is all Pine Ridge Reservation land. He used the bodybuilding interest to get on my good side with the promise of money for training."

"Did you take him up there?"

"Yeah, spent a half day on a Sunday watching him sift through dirt and chip away slivers of rock."

"Then what happened?"

"He died. He told me he was having health problems and the next thing I hear is that he's in the morgue. I don't want anyone to know that I took him onto Indian land. I'm asking that you keep that a secret. But maybe it's important that someone had samples from that area assayed. I don't trust anybody to tell the truth right now."

Ben agreed; lots of things were happening. And he promised not to share Two Shoes' secret. Then, he said goodnight and watched Two Shoes cut across his backyard to the street behind. Two Shoes said he'd pick up his car in the morning even though Ben had offered a ride if he wanted, but he declined. It seemed his brother worked at the local grocery and could give him a lift to the Moonshine.

Ben closed the door and noted the time—four fifteen.

Before he collapsed in bed, he went through the pockets of the jeans he'd worn when helping Nathan bring the horses down from pasture—he'd forgotten about the several pieces of rock carefully shaved from a larger boulder next to the creek's edge. Maybe he should have these assayed himself—along with the folded Kleenex of topsoil—another sample that needed attention.

Were they of importance because a company was considering fracking but needed to assess the content and availability of oil? Would these samples definitively prove whether the area was lucrative enough to pursue fracking? The past Government administration had allowed fracking on reservation land in more than one state. Could this be a precursor to more legal struggles for the Lakota?

Chapter 20

Morning came way too early. Ben had a nine o'clock sharp meeting with the tribe's fiscal officer concerning a budget for the additions to the proposed substance abuse program and then following that, a group meeting over Zoom to exchange ideas shared by personnel from several other reservation programs around the state. Last order of business for the morning was to put the finishing touches on the proposal that would be sent to Indian Health Services in Washington, D.C.

Directly following lunch he planned to get a copy of Two Shoes' explanation of the evening's events at the Moonshine to Sheriff Sterling. Ben had put the original signed copy in an envelope and planned on leaving it with the receptionist at the tribal offices, asking her to contact Red Bull to pick it up. That should be everything. He was cutting it close on time but he'd already made coffee, filled a travel cup, and gathered the printouts of information that Julie had sent last week. He was glad the office was only a two-block jog away.

Other than numerous questions, the morning budget meeting went smoothly. There was seldom, if ever, an argument against implementing further programs dealing with alcohol or drugs; it was always the funding, never *if* but *how*. Rent was usually not the most expensive thing to consider, but training people to man the programs or bring in outside help was. They would need a fulltime psychologist, several social workers trained in the area, and a skeleton crew of office help.

The tribal registry listing headcount warranted the number of personnel planned and overall size of the program. Government contracts always demanded a lot of t's to cross and i's to dot, and Ben was pleased that he was able to offer his expertise. It helped to have experience.

Just before the lunch break, he got a text from Red Bull asking if he had time to meet him at the Guadalajara Grill on West 14th. Ben made sure he wouldn't be needed until the following day, when he'd offered to help interview prospective employees, and texted back that he'd be there by twelve-thirty.

To say the Pepto Bismol pink building stood out from anything else within a half mile might be an understatement. It screamed 'look at me.' There wasn't much of a chance that Ben might miss it. Red Bull was sitting in a booth at the back next to a young woman who was probably older than she looked, but still younger than Ben.

"Ben, I'd like you to meet Micki Sterling. I think you've met her father."

It was still the time of elbow bumps and masks but Ben simply chose to nod and say it was nice meeting her. He slid into the booth on the opposite side.

"Is Spearfish home?" Small talk wasn't his strong point but Ben was curious.

"Used to be. I grew up here and only left to attend college in Billings."

"Montana State?"

She nodded, then laughed. "It was as far away as I could talk my parents into letting me go, and still have them pay. My mother lives between here and Pierre now. I've moved in with her for the time being. Between going through a messy divorce and the pandemic, I think she's glad for the company. Plus, my school closed because of the virus. All my work for the district is now online, nothing in the classroom. We've formed several committees on curriculum development. It's a pain in the elbow, but I'm kinda getting used to it."

A waitress interrupted to take their orders and the two locals ordered farmed catfish tacos with a side of guacamole. Ben wasn't so sure—this wasn't New Mexico. But red or green chicken enchiladas won out—red sounded good with extra sauce on the side, guaranteed homemade.

"Thanks for working with Two Shoes," Red Bull said. "I honestly didn't think he'd pulled a trigger. He's a good kid, works hard; I don't want to see his reputation compromised. I'd say he's free to go—I won't be detaining him."

"Red Bull said you're from New Mexico—aren't you a little far from home?" Micki asked.

"Ben's guardian to a young Navajo kid whose school in Bellingham closed until the first of the year—gave the two of them some vacation time on their way back to New Mexico. And lucky for me they could stay over and I now have some expert help on the proposed extended substance abuse clinic."

"And Nathan is lucky because Red Bull got him a spot in the Spearfish Creek Boys Camp on the reservation. It's a great learning experience. Of course, it is cutting into our fishing time together." Ben smiled.

"Spearfish Creek is a famous fishing spot. Maybe Nathan can sneak away? My ex spent a lot of time up there. He always said it was a beautiful part of the country."

"Did he work in the area?" This would be as good a time as any to check Two Shoe's story.

"Sort of. He was a geologist. He represented a large investment firm that had been hired to determine the mineral and ore content in the vicinity of Spearfish Creek's upper origination point. I guess you would call that the mouth of the creek?"

Red Bull nodded. "Was any of his exploration done on Indian land?"

"I have no idea. We weren't together and then he got sick. I would be the first to admit I was shocked at how quickly he died. I never expected that. I know he was in the middle of the project. In fact, the University—South Dakota State—left a phone message this week saying they had the results from analyzing the samples he'd sent. Someone in the Geology department wanted to let me know that he'd analyzed them and sent them back to the last address he had for David, which was mine. I received the package yesterday just before I left to come to Spearfish, only now I have no idea what to do with it. I'm only here overnight which doesn't give me much time to figure out who'd want it. Here, I brought it thinking you could help." She turned to Red Bull as she reached into an oversized tote, pulling out an envelope marked Priority.

"Ben, I'm going to punt this one to you. Should give you some good contacts for getting a read-out on the samples you collected."

He handed Ben the postal envelope. Slipping a dinner knife under the top flap, Ben pulled out probably five pages that looked like a report in a plastic binder, and a four by four by one inch cardboard box, possibly David's original samples.

"I'd be glad to check it out." Had they been taken from the spot where he'd collected his samples? He bet they had. Now that the garden topsoil story appeared to be a cover-up, it would be nice to know what was really behind collecting and analyzing soil and rock from the area. Especially because there seemed to be such a lot of interest in the place.

The red chili enchiladas were better than he could have hoped for, and conversation turned to things he missed about New Mexico. Ben even threw in a couple stories about Zac and Alaska. Dessert was flan and cinnamon coffee. Ben was stuffed but glad he'd had the invite to lunch.

"My mom and I are thinking of making use of the shutdown for a road-trip. My aunt Helen lives in Colorado. We were thinking of stopping in Colorado Springs, but maybe we should keep going—visit New Mexico while we're at it."

"I think that's a great idea. New Mexico has done well

with meeting and maintaining pandemic safety criteria. Lots of venues aren't open but I think there's enough to see that you'd enjoy it. It's a shame they cancelled the hot air balloon festival this month."

"And if you're traveling, I won't worry." Red Bull signaled the waitress for more coffee. "It's becoming dangerous to be around here. What's worse is that I'm not sure I can tell the good guys from the bad."

"Just don't tell my father what I'm planning. I know him. He wouldn't want us out on the road—out of his sight. It's a conscience thing. He might not have been the best father while I was growing up—mostly, he was seldom home, and he divorced my mother when I was twelve. So, now he tries to make up for lost time. But I agree with Red Bull; I think we'd be safer on the road and away from here. I don't think David's death was because of his health. We hadn't been together for months but I'm afraid people might think I knew more about his work than I actually did. When I met him, he was sort of undercover pretending to be a protester. He let me believe that he worked for the company in charge of bringing the pipeline across the reservation, but said he needed to infiltrate the other side. I have no idea who the 'other side' is. I just know all the secrets made life intolerable, and dangerous."

Just as Micki had finished sharing why getting away felt like the best thing to do—in walked her father. The timing couldn't have been more perfect, but that probably wasn't the right word. This wasn't a good time to meet up with Sheriff Sterling. And Ben didn't think this looked like a friendly visit. Mac Sterling's eyes were almost squinted shut, and his mouth was drawn back into a thin line. He fairly glowered at Micki as he was striding up to the table. "So,

what's this about running off? You and your mom. I have
to find out about it from the pharmacist at Walgreens. I
pick up my prescription and old Ed Tucker steps out of his
office to see if I could deliver the prescription that you'd
asked him to fill yesterday. Says it's wonderful to see you
back home but he's heard that you and Debbie are hitting
the road. Says it's a shame that the two of you can't stay
local but he understands that under the circumstances with
your dead husband and all, how that might be a problem.
Apparently, he put a rush on these, thought the two of you
were taking off today."

Mac tossed a bottle of 800mg Motrin on the table.
"So, share. Tell me what's up? Have you been harassed?
Threatened? Someone blaming you for something that
David fellow might have done? Some reason that you can't
let your old man know? I asked for information once and
was told to butt out. But now it seems that you have some
reason to try and disappear. Might have worked out better
if you'd shared a few things with your dad. He might just
be able to keep you out of harm's way. Did you stop and
think about that?"

"Mac, this isn't the place." Micki saw several people in
the restaurant staring. "Yes, I told you once to drop it—
David is dead. For all intents and purposes, his death was
brought on by natural causes. I divorced him six months
ago. I've seen him twice in that time. I don't know why he
was here. That's it. That's all I'm saying. Final word—the
end."

"Ah, and you're running off because? Just need a
little change of scenery? Tell me another lie while you're
at it. You and Debbie wouldn't take off unless there was
a reason—you'd been scared into it. By the way, I would

have thought the boyfriend here could protect you."

Snide. If it wasn't two lawmen facing off, the next move would have been a thrown punch.

Actually, it might be anyway. Ben almost smiled. So that was it. Mac had a problem with his only child dating Red Bull. Now his concern made more sense. All the chest beating and male trumpeting was directed at another male and probably didn't really have that much to do with the two women leaving the area. Encroachment of territory. My daughter. My responsibility. I can do better.

"We're adults here. There's no need for this kind of talk." Red Bull kept his voice just above a whisper. "Your daughter's a grown woman; she can make her own decisions."

"Like marrying that piece of shit from south of the border who only wanted a green card. Yeah, that was smart. I'd for sure trust her decision-making after that one."

"Sorry, Mac, that's over the line. I don't care if you are my father. I won't be psychologically abused."

Red Bull stood to one side as Micki scooted out of the booth, paused, turned back once to look at her father, then just shook her head before continuing out to the parking lot.

Red Bull nodded to Ben before following her. "I'll give you a call later."

Chapter 21

A person could get lost out here. In New Mexico, on the Navajo reservation, the mountains were always to the east. Here, the creek was his compass. As long as Nathan kept it in sight, he could get back to camp. Today, he'd brought the horses up to pasture by himself.

The instructors set aside one afternoon a week for contemplation. Actually, they called it meditation. They didn't care where he went or what he did as long as the activity would lend itself to a quiet time to look inward. The first week he'd chosen to sit by the creek but he'd fallen asleep which, according to the instructor, was a way for spirits to channel information his way. But he felt he'd flunked. He couldn't remember one thing that had happened. And he certainly didn't think any spirit had told him anything.

His instructor said he needed to try harder by not trying at all. Yeah, that was confusing. But Nathan thought he understood. He needed to work on clearing his mind. Letting random thoughts in, letting them take the lead by not trying to control them. He was going to give it a try.

If he got up high enough, he wouldn't lose sight of the creek. He had his eye on an outcropping of rock above the pasture. It would be a couple mile hike but even that seemed to meet the criteria for being alone to contemplate. He turned all three horses loose to graze, even the one he rode up on, and carefully hung bridle and saddle blanket in the branches of an oak.

He was glad he'd worn sneakers and not his favorite Ropers. He liked being above the valley. Trees outlined the creek as it snaked along the edge of the pasture, twisting around outcroppings of rock before dipping out of sight in the distance probably very close to the village. The brightest green vegetation thrived closest to a water source. He could even see how, here and there, water was diverted to the adjoining fields. An irrigation system, dammed now and inoperative, it was ready to feed the fallow land come spring when it would be prepared and brought back into production. Spent corn stalks littered the area, hinting at what next year's crop might be.

Nathan found a smooth rock among the boulders stacked hit-and-miss along the edge of a steep ravine. He stretched out, leaning back against the warmth of granite and willed himself to not give in to closing his eyes. He let thoughts of school float across his memory. He was anxious for school to start again. Soccer, the swim team, basketball—he'd had a great time. And Zac? The best friend ever.

He wasn't sure what jerked him back to the present. Had he heard the Jake Brake of the semi as it rounded a turn in the road and rolled to a stop below? The road was at least a football field, maybe almost two, in length away from him but the explosion of sound reverberated in the clear, windless air. He knew the brake was used to slow the big vehicle but as this one came to a stop, Nathan wondered what an oil tanker was doing here—out in nowhere.

As if on cue, two men jumped from the cab and one walked to the back of the tubular cargo-carrier while the other climbed up a ladder on the side of the tank and hoisted a banner-like flag waving it back and forth. Pickup trucks, eight in all, suddenly appeared in a cloud of dust, racing up the road to skid to a halt behind the tanker. By now the driver had opened what was, strangely, a door in the rear. Wasn't there supposed to be oil in a tanker? No oil spilled out. Only people. Lots of people.

Then he looked again. They were all men. Nathan leaned forward and counted. Fifteen men literally tumbled to the ground, some jumping then stumbling to remain upright from the six-foot drop. After gathering on the ground, they broke up into groups of two or three as men swarmed out of the trucks and the newcomers were steered to the pickups by their drivers. Most hoisted themselves over tailgates to land in the open beds of the trucks, then lay flat while someone covered them with what looked like tie-down tarps. Others threw open passenger-side doors to ride shotgun.

Nathan didn't have a watch but he'd bet the tanker was on its way in under ten minutes. Within another five, all activity in the area ceased to exist. It was as if it had never happened. The area alongside the road was scuffed up but that was it, the only testimony to any kind of activity. The tanker had accelerated and rumbled out of sight in one direction and the vehicles carrying passengers left in the opposite—off-road, across choppy ground that quickly took them out of Nathan's sight.

He waited but that was it. A tanker full of men had pulled to a stop, signaled that they had arrived, dumped their cargo and took off. That made no sense. Especially when the cargo jumped into prearranged vehicles to take them … where? That was the question that bothered Nathan. Where were these people going? Why couldn't they just fly into the state or come in by car or bus like everyone else? Did that mean they were doing something wrong?

Probably. You didn't sneak around if you didn't need to. He was old enough to know that.

And, he was feeling a little uneasy. He didn't need someone to tell him that he'd seen something he shouldn't have. Something that could put him in danger. He carefully dusted off his clothing and brushed away the indentation left by his sitting in the dust littering the surface of the boulder. He wasn't even sure why he was doing this. No one had seen him climb up. But just in case.

Suddenly the countryside had lost its mesmerizing beauty. He didn't like being isolated. He was pretty sure he was still on Indian land, but what if he wasn't? What if this low strip of rocks marked a boundary? And standing up here in a bright red flannel shirt could mark him from a distance—a telescopic lens would pick him up in a second. And no one would mistake him for a deer.

If he really let his imagination run wild, he'd keep an eye out for drones. Whatever was going on out here needed some surveillance—hadn't the guy in the tanker sent a signal? One that was answered pretty quickly. Another question: what was the need for secrecy? Why had all those pickups stayed under cover until they knew the tanker had arrived? Hadn't just lined up along the road to wait? That would have been the easiest thing to do.

This wasn't exactly the kind of meditation his instructor wanted, but it was difficult to shut his mind down. He slowed to a walk and took a couple breaths. What he needed to do was climb back down to the pasture, saddle his horse, gather the other two, and ride back to the village.

And that's when he saw it.

He'd almost reached the bottom of the hill in an area where at some time sand and topsoil had washed against a rock border and back out again, leaving cleavage between the larger rocks, sharp divisions with straggly vegetation wedged between. He couldn't be certain until he got closer, but from a distance it looked like a flesh-colored glove peeking out from between two narrow, rounded granite outcroppings. Something dropped by workmen probably. But as he got closer, he could see that it was a hand. A real hand with painted pink fingernails.

It had been the sun glinting off the watch crystal on its wrist that had caught his eye. And as he got closer, he knew another thing for certain. With or without a body attached—and he couldn't tell for certain what there was beyond the hand—this person was very dead. He looked around to make sure he could find this exact spot again, and then he knelt and unfastened the strap holding the watch in place.

The wrist was stiff, rigid and wooden. He thought of all the taboos of his people. He wasn't even supposed to be looking at the dead. But he would need to prove what he'd found. And he could tell this wasn't some cheap piece of jewelry. The watch's face was surrounded by glittering stones. He didn't know anything about jewels but these could be diamonds. He turned the watch over and saw the inscription: *To D.S., with love.* Someone would surely know this D.S. person or be missing her.

He tucked the watch into his shirt pocket and slipped and slid hurriedly down the rest of the incline. He grabbed the lead rope from the tree where he'd left it and dug three withered pieces of apple from his jeans' pocket. The three horses stopped eating and watched him approach.

Nathan smiled as the horse closest to him nickered and walked up, waiting patiently for his treat; the other two made him come to them. Once Nathan was on the lead horse's back and starting forward, the other two would follow. But just in case they had other ideas, he slipped a lead rope around each neck before starting out. He'd been smart enough to use lead ropes when bringing them up to the pasture, and now they were necessary to discourage any more grazing. Pulling them away from lush green grass wasn't a popular idea. But Nathan was beginning to feel safer as he headed back to camp. The very first thing he had to do was contact Ben. That is, after he brushed down, fed the horses, and got permission from his counselor to leave the camp.

Chapter 22

Village of Pine Ridge on Reservation

Almost seven and it was past dinner time. Ben had just finished making a ham and Swiss on whole wheat, mayo, and Dijon mustard when he heard a very soft knock at the door. In fact, at first, he thought he'd imagined the sound. But when he opened the door, there was Nathan.

"Hey, great timing. I can make another one of these." Ben hadn't even put his sandwich down to answer the knock.

"Okay. That looks good." Nathan followed Ben back inside.

"Why don't you pour us a couple glasses of milk and dig that bag of chips out of the bottom drawer." Ben pointed to the cabinet beside the stove. "I'll make your sandwich. I'm glad I have some company."

But he wasn't sure Nathan shared his enthusiasm. Something was wrong. Nathan seemed distracted, worried, and kept biting his lip.

Ben pulled out a chair at the table. "Rough day?"

"Yeah, I guess you could say that. Maybe just a strange day."

Ben didn't push. He sensed Nathan was gathering his thoughts, maybe trying to decide how to proceed? He could only hope that the young man wasn't in some kind of trouble. They ate in silence until the sandwiches were gone.

"There's a half gallon of Cookies 'n Cream in the freezer. Can I get you a bowl?"

"That's my favorite—a big bowl if there's enough." Finally, a smile.

Ben was feeling somewhat better—at least Nathan's appetite wasn't affected by whatever might be bothering him. After two spoonfuls of ice cream, Nathan began. Taking the horses to pasture, finding a place to meditate, seeing the strange delivery of men in an oil tanker ... Ben didn't interrupt. There would be time for questions but when Nathan pulled the watch out of his pocket and explained how he'd found it, Ben picked his cell up off the counter and called Red Bull.

Thirty minutes later the three of them sat around Ben's table. Red Bull seemed most interested in the watch. He stared at the inscription then got up, turned the chair to rest with its back against the table, and sat back down.

"I almost didn't come over. I had been called to help investigate an accident at the edge of reservation land, on a dirt road considered a back way into Spearfish. It's pretty much a forgotten artery and washes out every time we have a decent rain. But late this afternoon a Toyota sedan was found wrecked about five miles from here. It had rolled. Whoever was driving lost control on loose gravel coming around a sharp turn ..." Red Bull picked up the watch. "The assumption was, someone saw what had happened and gave the driver a ride into town—maybe to the emergency room or an urgent care. But after calling around, no one had reported an accident victim checking in."

Red Bull placed the watch on the table. "Now, this says something different." He continued to look at the watch before turning to Nathan. "I want you to tell me the story again—of exactly how you found the watch. Give me as many markers as you can remember. Estimate the number of feet the spot is from the creek, the number of footsteps maybe—a guess is fine—and how far down the slope from where you sat when you saw the tanker. And, Nathan, tell me again why you took the watch."

"I took the watch because someone needed to know who it belonged to. Evidence—it will be important to the Sheriff."

"That's the other thing I need to tell you. The wrecked Toyota belongs to Sheriff Sterling's ex-wife, Debbie. She was on her way here to meet Micki who's been staying with me on the Rez before they took off in the morning. I'd put money on the DS that's engraved on the watch standing for Debbie Sterling. We're going to have to go back to the site but first I need to call Mac."

But then the door burst open. "Mom's insurance company just called me. Something about an accident, and they had been called to tow her car to the nearest garage. I've been trying to reach her but she's not answering her phone. She was coming over this afternoon to get a manicure at an old friend's shop and then pick me up."

Red Bull got up, blocking a view of the table, but not before Micki saw the watch.

"Mom's watch. What are you doing with my mother's watch?" There was the beginning of hysteria in her voice.

Red Bull's arm quickly went around her. "I'm going to tell you all we know. I'm afraid we have a lot of questions and very few answers. Sit here." He turned his own chair back around to face the table and then handed the watch to Micki. "Keep it safe. I'm going to call your father."

Forty-five minutes later Ben's living room was packed—or so it seemed. Red Bull had called two of his deputies to join them and Mac had brought Sally Haines, making it nine in all. Everyone was briefed on the story.

They would go as far up the road as possible before hiking the rest of the way over the rock outcropping to the place where Nathan had found the inert hand. The sheriff's vehicle was equipped with lights, even a spot that would illuminate the climb up from the road. There were ropes and shovels and tarps—everything needed to bring a body back down the hill.

"I want the Indian kid with me in the cruiser," Sheriff Sterling said. "And I suggest we put these on." He tossed a pair of handcuffs to the deputy nearest him.

"Why? What's wrong with you?" Ben could feel the anger bubbling up. "Nathan is riding with me. And you'd better have a damned good reason to be treating a thirteen-year-old kid like a killer."

"Well, to my way of thinking, if you know where the body's buried, you're either the killer or linked to the crime somehow."

"That's bullshit." Ben stepped forward, not stopping

the anger that washed over his body. "I know this kid. Nathan is being honest with us. And we don't know what really happened. We don't even know if there is a killer or if there's even been a crime. What happened to 'innocent until proven guilty'?"

"Back off, Mac, this isn't the time to throw your weight around." Red Bull added, "I know you're upset. We all are. Before you go pointing fingers, think of Micki. Try to understand her feelings—how crazy this is, not knowing. She's going to need her dad."

Red Bull had put his arm back around Micki's shoulders, which probably further irritated Mac, Ben thought. But there was no call to attack someone who was trying to help.

Chapter 23

Pine Ridge Reservation

Nathan got into Ben's SUV and kind of slumped against the seat.

"People say things they don't really mean when they're upset. Give Mac another chance; he's not good at holding his feelings in."

Nathan nodded but didn't look convinced.

"Look on the positive side; you'll always know what he's thinking—he's not secretive."

"And that's good?"

"Okay, I'm not the one being attacked, but I know it hurts not to be believed or, worse yet, suspected of wrongdoing. But you've kept your cool. That's admirable—not everyone could."

"Can he put me in jail?"

"Not the way I see it." Of course, juvenile detention was a possibility but Ben chose not to go there. "Mac is scared. We're going out there to see if his former wife and mother of his only child is dead, possibly murdered. That's a shock. To relieve the pressure on himself, he lashes out. I believe he'll do the right thing, seeing that you've helped and not hindered the situation or in any way caused it. I think you'll get an apology."

"Maybe. Oh yeah, I almost forgot. There's a four-day camp retreat starting tomorrow. It's up in the foothills. I need your permission to go. I have the papers back at the teepee."

"Sounds like a fun time. Remind me later when we go back to the village and I'll sign." Ben marveled at what appeared to be perfect timing. Nathan needed some distance to put all this behind him. A retreat fit the bill.

* * *

The countryside was bathed in light that every few minutes was obscured by clouds drifting across the moon. Rocks took on menacing shapes, looming over the group of men and two women climbing upward. Everything was half hidden in shadows adding a surreal fuzziness to reality. The cruiser's spotlight pinpointed the ridge and probably saved a lot of missteps and falls.

They were halfway up when Jake Tully's F-150, the modified hearse, skidded to a halt behind the double row of pickups, Ben's SUV, and Mac's cruiser. Everyone waited at the top of the ridge for the coroner to catch up before proceeding to the site. He was carrying what looked to be a camera pack and a larger backpack of what probably contained instruments and sample vials—everything he would need for analysis before the body was moved.

"Sally called for a forensics team, but that's just me today. I can, however, make sure this search and rescue mission meets federal standards. We're in the gray zone up here—I mean it's not clear cut when it comes to topography and who this land belongs to. The road and side areas are county, the creek and other side is reservation, and to the east this land meanders over to join Judge Udahl's acreage. I'll do a mini survey and document with pictures of landmarks and the area we'll be working with. That will help decide jurisdiction. So, the less anything is disturbed the better. Okay, let's go see what we have."

Ben didn't mind but found it interesting that Coroner Tully stepped in and took over. The look on Mac's face said the intrusion wasn't welcomed. Too many drum beaters and not enough drums—wasn't that what his grandmother used to say? Looked like there was only one drum today. He stepped to one side as the coroner walked to the front of the group.

Once the site came into view, everyone was ordered to stay back until Coroner Tully needed help. He warned them that this might take a while.

It was easy to miss the hand unless you knew what you were looking for. Nathan was the one who pointed it out. Ben knew it would be necessary to remove the body and take it to Spearfish, no matter how late they might have to work. One night up here, exposed to animals, might have meant the corpse would be dismembered and spread over a wide area. But then couldn't that have been what those who put it here had hoped for? It wouldn't have lasted long and lots of evidence would have been lost.

Nathan did the right thing. Ben hoped he'd get credit for it.

More proof of what happened seemed to be the fact that the body was in a shallow grave, barely covered. An open invitation to predators. Coroner Tully asked for a whisk broom and a camping shovel. One of Mac's deputies stepped forward. Red Bull was holding a quietly sobbing Micki and stayed toward the back of the group. It was a solemn tableau of bystanders. Finally, some forty-five minutes later Coroner Tully stood, snapped off the blue latex gloves, and moved to stand in front of the group.

"I'll share what I know so far. First, my deepest condolences to Mac Sterling and his daughter, Micki. It's always difficult to lose a family member, but under these circumstances it's unthinkable. Because of the bruising to the body, Ms. Sterling apparently was in the rollover accident discovered earlier today, and according to the stage of autolysis, the death occurred approximately four to six hours ago."

"English, Tully," Mac boomed out.

"Sorry, that's the first stage of *rigor mortis*. It starts immediately upon death. The cells can no longer receive oxygen and become rigid. The accident itself was most likely caused when Ms. Sterling was struck in the neck by a bullet, probably from some distance. Was she targeted or was this random road rage, or maybe a hunter's bullet gone astray? Our county road seems a little remote for a highway shooter. But those are questions for our law enforcement. I will ask for help in bringing the body to the morgue for further testing. I will have more definitive answers over the next few days. But that catches you up for now. I do want to thank the young man for reporting what he found so quickly. I know interaction with the deceased is a taboo for your tribe. Thank you for stepping outside the boundaries of your Native beliefs to help us here."

Yes, finally, recognition for doing the right thing. Ben was pleased. He saw Nathan stand up just a little taller. No one had asked the coroner to single Nathan out for praise, but it couldn't have come at a better time. Plus, a long-range rifle shot pretty much eliminated Nathan as the killer. Micki asked to escort her mother's body to the morgue and Red Bull said he'd take her. There was no comment from Mac. He helped set up the body sling, a cot with handholds, to keep it from shifting on the trip down the hill after attaching ropes and poles. He asked his deputies to help dislodge the body, wrap it, and place it in the sling. Within an hour, everyone was ready to go.

Chapter 24

Spearfish Creek Morgue

Ben followed Red Bull and Micki back to Spearfish but first he dropped Nathan off at the teepee camp and signed the parental or guardian assent agreement allowing him to attend the upcoming retreat. Once again, Ben applauded the boy's quick thinking and time-saving decision to share the discovery of a body on the ridge. That showed clear, unbiased thinking. He was pleased at how Nathan had handled himself.

"At least I don't think I'll be going to jail." Nathan turned toward him with a sly smile. "The coroner kinda put the sheriff in his place, don't you think?"

"Didn't seem to be a lot of love lost, but the body *was* of his former wife. That can't be easy. Anyway, the rest is up to the law now. You have a good time this week." Ben watched Nathan wave to two other boys and take a seat around a pit fire outside his teepee. He was glad that Mac's accusation against Nathan was defused. He watched the boys load marshmallows on sticks. Nothing like a round of s'mores to make an evening turn out right.

When he got to the morgue, Red Bull and Micki were standing alongside Red Bull's pickup deep in conversation.

"Hey, I don't want to interrupt." Ben started to turn away.

"It's okay. Micki has just shared a new wrinkle in all this. Debbie Sterling was coming to meet Micki at the village offices on the Rez when the accident—I guess I should refer to it as an ambush—occurred. Micki had left her car at the garage in town for some basic service and parked there while she and her mother visited an aunt. But no one knew that. Not seeing Micki's car on the streets, one could have assumed that Micki had borrowed a car and was on her way to see me—"

Micki interrupted. "Dr. Pecos, I think I was the target. I think someone expected me to be driving to the Rez. At a distance my mother and I could pass for sisters. I can't bear to think that I somehow got my own mother killed." Fresh tears as she turned back to lean on Red Bull.

"I think David Gonzales is the key to the killing. Someone thinks you know more than you do, and someone is afraid that you'll share this knowledge," Red Bull added.

"And I don't even know what it is."

The back door to the lab opened and bright fluorescent light spilled into the parking lot. From the doorway, Coroner Tully was motioning for them to come in. "Got a minute? I won't take long."

"The evening's already a waste—might as well decide on our next moves. Do you feel like making some decisions? I know Tully's going to want input on what to do with your mother's body. Would you rather he contact Mac?" Red Bull asked.

"No. I'll be fine. I think I know what she'd like done. He can probably help me with arrangements. I think I'm just numb."

"Tell me if you need to leave." Micki nodded and slipped her arm through Red Bull's, and the three of them followed the coroner inside.

The room was immaculate. You could eat off the floor … well, maybe that wasn't the picture Ben wanted to remember. What was troubling was the half-eaten, loosely wrapped burger and very cold fries sitting next to the metal sink that had some containers of fluids lined up on a rubber pad. Unappetizing wasn't even the half of it. If he ever needed to lose weight, working here would be an automatic diet.

"Let's sit over here at the table." Red Bull pulled out a chair for Micki and waited for Ben and the coroner to follow suit.

"I got some coffee over there that I can warm up. Afraid it's a day old, though."

"I'll pass," Red Bull said.

"I'm fine," Ben added as Micki just shook her head.

"Well then, I'll share the new bits that I know. The bullet shattered her spine at C5 and C6. Death was instantaneous. My guess is that the marksman was over a thousand yards away. That puts him on Judge Udahl's land."

"A thousand yards?" Ben was surprised.

"Not even a stretch for a good sniper. Special Forces

personnel brag about hitting targets from almost four thousand yards, but I have my doubts."

The sniper was on the judge's land? Ben had a queasy feeling in the pit of his stomach.

No one knew the man was his father but what if he was involved in some way? No, that was unlikely. The ranch was so vast, the man couldn't know what was happening in every corner. Still, a visit might be in order. Maybe he should warn him. He hadn't forgotten the tanker truck full of men that Nathan had seen. Surely the judge needed to know about that. Someday he had to return the pen that he'd sent to Julie. That is, once he got it back.

The remainder of the evening included Mac showing up with sharp words between him and Micki as to what her mother would want in the way of a service. Mac was dead set against cremation and Micki was adamant that that was what her mother would want. An open casket service was out of the question because of the accident, but Mac didn't want a bunch of people at the church paying last rites to a vase of dirt, as he put it.

"Ashes, Dad, ashes. Do you know where she wants those ashes to be kept?"

"No idea."

"She wants to be taken back to North Carolina—Beaufort to be exact—and the urn placed on a shelf in the mausoleum between her parents. That's been the plan for many years."

"Not when I knew her."

"It's in writing. And I plan to honor those wishes." Micki looked defiant. It gave her something to take charge of and that was probably what she needed, Ben thought.

"We'll talk about it." Before any more could be said,

Mac walked out, letting the door bang behind him.

"Trust me, there'll be no talking about it," Micki called after him.

"I think we all should call it a night. I'll organize my notes and get you a copy," Jake said, nodding to Red Bull, "and give you time to take a look before I send the report off. We'll need to keep Ms. Sterling here for the time being."

Ben felt drained. Midnight and he needed to be at a meeting by eight. The only plan for the day was office work—no running around, and that was a relief.

Chapter 25

Pine Ridge Reservation Tribal Offices

It was one of those mornings when even a sixteen-ounce cup of coffee didn't clear the brain fog. Ben walked the two blocks to work, hoping the brisk fall air would infuse him with energy. But walking up the front steps to the offices, he realized the experiment hadn't worked—he was still dragging.

He poured another cup of coffee from the community pot in the break room. Thank goodness the receptionist got in before seven-thirty and this pot was fresh. Then he shut his office door before he sat down. It was still a half hour until the place filled up, but he didn't want to be disturbed. He needed to follow up with the assayer at the university. He rummaged in a desk drawer and brought out the package that had been sent to David Gonzales at Micki's address.

He pulled out the letter of explanation first, but wasn't sure the guy's findings made sense. Of course, it wasn't his field of study; if Ben expected something to jump off the page, it just hadn't happened and probably wouldn't. To him, a collection of granite shards remained just that. Ben knew he needed an interpretation.

His first phone call, directed by the department head's assistant, went to voicemail. It was exactly eight—time for the business day to start, Ben would have thought. There was always the possibility that the virus had closed the university to in-person classes but faculty should be on hand. Ben could only hope that the department head was in; his assistant hadn't said otherwise. At eight-fifteen, he tried again and didn't have to wait.

"Dr. Dayton here, how can I help you?"

Ben explained in detail who he was and how he'd come by the material he was calling about. At first, there was only silence. Had he lost the connection? No, Ben could hear breathing.

"Do you have access to reservation land?"

"Pine Ridge?"

"Yes."

"I'm not from this area but I am Native and am currently working on the reservation in community planning. If you need access, I can put you in touch with the head of law enforcement for the tribe. Could you tell me why you asked?"

"I'd prefer we set up a meeting with this person—face to face. I'd like to keep it to just the three of us. Someone from law enforcement would be a good addition. I'm not comfortable discussing issues over the phone."

"Of course. Are you available this afternoon? Perhaps, four o'clock?"

"That would work. I'm out of here most afternoons by two."

"Then, I'll contact Officer Red Bull and will call you if that time doesn't work for him. Otherwise, meet us here at the tribal offices at four."

After thanking the man for his time, Ben pulled up Red Bull's number on his phone and then just sat there. Why the secrecy? A geologist's report and some rock shards? What could be so important that it would take an in-person meeting? But he guessed he'd find out soon enough. He dialed Red Bull who had the same questions but agreed to meet.

Should they include Sheriff Sterling, Ben asked; the geologist had welcomed involving law enforcement. But Red Bull was cautious. If there was information that shed light on Debbie Sterling's death, there would be time enough to catch up the local law. But right now getting as much information as they could before sharing it precluded making a misstep. Mac Sterling was just a little too close to the situation to approach it with a cool head, Red Bull mentioned, and Ben could see his point. There would be plenty of time for follow-up.

The afternoon flew by. Ben met with two docs and a nurse from the community health center, along with the tribe's fiscal officer. They had questions about the budget Ben had proposed but by the end of the meeting, it had passed by a vote of five to two.

It was time to put personnel in place—social workers with substance abuse experience, preferably in a clinical

# 180

setting. Social workers would be able to get the program up and running; a psychologist could be added later. Ben had offered his time to interview applicants. No fewer than eight experienced or newly graduated sociology students had already applied. The next week was going to be busy.

Red Bull got to his office first. He was alone. Micki was on her way back to Pierre to make arrangements for her mother's cremation and subsequent trip to North Carolina to honor her wishes for interment.

Ben was hoping they wouldn't have long to wait. And they didn't; Dr. Roger Dayton was prompt. His jeans were bunched up around his ankles and his knit pullover had a splash of something that probably landed there during lunch, but the sport coat was a vintage wool tweed with leather elbow patches and leather-covered buttons in pristine shape. Ben thought he caught a whiff of mothballs as the man walked by. The jacket must be a part of special-occasion apparel. And the outfit fairly screamed, 'man lives alone.'

Ben closed his office door after the men were comfortably seated at a small conference table and refreshments had been declined. Ben placed the contents of the package that Dr. Dayton had returned on the table.

"I want to thank you for humoring me and meeting under somewhat cloak and dagger circumstances. I trust my instincts and after Doctor Gonzales died—"

"Wait, *Doctor* Gonzales?" That elevated the man's credentials, Ben thought. At least, gave him some much-needed credibility.

"Yes. David Gonzales was a student of mine. I taught a summer in Mexico—at the National Autonomous University of Mexico in Mexico City—some ten years ago.

David was my teacher's aide, finishing a degree in geology. I lost track of him for a number of years, then year before last he got in touch. He was in the States but not as a member of his chosen profession. He was basically undercover."

"Undercover? For whom?" Red Bull sat forward.

"I'm getting to that. I'm not sure I have all the particulars, but I need to share what I know."

"Sorry for the interruption." Red Bull continued to lean in, forearms on the table.

"Apology accepted. I think you knew David as a rabble-rouser, professional paid picket line agitator. His disguise was so complete that he joined a gang, members of a cartel that give homage to Pancho Villa through tattoos. I don't know who hired him out here. I only know it was big money and he was part of a group of undercover men. My understanding is that those who paid him weren't happy with his marriage to a young local woman and had him divorce her within a few months. He was completely under their control. He never really said that, but I felt it was implied."

"What was the purpose of his coming to South Dakota? What was he being paid to do? You're seeming to indicate he *wasn't* here to protest the pipeline after all?"

"Far from it. He was here to determine the worth of what was suspected as very rich mineral deposits—the new gold, if you'll allow my hackneyed analogy. He was here to prove someone was going to be very rich if his preliminary analysis proved to be correct, and if the area was large enough to make mining profitable."

"Mining?" Ben asked.

"Exactly. Not an endeavor everyone would welcome

into their backyard. Dirty, disruptive, land-altering … but the potential for riches beyond the wildest imagination, *if* David could prove the extent of the deposits."

"And you're saying he was successful?" Red Bull asked.

"Very much so, and I'm convinced he lost his life for it."

"It's my understanding that his death had been ruled natural, brought about by a health condition." Red Bull thought he could trust Coroner Tully.

"I don't believe that."

"I'm still at a loss here. Why was he killed as you think?" Red Bull asked.

"Simply for knowing too much. The land in question borders the reservation and would include, as a water source, Spearfish Creek which would quickly become contaminated. Any wells in the area would draw upon the rich underground aquifers that also provide water to Pine Ridge."

"Did I miss what was being mined?" Ben asked. "What could be so precious as to cost lives?"

"Oh, sorry, lithium—meant to state that earlier. If we end up with the number of electric cars that's predicted worldwide, we're sitting on top of the next Sutter's Mill."

Chapter 26

Pine Ridge Reservation

"Oh my God, did you hear?" The door to Ben's office burst open, no knock, just the receptionist hurriedly stepping into the room. She was slightly out of breath, but obviously giddy over her information—"it has just been announced out of Washington, the pipeline project has been permanently cancelled. It will not cross our land. We have Judge Udahl to thank. He even went to Washington to lobby for indigenous people—to protect our land and maintain its sacredness. Bless that man. This is such an important day."

"When did you hear this?" Red Bull asked.

"Right this minute. It's just breaking."

Red Bull pulled out his phone. "Not a fib. It's on the

news networks now. Project L is no longer on the books. I think we may have dodged a bullet. There are probably a hundred people congregating along the highway right now, lining up to protest the pipeline. They've been uppermost on my mind for weeks—how many would there be? Would they be armed? Did we have the manpower to handle that kind of crowd?—and now they're left with enjoying some great South Dakota weather instead. And I'm left with peace of mind—until we face the next crisis—God forbid there's one waiting for us. Great news, Pecos, no?"

Ben nodded. "Absolutely." But he noticed that Dr. Dayton didn't seem to share their enthusiasm. "Dr. Dayton? The cancelled pipeline takes some pressure off, wouldn't you agree?"

Dr. Dayton shrugged and waited until the receptionist had stepped back into the hallway and closed the office door. "I think you've dodged one problem only to find yourselves standing in the line of fire of something far more insidious. That next crisis is already here. Something that could change life on the reservation for years to come."

"The mining for lithium?" Ben asked. "I take it the samples you received from David Gonzales more than assured those concerned of the richness of the deposit?"

"And by richness I took you to mean people getting rich?" Red Bull turned to Dr. Dayton who nodded. "But those monetary gains do not include the Lakota?"

"Not as I understand it. Reservation resources will be siphoned off but a move needs to be made now to keep the greatest amount of damage from being done. The land is in jeopardy of being raped, plundered actually. David Gonzales had indicated to me that he was going to report what he knew and not stand by while the inhabitants of

Pine Ridge were taken advantage of. He was only waiting on my final report. You know how far his good intentions got him."

"I've seen the autopsy. I don't think Jake Tully would misdiagnose. Not to mention, the lab that found evidence of excess insulin wouldn't falsify a report. The insulin overdose made sense and led to a decision and pronouncement that cause of death was due to natural causes. Are you disputing this?"

"Yes. The death was not natural. I think it was murder, hidden quite nicely. Someone who knew his condition set it up. I tried to reach him daily for about five days before his body was found. I think he was kept locked up, with sustenance either refused or greatly restricted. When he was finally injected with much-needed insulin, death was immediate."

"Tough to prove," Red Bull offered.

"Impossible to prove now," Doc Dayton added. "I don't think anyone knew he'd already talked with me. I believe they thought any information about the project stopped with him. They assumed killing him bought them time. What I'd like to do is survey the area—see if David knew what he was talking about, that the mining was going to negatively impact the reservation, and I'd like your help."

"You've got it. I'll bring my truck around. Let's check this out."

* * *

They took the back road that bordered the county line and snaked along the edge of reservation land. Ben wouldn't have known where he was if he hadn't seen the *descanso,* the roadside memorial of a cross and plastic flowers so prevalent in his home state of New Mexico when an accident took a life along a roadway. Erected at the site of a death, family members or friends of the deceased paid homage with these small but colorful shrines. At least Micki's mother was being remembered.

Maybe three miles farther and the road turned to the left just beyond a steep incline. "That's where we're going." Red Bull pointed to a thickly wooded area above them. "I can get close with the truck, but we'll have some walking to do. Everybody good with that? We'll hike up to an old logging road and then circle around until we come to Spearfish Creek. That'll put us directly on the reservation, but right at the edge of the land we want to take a look at."

The trek up the hill was a little more arduous than it appeared from below. Ben made more promises to himself to hit the gym the minute he got back to civilization, as in home. He wished he'd grabbed a bottle of water. But if he quit complaining, he'd have to admit that the afternoon was once again, picture perfect. Not a cloud in the sky, not even the whisper of a breeze, just the prevalence of cool air—invigorating, not chilling.

"Hey, look at this." Red Bull was pulling tree branches away from a distressed area to reveal a roughed-out road connecting to the county one they'd driven up on. "Looks like this goes all the way to the top and will intersect with the logging road. Interesting that someone thinks it's necessary to keep it a secret. These branches are fresh—haven't been here long at all. And it took some heavy-duty equipment to scrape this artery out—they even banked it on each side. Somebody's already put time and money into being able to reach the top of the ridge from here."

"And that looks like the one thing they don't want us able to do." Red Bull was pointing to a sign that had been knocked on its side. It looked official, a county erected warning to stay out of the area. Another sign farther up warned of the operation of heavy equipment and unstable ground. No private vehicles beyond this point.

"Had you heard about this?" Ben asked Red Bull.

"Nope, not a word. The reservation has a contractual agreement with local government to share information that would impact the county—that's supposed to go both ways."

"I'd still like to hike up as far as we can." Doctor Dayton had walked ahead. "I think we'll be okay if we stay aware of our surroundings."

By the time they reached the logging road, they had walked and climbed a mile and a half. And it was obvious every step of the way that a concentrated effort had been made to move equipment along the same path. Now, Ben would have given anything for a breeze. He'd taken off his sweatshirt and hung it over the lower branches of a large Black Hills Spruce. The t-shirt underneath was more than enough. He'd pick the sweatshirt up on the way back down. He didn't need the extra weight of the thick, cotton material. Even tied around his waist, it would have been too hot. Once they had entered a clearing of sorts, signs of recent activity were everywhere, right down to remnants of what had probably been several lunches now scattered thanks to wildlife.

"Looks like they've completed the exploratory stage and are moving toward production if I'm any good at identifying machinery." Dr. Dayton moved toward a large earth-moving, metal behemoth. "We're looking at the investment of a few million." He turned to point at four other large pieces of equipment. "Just getting all these up here must have been a huge challenge. And probably carried out in the dead of night, or maybe they just temporarily closed the road down below. Whichever, I'd swear that it's been here less than a week. And it hasn't been used. There's not a trace of dirt on any of it other than the tires. Looks like it's sitting in a showroom. This is all in the name of preparedness."

"I'm beginning to think Debbie Sterling wasn't mistaken for her daughter but rather killed because she saw something—was coming down the road and got stopped by all the activity." Red Bull pulled out his phone and took snapshots of the road and equipment. "I'm surprised they haven't posted guards. But I guess they feel pretty safe that no one knows what's going on up here. The brush allows a fair amount of cover. But the tribe needs answers."

"I should share with you that I'm on the State Board of Land Use Licensing for mining operations. I can maybe answer a few questions from a legal standpoint."

"So, who owns all this?" Ben asked.

"Unless I'm mistaken—and that includes the fact that this portion may have been sold or deeded to family members—this is all a part of Judge Udahl's spread," Dr. Dayton said.

"But you don't know for sure? You think this area may have changed hands?" Ben pressed.

"Well, this is hearsay, but his mother died last month and gossip has it that two of her brother's children have made a pitch to sue for part of the judge's inheritance. Which is plenty, by the way. It's another case of vultures gathering at the time of death, that sort of thing. And maybe that's unfair. This project has been in the planning for months. It's been disguised but it was the judge's money that got all this started. Dr. Gonzales was hired over a year ago. But recently there has been a hold placed on the paperwork until ownership is established. I doubt if his cousins have a case, but it's got to be a touchy situation for the judge—as long as he's on the bench, that is. Someone could clearly make a case for his overreach, using his position for what might be interpreted as favors."

Ben was quiet. If he was going to suggest that his father set up a college fund for his grandson, he'd better do it soon. The judge getting disbarred and having his assets frozen wouldn't help Ben's cause. He made a mental note to visit the judge ... soon.

The air-piercing crack of the rifle was almost simultaneous with the splintering of the tree branch just above their heads.

"Down!" Red Bull screamed as he threw himself prone into tall grass. Crawling forward, shielded by a huge boulder, he pulled himself to a seated position, yelling, "Law enforcement here, Pine Ridge Reservation." The silence seemed as ominous as the gunshot had been. Nothing.

All three men scrambled to their feet as a lone man holding a rifle out away from his body and slightly above his head walked toward them from the rocks above.

"Didn't mean to scare you. I was taking a dump or I would have met you out on the road. This here's private land. I don't know about no reservation, but where we're standing belongs to Judge Rex Udahl."

The man, probably somewhere in his fifties, was almost out of breath by the time he'd joined them. He took a couple deep breaths before he leaned his gun against the trunk of a tree and continued. "As you can see, we got some pretty expensive equipment up here—don't want anything stolen or defaced. We've got three shifts of guards on duty. Oh, sorry, meant to introduce myself. Sam Olsen here." He held out a hand and Red Bull offered his.

"Any idea when the work is going to start?" Dr. Dayton stepped forward introducing himself as a state representative from the mining and minerals division.

"Nope, scheduling's above my paygrade, as they say. I just walk around holding a gun and drawing a paycheck." He chuckled, then added, "Didn't mean to startle you guys. Just doing my job."

"Understood," Red Bull said.

"Hey, I don't think you're supposed to be taking pictures."

Ben pressed his phone off and slipped the case in his back pocket. "I'm Ben Pecos, a consultant to the Pine Ridge tribe. My pictures will only verify that Indian land hasn't been encroached upon. Keeps us all honest." Ben offered a congenial smile that hopefully conveyed 'I'm just a paid employee, too' vibe. He hoped the guy wouldn't demand to know what he did exactly. A mining expert being up here made a lot more sense than a visiting psychologist.

He thought Red Bull was trying hard not to grin.

* * *

The trip back down the hill went quicker than the climb up. Of course, being shot at would hasten anyone's pace, Ben decided. Had they been lucky? Or was it just a case of safety in numbers? He couldn't shake the feeling that the incident might have had a different outcome if there had been just one of them.

They piled into Red Bull's pickup and before starting the truck, he turned to his companions. "So, what'd we learn, if anything? And what happens next?"

"They're going to be using rock crushing equipment, but I could have predicted that, based on the samples of ore Dr. Gonzales collected. It had also been his conclusion."

"Which means greater or lesser degradation to the land?" Ben asked.

"Depends. Salar brines are often the first choice to retrieve lithium, but mineral ore deposits are often richer. The cost to extract from hard rock formations is sometimes prohibitive—certainly for the small-time operation—but it does prove lucrative in the long run. Cutting to the chase here, the recovery process entails removing the mineral material from the earth and rock, heating and pulverizing it. The resulting powder is added to chemical reactants—sulfuric acid is a favorite—the resulting slurry is heated, filtered, and then through evaporation, it's concentrated. The result of this evaporation process is a saleable lithium carbonate."

"Of course, waste is a result, too," Red Bull commented. "How much, and what happens to that?"

"Really good question. Wastewater has to be treated in order to be reused or simply disposed of. I don't have to tell you that adds tremendously to the cost of spodumene lithium extraction. There are over a hundred different minerals that contain some lithium, but only five are actively mined. Dr. Gonzales's samples contained spodumene crystals known to exist in South Dakota and known to be the predominant, much sought-after deposit medium."

"Would you wager a guess as to how disruptive mining lithium will be to the reservation, to our way of life—sustaining our water sources and making certain water for the tribe, as well as our animals, won't be poisoned or used up?"

"I'm going to sidestep the guessing game. Lithium mining is a dirty business ruled by a very hefty bottom line. The bigger the payoff, the less restraint, the more destruction."

Red Bull didn't comment but started the pickup. Conversation had run its course and Ben was left with his own thoughts, facing the fact that his father was in all probability taking advantage of a money-making proposition at the expense of sustaining and protecting the life of several thousand indigenous people. He found himself wishing he'd never found his father. No wonder his father had done what he could to stop the pipeline. If he understood correctly, even oil could never match the demands for lithium in upcoming years.

Chapter 27

Pine Ridge Reservation

Even though it was after seven, Red Bull asked if they could use Ben's office to discuss a plan of action. Ben readily agreed. He wasn't even certain he knew what would be legal, let alone doable. And there was a real feel of unfinished business to the afternoon, unfinished and possibly dangerous if not handled quickly.

Dr. Dayton spoke first. "I suggest that tribal leaders get an injunction. That will stop any work before it begins. I'd also suggest a new survey. I'll bet the survey on record could be a hundred years old. But we need to know if the proposed mining is within the confines of the Udahl ranch. Where does reservation land start and stop along that ridge. We need that information before going forward.

Knowing the boundaries will also tell us the possible impact of the inevitable use of water that the reservation depends upon."

"What about the judge? He needs to recuse himself," Red Bull said.

"As the tribe moves on this, absolutely, but I'd let the legal system handle it. I don't know the man but by reputation he's known as a no nonsense, throw the book at you type. I wouldn't want to approach him."

"Ben, any thoughts?" Red Bull asked.

"I've had reason to look at tribal finances recently as part of the planning for a drug rehabilitation center. After careful research, the tribe might want to sue for compensation, some contractual sum for water use or maybe an easement across reservation land to transport equipment. Possibly a monthly fee for this use. A contract might also include the guaranteed hire of a certain number of tribal members. There's nothing to say, if all else fails, it can't be consensual and lucrative for both parties if safe practices can be put into place."

"Good points. If the mining can't be stopped, then make it work for the tribe. I like that," Dr. Dayton said.

Ideas were discussed as to how to proceed. All thought the tribal lawyers who represented the seven reservations in the state should be consulted. Dr. Dayton offered to go to the capital and intercede on behalf of Pine Ridge. He also had the name of a surveyor in mind and would email the pertinent information to Ben in the morning to be shared with those in charge at Pine Ridge.

"We need to be careful. I'm not convinced that Dr. Gonzales' death was accidental, and unless you have a reason to hide it, no one is going to drag a body up to a ravine hoping nature will disperse evidence." Red Bull concluded, "The stakes are big. Worth it to somebody to take chances and safeguard their investment at any cost."

"I agree," Dr. Dayton added.

"We all know more than we should. That knowledge could put us in danger. Keep your eyes open and remember, I'm only a phone call away." With that, Red Bull walked down the porch steps and out to his truck, followed to the parking lot by Dr. Dayton.

Even though it was getting late, Ben knew he couldn't sleep. Was nine too late in the evening to pay the judge a visit? Getting some feedback on what he would do for Zac was becoming pressing, now that he knew other family members had their eyes on the prize. But in clear conscience, could he approach the man with his hand out? Didn't it make him one of the vultures? Or did it make him the one with the most legitimate request?

* * *

Turning onto the county road, Ben began to have second thoughts. This whole idea of a late-night visit was probably stupid. The judge might not even be home, but if Ben remembered correctly, this was the part of the week that Judge Udahl wasn't traveling the circuit. Peace of mind was worth a chance.

The minute he got into the SUV, he turned the heat on low. The nights were getting cooler; they were probably less than a month away from the first snow. But he would be gone by then. Home for Christmas had a nice ring to it.

He hoped Nathan had adequate clothing and bedding on his retreat. Ben looked forward to hearing about his adventures, but knew Nathan would miss his newfound friends. If the judge agreed to support his grandson's college aspirations, then this trip would have been more than a success on several fronts. In addition to Ben being able to fill in the blanks on his own parentage, he'd give Zac's grandfather a chance to be supportive—make some atonement for his mother's callous dismissal of a cry for help. In some ways Ben was glad he'd been spared meeting his grandmother. Forgiveness would have been difficult.

Other than dodging what was probably an amorous elk strolling across the road, the evening was moonlight bright and it was pleasant to just be out. He made good time and pulled into the long drive leading up to the judge's house in forty-five minutes.

It looked like someone was still up—the living room and dining room lights were on. The large leaded glass panels on each side of the front door distorted a view of the house's interior, but Ben distinctly saw what appeared to be two people in an embrace. Hmmmm, his old man must have a friend.

There were several cars parked to the side of the three-car garage. Two pickups probably belonging to help ... then Ben did a double-take. The red Mustang GT fastback looked familiar. That day at lunch when he'd met Micki and Red Bull, wasn't that what she had been driving?

Of course, there could be more than one in the area, but not likely. It wasn't your everyday Mom and Pop choice of transportation in a small and older community. And Micki was in Pierre seeing to burial plans for her mother. There was no way she was out here at the judge's house.

He could hear two people talking on the other side of the front door when he walked up, but it was the judge who opened it.

"Why am I not surprised?" The judge didn't try to hide a smirk.

"May I come in?"

"Why not? You seem adept at inserting yourself into situations that don't involve you. Did you mean this to be a donation to Goodwill or did you come to pick it up?" The judge swiped the sweatshirt from off the back of a nearby chair and tossed it to Ben.

"Thanks. I'd totally forgotten where I'd left it." Ben followed the judge into the living room. He knew he'd heard voices but they were alone. He was pretty certain that his eyes hadn't deceived him; the judge had had company.

"Now, what is so important that you had to come out here at this hour?"

"I apologize for that, but we both have busy schedules; this seemed the most opportune time."

"Ever consider using the phone?"

Ben ignored the jab and remained standing. "I'll make this quick. I think you would be more comfortable if our genealogy—the boundaries of which—were spelled out. I know it's crossed your mind that I might make demands on your estate. I'd like you to know that the only demands that I'll make are on behalf of your grandson."

"And those would be?"

"I'd like you to put one hundred thousand dollars in trust for Zac's college. In so doing, I will forego any entitlement that I would have as your son to any property or other assets that you might have."

"And I'm supposed to believe you?" The sarcasm tapped into feelings of anger that Ben stifled quickly. He hadn't come for a fight.

"You know how to protect yourself legally. In fact, you might suggest someone who could draw up the papers for us."

"This has become a rather expensive toss in the hay, wouldn't you say?" Ben didn't react. He was being goaded by the judge, by his father, and a reaction would only give the man the upper hand. "And if I refuse to entertain such a request?"

"Then I would consider legal action and not remove myself as a recipient."

"In legalese I believe the saying is 'I'll take this under advisement.' Are you finished now? I have a rather full day ahead of me tomorrow."

"Just one more thing. The lithium mining operation at the top of the ridge—there might be legal ramifications to not seeking the tribe's support. The lack of notification would seem to indicate some need for secrecy. Possibly something nefarious? The ramifications of defiling the land of a sovereign entity under government protection might be costly." Ben saw a twitch start then stop, just below the judge's left eye. He'd struck a nerve.

"You need to go now." The judge brushed past him to hold open the front door. "Do not come here again unless you're ready to apologize for your insinuations, your callous finger-pointing, and brazen demands. I don't even want to think that you're my son. My mother was right; I never should have met you." The slamming of the door reverberated into the night. Ben didn't turn back and didn't hold back the grin, but he did notice that the Mustang was still there.

Chapter 28

Pine Ridge Reservation

"Stupid. And dangerous. You're out of your mind confronting that man on your own. Not to mention that you were asking for money then forcing him into a corner over the lithium mining." Julie was fairly shouting into the phone. "You scare me to death, Ben. I've never met the man, and I don't trust him just from what you've told me. I'm convinced your being his son holds no meaning for him. Emotionally he's unable to show any caring and certainly no love for another person. I think that toss in the hay remark was cruel."

"In hindsight I'd have to agree with you. But he has no right to get away scot-free. His mother made lives a lot more difficult than they had to be. I think he's the product of her control and meanness. I want to think he's bigger than all this—that he wants to do what's right."

"But you don't owe him an invitation to a second chance now. I don't think he's capable of doing the right thing. I don't trust him—didn't I just say that?"

"Hey, I'm sorry I upset you."

"I miss you. I think you need me there to pound some sense into you." They both laughed and the tense moment was averted.

"I should be home in ten days—two weeks at the longest. Still makes the most sense to turn the car in here and fly into Albuquerque."

"What about Nathan?"

"One of the tribal leaders offered to have Nathan stay in Pine Ridge until his school opens up again in Bellingham. Along with me, Nathan was vaccinated just after we got here. Being vaccinated, he should be able to be in the first group returning to campus. They're still planning on opening January fifteenth. At least, I haven't heard otherwise. I need to give them a call to make certain, but it looks like we'll have the holidays all to ourselves."

Another fifteen minutes of catching up and more than one 'I love you' and Ben was ready for bed.

* * *

The community meeting had been called for one o'clock. It was held once a month as just a heads-up, Q&A opportunity for townspeople to know what was going on. Ben was on the agenda to share the plans for a drug rehab center on the reservation and its implications for the county. Alcohol and drugs weren't just a reservation problem but spilled over into Spearfish and the surrounding area. As part of his interviews with two possible hires, social workers from Rapid City interested in relocating, he brought them to the meeting to get a feel for the working conditions and the community's expectations for his proposed program.

Ben counted forty-seven people in attendance. Most seemed to be county officials of one kind or another, shop owners, two pastors of local churches, a local newspaper reporter, and the recently elected mayor and the city manager, plus the curious. The hall held approximately seventy-five so there was a feeling of intimacy. Those in attendance felt more at ease to talk in front of a smaller group.

Mac Sterling was up first and recounted the good fortune of being able to ward off any disturbance by protesters. The pipeline project was indeed dead for the time being. There was loud clapping and cheers. The project certainly had not been popular. He ended with the announcement of a soon-to-be listing for a fulltime deputy and passed out a list of requisites.

The chairman of the water board asked for the floor next and reported on the recently published drought numbers using the white board on the dais.

"I know this isn't new news. We're depending on a good snow cover this winter, leading to an ample spring runoff. Spearfish Creek is especially vulnerable, currently being down twenty percent of capacity. Our adjoining farmlands are desperate for irrigation water." The man paused to look at his notes. "This next bit of information that I'm going to share is alarming. Just this morning I received a request from the State Mineral and Mining Program. As the regulatory arm of the DENR—for those of you who might be new to the state, that's the Department of Environment and Natural Resources—they are being petitioned to permit mining just outside our town's boundaries. I'm meeting a part of their request by announcing the proposed land use at this public meeting. In addition, I'll arrange for a separate use hearing very quickly. It's my understanding that mining equipment is already in place and work could start immediately unless we take measures to at least slow it down."

"What type of mining?" someone yelled from the back row.

"Lithium; the dirty, disruptive type."

"Then that's easy, petition the state to refuse to grant a permit."

"Not quite that easy. The proposed mine is on private land. In this state, as in so many others, a landowner has mineral rights—ownership above and below the surface. The project I'm talking about could possibly contaminate our water supply, as well as that of the Pine Ridge Reservation."

"So, who's the owner?" Another voice from the back row. "The person can't be much of a good citizen."

"That's just it. The land belongs to Judge Rex Udahl." The commissioner paused to let that sink in. Ben noted the buzz of discussions that broke out almost immediately.

"This all sounds like it's going to cost this county a whole lot of money, with no guarantee that things can be turned around," a man in the front row called out. "Who's paying for us to try and stop it?"

"I'm hoping to get tribal officers involved but it's way too premature to make any promises," Red Bull answered. "We're willing to entertain any ideas as to how to proceed."

Ben knew there would be lively discussions around several dinner tables that night. If anything, this was a tight-knit community that took its citizenship and good neighbor policies seriously.

The rest of the meeting was anticlimactic. Other announcements seemed nonessential in comparison. A sign-up sheet for volunteers to help with Christmas decorations was circulated, and other new business involved establishing the locations of three new vaccine centers that would be opening by the end of the week. It was after three o'clock when the meeting adjourned. Ben followed Red Bull, Mac Sterling, and Bill Turner out into the parking lot.

"I feel better with the information out in the open," Bill Turner said. "I don't have a good feel about this. If there's a misstep, we could have problems. And it would be too easy to say or do the wrong thing. We have to be prepared. We have to be on solid ground before we make a move and time isn't on our side. We've needed lawyers and legal help as of yesterday and didn't know it."

Red Bull turned to Ben. "Any chance you could give us a hand with help from the top? Surely, IIIS or other source groups for indigenous peoples would have some clout. At the very least, money and legal power—basically, I don't want to get sideways with the Feds. But I don't want our way of life ruined, our lands stripped of nutrients. I can't imagine they would turn us down. They've stepped in before, in other situations."

Mac was shaking his head. "I can't believe I had five minutes to think I'd dodged a bullet with the pipeline, only to realize I'm actually already in front of a cannon. I'll put my extra help on standby just in case this new twist turns ugly, too."

"Good idea, Mac." Red Bull then added, "I think the three of us need to stay in touch."

Chapter 29

Mac pulled into the Mobil station to gas up the cruiser and get a Mountain Dew. That was his second favorite drink but no one stocked ginger ale. He had a mound of paperwork waiting for him at the office and a couple more errands like this one. He'd gotten the okay to add a deputy and needed to post qualifications in the town's newspaper, the *Black Hills Pioneer*.

He'd called them but they had suggested he visit their website. In the old days you typed out what you wanted an ad to say and hand-carried it down to the news office. He was glad he had Sally to help him with the online stuff. He expected some response from the city meeting; thank God he'd thought to hand out notices. It wasn't totally a thankless job and the pay beat out the local Walmart. He expected several people to put in applications now that the pandemic was losing its grip. Vaccinations seemed to be turning the nightmare around.

"Hey, Mac." The station's owner waved to him from the doorway. "Got a minute?"

Mac nodded, finished filling the tank and walked inside. "Rudy, how's it going?"

"Listen, I was over at your office earlier but missed you. I shoulda probably come to see you earlier but what I got ain't much. Maybe nothing at all. But because of what happened, I think I need to say something. You guys always tell people to keep an eye out and if it's something weird, let you know."

Mac felt himself losing patience. "Just spill it. I'm listening."

"Well, yesterday, your ex-missus pulled in to gas up and I don't know if she pulled up to the front pump and didn't see the guy getting ready to roll into the same spot—I mean I can't think she intentionally cut him off—but you know Debbie, always a little spacey. So, I tend to think she just wasn't paying attention to what was going on around her." Rudy stopped and began to chew on his lower lip.

"And?" Mac tried to not make it sound threatening but the guy always got on his nerves—even back in high school.

"Well, this man gets out of his truck, waving his arms and yelling. It wasn't just because he called her a '*puta*' but he also kept calling her Micki. Well, after I heard what happened, I mean I am so sorry for your loss, I thought I better say something. You know, the guy had mother and daughter totally confused."

"The guy spoke Spanish?"

"Well, yeah, *puta* isn't English."

"What finally happened?"

"I guess nothing. I don't think the guy followed her when she left."

"But you don't know? You didn't watch to see what happened? It didn't cross your mind that a little road rage might be in the making?" Mac willed himself to calm down.

"Mac, I know this may come as a shock, but I don't have time to stand out here and stare at the pumps all day. It's just when I heard about the accident that I remembered ... but like I said it could be nothing." Rudy's voice was rising.

"Thanks, Rudy. Hey, I apologize. Sorry to be a little short. A lot's going on and then losing Debbie that way ... it was shocking. Your information could be helpful. I appreciate you telling me."

"No hard feelings; it must be tough."

"You didn't notice a tag, maybe get a number?"

"No, I do remember the tag said Chihuahua though. We usually don't get many Mexicans way up here. But lately there's been a lot of strangers. And then that Gonzales fellow was found dead ... this used to be a nice quiet, safe place to live. But not anymore, I guess. Sure doesn't make your job any easier."

Mac thanked him, signed the city voucher for the on-duty gas-up, and left. Yeah, he had to agree with Rudy, the whole place had a different feel to it—edgy, for lack of a better word. Mac felt like he was just waiting for the next shockwave.

* * *

The day was a little disjointed but Ben had time in the afternoon to finish the interviews with the two applicants from Rapid City. A young man and woman, both just out of school. Both were interested in working in an addiction clinic setting on the reservation, and Ben liked their credentials. Ben always marveled at the eagerness of the young. But that attitude was what he looked for—good grades, community experience, but most importantly, a willingness and dedication to healing. These young applicants were change agents. And that's what the reservation needed. They had his recommendation and he would forward their applications to those in charge of hiring at Pine Ridge. He was looking forward to a quiet evening after picking up a pizza for dinner.

But first, his next major bit of business was contacting the Bureau of Indian Affairs. The BIA oversaw many aspects of reservation life and was the one government office that should, and hopefully would, respond to Pine Ridge and the mining threat. As a federal agency that managed over 55,700,000 acres, it was responsible for all lands held in trust by the government for indigenous tribes.

Ben recalled that more than two million tribal members from 574 recognized tribes currently received some kind of services via the BIA. They would have the big guns and the power to know how to handle a threat to a reservation's natural resources—especially since that threat was being orchestrated by a circuit court judge.

As a part of the Department of the Interior and one of the oldest federal agencies, if any federal office had clout, it would be the BIA. Ben knew putting them on alert would be the right thing to do. The BIA was developed to promote agriculture, oversee needs of infrastructure, regulate tribal management, and most importantly, guard and manage natural resources and encourage the quality of life in tribal communities. Bingo. Their very reason for being made them the perfect go-to entity to protect the people of Pine Ridge.

He picked up the receiver on his office phone and then hesitated. He was about to implicate his father; until he found out otherwise, he had to treat this person as the one who made up half of his genes. And that added a certain gravity to the situation. Would people understand? Wouldn't Natives recognize the judge for what he was? A get-rich-quick manipulator in what Natives would see as a bold scheme to enrich himself while harming the lives and livelihood of others. Ben wasn't worried about the backlash once his position was known—a son angered by years of neglect and finding only refusal to recognize him now. That might be what it looked like on the surface, but that wasn't it; that wasn't what he was about. Ben simply couldn't abide the taking advantage of, let alone the harming of others.

The judge was wrong. Ben had to look past who he was and concentrate on the damage he was about to wreak on innocent, unsuspecting, Pine Ridge residents. The kind of damage that couldn't be reversed once set in motion. He checked the federal directory and dialed the phone.

After introducing himself and explaining his concerns to three different department assistants, he was connected to a Lawrence Standing Hawk, a commissioner and person who was in charge of natural resources on government trust land. He listened quietly as Ben gave him the particulars of what was happening in Pine Ridge.

"Have the Pine Ridge tribal officers put exactly what

you've told me in writing. I'll need the exact locations of the proposed mine, pictures of equipment that's in place now, and anything else that pertains to the project—such as a copy of the assayer's mineral content analysis. If we move quickly on this, I can have a team out there to follow up and propose a plan of action next week. At least, at first, we can stall any work—either planned or presently ongoing—even before we have concrete conclusions. But I have no reason to doubt you. This is a serious overreach by locals in the area and certainly takes advantage of the indigenous people of South Dakota. I think we're on solid ground here. A mine that would ruin drinking water and halt irrigation has to be dealt with. I look forward to working with you and the people of Pine Ridge."

Ben offered his thanks before hanging up. He then made a list of what Lawrence Standing Hawk had requested and added a brief note of explanation before forwarding the request to the local tribal leaders. Finally, done for the day.

He'd driven to work because of the early meeting in town and parked the SUV in back. He'd barely rounded the corner of the building, heading toward the parking lot when Red Bull skidded to a stop and lowered his driver-side window.

"I need you to follow me. You'll want to take your truck. We need to get to Rapid City—to Black Hills Surgical Hospital. Nathan took part in a Sun Dance and there were complications. Stay close; I'll use the lights—that should clear us a path."

No time for questions, the window whirred upwards and Red Bull backed up and pulled forward ready for Ben to follow.

Chapter 30

Rapid City, South Dakota, Black Hills Surgical Hospital

Ben couldn't allow himself to think. He jumped into the SUV, peeled out and hit I-90 on Red Bull's tail. The siren and lights helped; they made it to the hospital in forty minutes. And then had to wait. Red Bull needed to get back to the reservation but postponed leaving until he could hear how Nathan was doing. He pulled up a chair next to Ben.

"Don't be too hard on him. The camp counselors tried to dissuade him but Nathan was adamant. He felt he needed to subject himself to the ceremony. I don't know how strong your Anglo side is—whether you follow traditional Indian ways at all—but he told them he needed to be cleansed, in addition to offering himself in prayer. He felt contaminated. He'd touched the dead when he found Debbie Sterling's body—that's serious stuff for a Navajo."

"I'm not sure that a thirteen-year-old boy from a far different tribe could have been thinking clearly."

"Indigenous peoples are all brothers and sisters. I hope you understand that. If he believed in invoking our god of spirits to help relieve his burden when he did so, he would have received solace."

"But the Sun Dance, the danger of it …"

"It's a great honor to take part. Do not forget that. Nathan showed respect and commitment to his brothers. He's strong. I believe that he will come through this."

"I second that." Ben and Red Bull turned as a man in scrubs entered the room. "I'm Dr. Bronson. You probably have less than an hour before you can see Nathan. He's out of surgery and doing great and being hooked up to several monitors at the moment. There was muscle tearing in the pectoral area and some blood loss that could have been worrisome. I congratulate those who got him to the hospital in a timely manner. That's going to make all the difference in his recovery."

"You expect a complete recovery?" Ben asked.

"Absolutely. Obviously, there will be pronounced scarring but no underlying damage. That's one strong kid. I want to keep him overnight. I've started him on antibiotics and a painkiller, and want to see how he's doing in twenty-four hours."

"I'd like to stay with him. Do you allow that?" Ben explained that he was Nathan's guardian.

"Absolutely. It will be helpful. I'll tell the nurse. I think Nathan thought he might be in trouble."

Red Bull stood up. "I'm out of here then. Ben, let me

know how things are going. I think we have a happy ending in the making. See you in the morning." He shook hands with the doctor before walking out the front door.

"Let me go check on Nathan. I'll have the nurse come get you when he's ready for company."

The wait wasn't long. Ben braced himself but the paleness of Nathan's skin next to the strips of white bandaging that covered his chest was still shocking. But Ben was proud. Nathan had honored his roots and followed his ancestors in seeking help. Did being half Anglo dilute his own beliefs? Red Bull had given Ben something to think about. And to think his Anglo side was less than compassionate and loving … well, more than once, he'd wished he'd never met his real father.

"Ben?" The voice sounded rough and scratchy.

"How about a few ice chips?" Ben had noticed the container on the bedside tray.

"Yeah."

"You hold still. Let me get some on a spoon." Not that Nathan could move very far, pinned down by an IV in each arm. Three teaspoons later Ben pulled a chair up to the bedside and sat down. "How are you feeling?"

"Pretty much okay."

"I don't think I could do what you did. Takes guts."

"You know the guy at school with the convertible? I don't think Alex will call me a pussy again."

"No, I bet not. How are you going to tell him what you did?"

"I'll show him. I'll take off my shirt like Red Bull did. Remember that night at the restaurant? That was badass."

"It was." Had showing up this Alex been the motivating factor in taking part in a Sun Dance? And not some show of altruism? Or deep self-introspection and redemption? Did it matter? Ben thought not.

To the almost-teen, he had been successful and was obviously proud of his accomplishment. Ben needed to accept that and not pry.

"I'm hungry."

"That's a sign of life getting back to normal. You should be having dinner served any moment." Ben had hardly finished the sentence before there was a knock on the door and a staff member carried in a tray.

"Let me get a nurse in here to undo you. You're going to need at least one hand free to eat." In ten minutes Nathan was sitting on the side of the bed, unhooked from any machines and drips, and attacking a mashed potato, green bean, Salisbury steak and gravy meal.

"Better?" Ben thought Nathan was starting to look normal, good color and strength returning with each mouthful. He only noticed him wince once when he reached for the carton of milk.

"I'm going to head downstairs to the cafeteria but I won't be gone long. Anything you'd like?"

"Dessert?"

"You got it. Don't tell me, something with chocolate in it?"

Nathan grinned and nodded then put down his fork. "Ben?"

"Need something else?"

"Sort of. I wish I could call you Dad."

Ben didn't hesitate. "Me, too. Why don't I make that happen? I'll call Julie and get the paperwork going. Nathan Yazzie Pecos. Sounds good."

Nathan barely lifted an arm and made a fist for Ben to

bump. "Now Zac will be my real brother."

* * *

"Ben, I think that's a great idea. And I'm glad it was Nathan asking, and not one of us pushing him in that direction."

"Sure this isn't too much motherhood in such a short period of time?" Ben had stopped in the hospital foyer to give Julie a call. "I need to know that you support the idea."

"I think I can handle it. Support it? I love the idea. Are you going to let Nathan break the news to Zac? He'll be thrilled."

"I'll let him use my phone the minute I get back to his room. I'm staying with him overnight. I'll call you from the office tomorrow morning. The doctor is pleased with how well Nathan is doing. He'll be released to go back to camp if the counselors give their okay to let him rejoin the group."

"Do you think that's a good idea?"

"I do. He'll enjoy a little celebrity among his peers—nothing like that to make pain go away."

Julie laughed. "I'm sure you're right. It's an impressive act."

Chapter 31

Pine Ridge Reservation, South Dakota

Fresh bandages, a warning that any cough or sneeze would be painful for a while, and Nathan was free to return to the reservation. All he could talk about on the way back was how excited Zac was to be getting a big brother. At the camp, both senior leaders assured Ben that everything would be all right.

Judging from the adulation of the ten or so boys gathered around the SUV as Nathan got out, Ben could see that they were telling the truth. Nathan must have been the only camp member to take part in the Sun Dance ceremony, and it looked like it gave him unlimited points with the group.

Ben waved goodbye and turned back toward the tribal

offices to begin his day. He was already getting a late start, but important things first. He'd call the Navajo agency governing native adoptions and make certain there would be no glitches in this adoption moving forward.

A call to the agency and then a call to Julie. Her name would be required on the papers, too. She would be able to handle the paperwork on her end and then overnight everything to him to sign and send back to be registered by the tribe. It would be finalized and recorded by the time the boys returned to school.

A father of two in under a year—a tween and a teen. And he liked the feeling. Before Ben could get to work, Zac called. He was beyond excited and wanted to tell Ben he already had his airline ticket to Bellingham for January second. Was Nathan returning then, too? Ben assured him that he was. Ben was going to New Mexico for Christmas, and Red Bull promised him that he'd have Nathan on the right flight to meet Zac at the SeaTac airport the day after New Year's.

He'd barely set up an interview for one o'clock when the intercom buzzed. Ben had a call from a Lawrence Standing Hawk of the BIA on line one. He crossed his fingers that the call would be good news—hopefully suggesting the next step they had to take in order to derail the mining plan.

"I just need to know that if I show up tomorrow, I won't be rushing things. South Dakota seems to be a prime location for more than one lithium mine. I'll be bringing along a couple of specialists—a geologist and a mining guru. We plan to get definitive answers on what the plan is when it comes to excavation. If we're looking at a lawsuit, then that will follow; but facts first."

After he hung up, Ben left a message for Dr. Dayton. He wanted him to be part of the team. Next call was to Red Bull. Again, he had to leave a message. But the field team was coming together and a trip back up into the hills was imminent. The ducks were lining up.

* * *

Lawrence Standing Hawk and his two associates flew into the Rapid City Regional Airport, rented a car, and were in the tribal offices of the Pine Ridge Reservation at one o'clock sharp. Ben was impressed. Standing Hawk was a man dedicated to his job. Lanky to the point that his clothes seemed draped over his body instead of fitting, it would be difficult to guess his age. Ben thought probably somewhere in his fifties but with a boundless energy that took years off.

A trip to the restroom where he had obviously run a comb through his thick, somewhat shaggy, black hair and he was anxious to get started. A quick sandwich and after sticking an extra bottle of water into his backpack, he was ready to trek to the site. Ben thought his two traveling companions looked like they needed a nap. Apparently, they had caught the red-eye out of D.C. and had been traveling for the most part of half a day.

"We're already behind when it comes to regulating lithium mining and choosing sites with something other than the bottom line in mind. But we're in a race with China, as well as other countries around the world. Argentina stands to become a leader in mining the ore. Here at home, sites are being mapped out and registered in several states—California, Nevada, the Dakotas. More than one reservation's land is being threatened with a disruption to its natural resources. When you figure lithium mining consumes over 3,200 gallons of water a minute and it takes up to 300 years to recover from waste being deposited in and around the sources of that water, our work takes on an urgency."

Dr. Dayton was enthusiastically nodding in agreement. He expressed his relief at the BIA taking this project so seriously. Now was the time to get on top of things—to slow, if not stop, the operation before the desecration had begun. Ben noted the six men were all in agreement.

Besides himself and Red Bull, each lead geologist had brought two others with him. Was there safety in numbers? Ben would bet on it. He fully expected to run into more guards at the site. Bringing the BIA into the mix was the right thing to do. Ben had a feeling that it was going to take big money to change what was happening.

Red Bull was in charge of the group. He'd alerted tribal officials to what was going on and Ben, including the BIA, were applauded. Now it was a matter of photographing the area, taking samples of water and ore, matching boundaries with the only survey on file, and waiting for the report that would outline a suggested plan of action.

Ben rode with Red Bull and filled him in on Nathan's progress, including the fact that Nathan would soon have a family.

"That's fantastic! I think the kid's lucky."

"Thanks. My own son is thrilled. Being an only child can be tough and a little lonely. Just ask me. I was glad this worked out. The boys are good for one another." He laughed, then changed tone. "Can I be snoopy? What do you think is going to happen today?"

"Not much, if we're lucky. I'm hoping we'll be able to match up the land to the survey map without any interference. Most likely, we'll have to get surveyors up here. The current map has got to be wrong in some places. Erosion along the creek bed has moved some boulders, even put an extra bend in the creek's boundaries—that I know for a fact. Plus, Mr. Standing Hawk and Dr. Dayton will want to explore Spearfish Creek themselves—estimate the force of flow, that sort of thing. Those measurements will have to be duplicated in the spring after runoff."

"I'd like to think we're ahead of the game just by getting the right people involved."

"Can't hurt."

Red Bull motioned for the two SUVs following him to pull to the side of the road and park. Everyone got out and waited for Red Bull to tell them what the plan was.

"Do you hear that?" Red Bull held up a hand for quiet. The sound of heavy machinery was faint but seemed to hang in the air. "Sounds like we'll get to see a little action— something's going on up there. We have a mile or so hike. Don't push it if you don't feel like it. Stop and take a drink of water if you need to. I don't want to have to carry anyone back down the hill." With that, Red Bull took off across the road and started upward.

It wasn't an arduous climb unless you weren't used to that sort of thing. Ben noticed that everyone seemed to be keeping up, even though Red Bull set a brisk pace. They were on county land but would cross over onto reservation land closer to the creek and then back. Somewhere near the top they would be on a part of the Udahl ranch. But they were nowhere near that area when they were stopped by three armed men who burst out of a thick stand of shrubs.

"Stop there." No one was pointing a gun at Red Bull and the others, Ben noted, but all three looked menacing and held rifles slung across their shoulders.

"Reservation law enforcement, Officer Red Bull here."

"Don't care about your credentials. You're trespassing." One of the men stepped forward. He seemed to be the one in charge.

"Sorry, but you're wrong. This is county land up to and including that stand of willow by the creek. I'll show you. I've got a topographical map and survey." Red Bull was carrying a cardboard tube with the documents and he held them out. "Want to take a look?"

Ben thought the guy looked confused. He shook his head, turned to his two companions, said something under his breath, then stepped back and waved them on.

"Looks like we just got a hall pass. Stay close together." Red Bull started out again.

Ben knew it wouldn't be the only time they were stopped, but they made it to the top of the ridge and walked along the creek without incident.

Several earth-moving machines were busy tearing up the earth about fifty yards to their right, bouncing along, pushing boulders out of their way. They must be on the Udahl ranch, Ben thought. As he watched, a dump truck emptied its bed of good-sized gravel onto an already twelve-foot-high pile. This didn't just happen. People had been up here working for a couple days at least. He watched as the empty truck went back over the far side of the hill and out of sight.

Standing Hawk had a camera and was busy taking shots of equipment, as well as the result of the work being done. Two more men from their group were using tape measures to assess the area from the creek to the worksite.

Ben walked up to Standing Hawk. "What do you think?"

"I'm glad we came. This is a disaster in the making for the tribe. I've seen enough and have what I need." He patted the camera case around his neck. "I think our next step involves our legal system."

The walk downhill was quick but what met them at the bottom was maddening—the rear tires on all three vehicles had been punctured. Red Bull was furious.

"In retrospect, I should have left someone with the cars. Too late now. Ben, can I talk to you for a minute?" Red Bull walked to the front of his truck and leaned against the hood. "I need a favor. First, I'm going to call one of my deputies. You're the only one with operable wheels back at the office. I'll have my guy take you to your car; I'm going to stay here until we have all three vehicles ready to roll. Now, here's my problem." Red Bull stopped and drummed his fingers on the truck's metal. "I'm not even sure how to say this—I so want to be wrong."

Ben waited and didn't interrupt but wondered what could be causing Red Bull to struggle for words.

"I'm worried about Micki. I know old man Tully wanted to do the right thing. He released the body of Debbie Sterling as soon as the cause of death was ruled accidental, or at least under investigation. He bypassed Mac and let Micki know. Micki immediately set up transport to take her mother back to Pierre for cremation. From there, Micki planned to ignore her father and honor her mother's wishes to be interred with her parents, Micki's grandparents. She would take her mother's remains to North Carolina herself. It was simple and straightforward, and I agreed that she needed that closure. Or so I thought.

"The funeral home in Pierre wanted three thousand for the cremation. It wasn't a sum that Micki readily had—but will, once she disposes of her mother's belongings. So, I offered to loan her the three thousand. I put it on a card and two days ago I saw her off. I kick myself that I didn't go with her, but with everything going on around here, that was impossible. She was distraught but holding it together. She assured me driving would be a relief, give her time to think, to reflect. We texted and I thought she was fine; she was in Pierre and packing up her mother's house, even planning on looking for a new place to live herself. Then the texts stopped. I called the funeral home and was shocked to learn that she had never shown up. As far as they knew, she had never made it to Pierre."

"But the first texts, didn't she say she was there?"

"I guess anyone could text if they had her phone. There's no proof that it was Micki."

"What do you want me to do?"

"Go to Pierre. Check out her mother's house. I don't want to involve local cops—Micki's been through enough. There's no need to make this an incident if it isn't one. She may have simply opted for some alone time to grieve her mother's passing. Being in her mother's house must be emotionally challenging—going through her things, deciding what to do with mementos. She's got to be reliving her own life, too. That's rough. I'm trying to convince myself that that's all it is. Here's the address and a map. Let me know the minute you get there."

* * *

Ben picked up his SUV, got gas, and headed out. The trip to Pierre was about three hours. And he was kicking himself all the way. Should he have mentioned seeing what he thought was Micki's car at the Udahl ranch? It would have been at a time that Red Bull thought she was in Pierre. But was it really her car? And what about the shadowy embrace he saw through the glass beside the front door? Would he have been comfortable sharing that? He had absolutely no definitive, concrete proof of anything that could have been suspect, and the information would no doubt have been extremely unsettling. No, it had been best to keep his mouth shut.

But wasn't his decision colored by the fact that he would have had to explain why he was there? Nine at night wasn't the usual, acceptable time to go calling. And what could he say? What if he told the truth? Judge Rex Udahl is my father. Or even further explanation—I'm here with my hand out to get my son an all-paid trip through a college of his choice. What did that make him sound like? How would that kind of info be received?

No, not mentioning anything about seeing the red Mustang was the right way to go. He was content with that decision, until he turned down the lane that held Debbie Sterling's house—it was swarming with police.

Yellow police tape outlined both the front and back yards; four cruisers were parked nose to trunk in the driveway next to an emergency responder truck. Several neighbors stood in the street talking with two uniformed cops who were taking notes. Everyone fell silent as four men, possibly EMTs, came out the front door, each supporting a corner of a stretcher. The white sheeting covering the body seemed to indicate that the person being carried was deceased.

Ben parked and got out of his car, which immediately

attracted the attention of a man in plainclothes who appeared to be in charge.

"Gonna have to ask you to move on. I'm not turning this into a stop and gawk."

"I'm Dr. Ben Pecos currently working on the Pine Ridge Reservation. I was asked by Officer Red Bull, chief of law enforcement for the tribe, to check on a Miss Micki Sterling who has been staying at this residence with her mother. I'll gladly share his cell number and he can corroborate my reason for being here."

"Sergeant Roy Cummings here. Glad to meet you. If you'd be comfortable—and it's up to you whether or not to slip a mask on—let's sit in my cruiser over there. I'd rather talk where there's some privacy."

Ben didn't have a good feeling about what was happening. Had Micki been attacked? The red Mustang was sitting tucked up close to the garage in front of him. So, she must have made it home. Hopefully, not to be ambushed.

He turned his attention to Sergeant Cummings who had slipped behind the wheel of his car. He waited for the officer to begin the conversation. His frown didn't instill confidence. Ben fought back a feeling of dread as he watched the man lick his lips, pressing them together before turning toward Ben.

"I'm just going to tell it to you straight out. About an hour ago, the neighbor to the north ..." He pointed to a house to Ben's right. "A Ms. Conklin came over to offer her condolences to Miss Sterling concerning the death of her mother. Apparently, the obituary had just been published in the afternoon paper by the funeral home. When she walked up, she found the front door open. Thinking this was more than odd, she entered the home, calling out for Miss Sterling. There was no answer. She continued on through the house, finally stepping out into a patio area at the back. That's when she saw the body. Miss Sterling was hanging from a branch of an oak tree just a few feet from the back door."

"Do you believe it was suicide?"

"At this point, I think it is highly likely. It appears Miss Sterling was under a lot of stress. Certainly losing one's mother would be cause for depression. I understand that she was an only child. I know her father, and I will be going to Spearfish this afternoon to apprise him of the situation."

"Did she leave a note? Any indication that she intended to take her life?"

"Not that we've found, but I can't say that we've really looked. I'm afraid seeing to Miss Sterling came first." Anything else that he might have added was interrupted by a uniformed man yelling from the porch for the sergeant to return to the house. "Oops, duty calls. Doesn't look like I'm going to get away any time soon. I hate to saddle you with sharing this kind of information but Mac needs to hear what's happened from a friend. Please tell Mac to expect us at his office late this afternoon. Offer my deepest sympathies from me and my missus. Oh, and good to meet you, Dr. Pecos. Sorry the circumstances weren't more congenial." With that, he got out of the cruiser and jogged toward the house.

Ben walked to the SUV. He was about to leave when he saw a tow truck maneuver to back up to the Mustang in the drive after an officer moved one of the police cars. Impounding Micki's car? Something must be going on. Or maybe it was just best to safeguard her belongings and allow room for official vehicles to pull up closer to the house. Not that that really made sense.

Chapter 32

Spearfish, Sheriff's office

Ben wasn't even twenty-five miles out of town when three patrol cars, sirens blaring, lights flashing, tore past him doing well over the speed limit. He hoped he wouldn't be delayed by an accident. He called ahead and left a message for Red Bull to meet him at Mac's office, but didn't say anything else. He wasn't about to deliver his news other than face to face. And it was going to be shocking. He didn't know what support he could give, but he would offer.

And then his thoughts went to Micki. Two deaths fairly close together of those who had been family—an estranged husband, and her mother. That was a double whammy, especially for someone not used to coping with adversity and convinced that the person shooting her mother had mistaken her for her daughter. Blaming herself could be demoralizing.

He made it to Spearfish without seeing any accidents, and the patrol cars racing past him seemed to be long gone—until he turned the corner to park in front of Mac's office and there were the three black and whites parked next to Red Bull's truck. They'd beat him here. Well, the news would be delivered by authorities and announced face to face. But why did it take three cars of officers to do it?

He was almost to the door when he heard the burst of shouting. And it didn't sound friendly. Taking the stairs two at a time, Ben jerked open Mac's office door at the exact second Mac lunged, with one hand doubled into a fist, at a handcuffed Red Bull who was standing against the wall with a cop on each side.

Ben didn't even stop to think. Before Mac's right uppercut could connect, Ben grabbed his arm and twisted it behind him, causing him to stumble backwards. Then both cops grabbed Ben and dragged him back, forcing his hands behind his back.

"You got him—assault on a law enforcement officer. You're all witnesses." Mac pulled himself up with a hand from the nearest cop.

"What the hell? That ok's your assault on this officer?" Ben pointed at Red Bull.

"That son of a bitch is a murderer. Plain and simple. And because of the stress, the terrible pressure he put on my poor daughter, she killed herself."

Ben looked at Red Bull. "What's he talking about?"

"It's bullshit."

Sergeant Cummings stood up from behind Sally Haines's desk with the phone in his hand. "This can wait. Everyone find a seat." He said 'thank you' to someone on the line and put the phone back in its cradle and scooted the desk chair out into the room. "After you left Ms. Sterling's home this afternoon, a note was found, apparently left by Micki Sterling. Here, I made a copy and had my office assistant send it here." He handed Ben a sheet of paper. "Take your time."

Ben unfolded the 8 ½ by 11 sheet of printer paper. The original note looked to be on a scrap of paper, about a half of a page, possibly torn from a journal judging by the perforations along the edges. It was addressed to Red Bull and began, "Robert." Ben paused and looked at Red Bull. "It's all right. Read it." Red Bull was still handcuffed, but at least was sitting down. Ben looked back at the note.

"I love you but hate you for murdering David. Yes, he was stalking me but the law could have handled that. I could have called my dad. But now, I hate myself for telling you how to do it. It was foolproof—no one else would have known about the insulin. But I cannot take the pressure of being an accessory. And then when Mom was killed, I think someone was trying to kill me and made a mistake. Someone from David's gang of friends wanted retribution. I know they all suspected me. Yes, I'm taking a chicken's way out. I know that, but my conscience will not allow me to live with myself. Please understand." It was signed *"all my love, Micki"*.

Ben handed the paper back to Sergeant Cummings.

"That never happened. We *never* discussed anything about David Gonzales's death. Nothing. Nada." Red Bull held Ben's gaze. "You have to believe me. I'm in shock. This isn't happening. I know Micki, *knew* her, maybe better than anyone in this room. We had plans. Our going out wasn't some casual thing. I loved Micki Sterling." Ben saw Mac turn away and stare at the floor.

The room was dead quiet until the sergeant broke the spell. "Would you recognize Miss Sterling's handwriting?" He held the copy in front of Red Bull.

Red Bull leaned away from the wall and peered at the page. "That's what is making me crazy. It looks like Micki's writing."

"Sheriff Sterling? What's your take?" The sergeant held the paper where Mac could read it.

"Of course, it's hers. I'd know my own daughter's handwriting." Then Mac wiped his eyes and added, "And my poor daughter had to hang for two days in the backyard of her murdered mother's home before she was found. The local coroner puts her death at forty-eight to seventy-two hours prior to discovering the body. My baby, all by herself …"

"Wait, that's not possible," Ben spoke up. It was now or never. He had to share what he saw at the ranch two nights ago. "I don't know where she died, but she hadn't been hanging for two days." Every eye in the room was on him. Ben cleared his throat. "I need to share something that I'd wanted to keep private."

"And this, whatever it is, has direct bearing on this case?" Mac sounded gruff.

"Yes, I believe it does. There's proof that Micki Sterling never made it to her mother's house two nights ago—at least not by driving herself there."

"Okay. Get on with it." Mac sounded exasperated.

Probably thought he had an open and shut case against Red Bull, Ben thought.

"Last month after Judge Udahl's mother passed, two

letters were found. One from a young woman whose affair with the judge in her college days had left her pregnant, and the other from Frances Udahl stating how she had kept the results of this transgression, as she called it, a secret. I'm the son that my father never knew about."

"Wow, man. That's unbelievable." Red Bull probably spoke on behalf of the entire room.

"So, what does this have to do with the suicide of Micki Sterling?" Mac asked.

"I am not someone standing around with my hand out, but I have a son. I went to the judge's house two nights ago at around nine-thirty in the evening to talk. I wanted him to be aware of his grandchild and ask that in lieu of my receiving anything from his estate, would he set aside college funds for his grandson. I believe Micki Sterling drove a red Mustang GT Fastback." Ben looked to Red Bull who nodded. "That model car was parked to one side of the first garage at the judge's estate. It was there when I arrived and hadn't moved by the time I left. I did not see or hear any evidence that Micki was at the ranch. And, of course, there could be other red Mustang GTs, but I find it highly unlikely in the town of Spearfish."

"Only one that I know of anywhere near here," Cummings said.

"I suspect the car has been impounded. I think fingerprints or DNA might tell us a lot," Red Bull offered.

"I probably don't need to be told my business. But I know you're anxious for some answers." Sergeant Cummings softened the reprimand by adding, "Because the purported crime happened in my jurisdiction, I'm willing to offer the following, contingent upon agreement by a judge from my district. I think we have enough information to cast some doubt on what appears to have happened. We know that, according to the funeral home in Pierre, Micki Sterling never arrived to complete the paperwork and pick up her mother's remains. The cremation had been paid for by credit card."

He glanced at Red Bull, who nodded. "Then, someone, if not Micki herself, arranged to provide circumstantial evidence at the mother's residence to provide a believable scenario of suicide. Whether or not the note is legitimate, it will be up to us to prove that Micki Sterling did, indeed, take her own life and did so at that residence. I want the time to submit the document found in the house of the deceased for graphoanalysis.

"The sighting of the deceased's car at a property some two hundred miles from the crime scene, at the time the incident was supposed to be happening, is yet another added question as to what exactly took place. It certainly casts doubt on the death occurring where the body was discovered. I need time to have our lab go over details. I do not believe that Robert Red Bull is a flight risk. I'm well aware of the officer's community work, on and off the reservation. I want him released under his own recognizance with the understanding that he is not to leave the reservation."

"Now, wait a minute—" Mac took a step forward.

"Personally, I understand your concerns—it's always tough to think clearly when family is involved. But feelings cannot stand in the way of good detective work."

"And you don't think it's possible that one Indian is going to cover for a brother?" Mac's face was red, Ben noticed.

"If that were true, bear in mind that Dr. Pecos would

be throwing his own father under the bus by implicating his involvement in possible foul play."

"Wouldn't anger account for that? Anger over the mistreatment of his mother, let alone him?"

"I know that Dr. Pecos can speak for himself, but I don't sense any vindictiveness. Until proven otherwise, I believe he is telling the truth about seeing a car matching one driven by Micki Sterling at the Udahl ranch."

"Thank you." Red Bull turned and held his hands away from his body and the officer nearest him unsnapped the cuffs. "I appreciate the vote of confidence."

Chapter 33

"I don't like it but being called 'a person of interest' sure beats being locked up." Red Bull and Ben sat at the conference table in Ben's office. Mac had grudgingly agreed to stay within boundaries and not overstep by making snap judgements as to what was right or wrong. Ben could only hope he would keep his word and not try to confront Red Bull again.

"We need a plan." Red Bull seemed to be thinking out loud. "Because maybe the question is why, or better yet, who wants me to take the fall for Micki's murder? And it is just that. She did not commit suicide and I did not kill Dr. David Gonzales. So, what would getting me out of the way accomplish?"

"Is it possible that you've come a little too close to the Spearfish Creek mining project? People probably thought you had involved the BIA."

"Could be, or maybe David's cronies were seeking revenge?"

"Any ideas as to what can be done?"

"We need someone on the inside."

"And you're looking at me?" Ben wasn't sure he was being complimented.

"Did you close any doors—I mean when you talked to the judge about scholarship money for your son?"

"He told me not to come back unless I could apologize."

"How good are you at groveling?"

"Not very, but what are you thinking?"

"We've got to know what's going on out there. We know that there's more than one Mexican National—at least two with tattoos of Pancho Villa. And there've certainly been rumors of cartel involvement. The men running the equipment yesterday up on the hill were pretty much all Spanish speakers from what I overheard. I can't begin to tell you when the last time ICE ran any crackdowns on illegals in South Dakota. We've always been just a little too far from the border."

"I'm not sure how I could convince the judge to let me into his home, let alone his confidence."

"You're going to be out of here next week?" Ben nodded. "That's the plan, home for Thanksgiving and Christmas."

"Then let's use that as an excuse. Time for face-to-face discussion is running out and you've had a change of heart."

"I doubt he'll believe that. He's a tight old bastard—I think he's relieved that he thinks he's gotten rid of me.

That I won't show up with my hand out again."

"Then let's come up with another plan."

"Such as?"

"Throw all your fishing gear and tent into the SUV and accidentally go fishing on the judge's land. Then your car breaks down, or you get stuck or something … anyway, you have to go for help."

"I think the judge is on the road this part of the week."

"All the better. See if you can find the camp of workers, check out the maintenance barns—"

"What am I looking for?"

"I can't even tell you that. I don't know. But you'll know something odd or out of place when you see it. Get into the house if you can—legally, of course, maybe to call a tow for your car. Then open drawers, take pictures—I'm sure you'll know what to do. And among your fishing gear? This is your most important piece of equipment." Red Bull reached under the table, then sat back and slid the holstered .38 across to Ben. "Take it. I don't think your life will be in danger with the judge gone. And, to be honest, I can't imagine him orchestrating his only child's death. Plus, I think he runs things with an iron fist—no one will act without his knowing. Are you game?"

Ben nodded.

"Good. I'm going to get copies of a couple maps from next door. We can get you on the ranch and make it believable that you're just following the creek or a narrow feeder stream that cuts across the northern corner of the reservation and intersects with Udahl's land. You can drive most of the way and it's all within two miles of the ranch house."

Chapter 34

Judge Udahl's Ranch

Ben had left the tent, camping and fishing gear in the SUV. He threw in a pair of jeans, added two jackets and a flannel shirt plus waders and sneakers, checked the map that Red Bull had given him, and then took off. He would be traveling toward the judge's ranch but veer off to follow a stream bed, a seasonal tributary, now dry.

He had to smile. In New Mexico many properties had what real estate agents referred to as a 'seasonal stream' meaning that after runoff, the property had a water feature for a few months. This feeder added water to Spearfish Creek probably six months out of the year. In the meantime it was a sandy-bottomed makeshift road going back into areas otherwise only available to persistent hikers—not to people on foot carrying a hundred pounds of camping gear.

The plan entailed disengaging the serpentine belt, dangling the belt from one pulley wheel at the back of the engine, rendering the SUV's alternator useless and, of consequence, robbing the vehicle of electric power. To any observer, he would be stranded. Ben would then remove a fishing pole, flashlight, put a couple lures in a creel along with the .38, sling it over his shoulder, and take off walking back toward the judge's house—about a two-mile hike, maybe three, if he could believe Red Bull's map.

It was late afternoon. Shadows were beginning to stretch across his path, obscuring low-hanging branches and rocks embedded in the sand along the stream's edge. It was a lot slower going than he'd anticipated. An hour simply crept by.

As Red Bull suggested, he tested his phone for a signal. None, not even one bar. That would be the reason to make it to the judge's house—a call for help using a landline. It was a simple cover and completely feasible. He tucked the phone back in his jacket pocket.

When the two men jumped in front of him, he was startled but had more or less expected there to be guards on the judge's property. At the first glimpse of the Glock aimed at his chest, Ben put both hands in the air.

"I was fishing but when I got back to the car, it wouldn't start. I thought I'd try to find the judge's house and get help. My phone is useless out here." The two men didn't change their expressions but turned to one side and conferred in Spanish.

"Okay, you follow." The man closest to Ben motioned for him to move ahead while the second man stepped in behind. Twenty feet to his right, the man leading pushed through a bramble of twisted shrubs revealing a Jeep. "You ride here."

Ben climbed into the seat behind the driver of the open-air vehicle while the second man jumped into the shotgun position. Within thirty minutes they pulled into the long drive leading to the judge's house.

"Dr. Pecos. It is doctor, isn't it? The judge was very complimentary. I was hoping we would get to see you again. He'll be back day after tomorrow—more state judiciary business. Now, how can I help you?" She dismissed his two companions with a hand wave, stepped back and invited him into the house.

Miss Rose Aguilar was, as he remembered, stunning. This time in a filmy knee-length, sleeveless dress in a pale aqua; flawless makeup and stiletto heels completed the look. It struck him once again that this was a lot of work to go to out here, perpetual date night polish, but for whom?

Ben explained his need for a mechanic and a land-line to get one out to help. "I'll be leaving next week and I'd hoped to get in some fishing. I wasn't planning on car trouble."

"I can certainly provide you with a phone. The lack of cell service drives me nuts out here. I love the openness of the ranch, the beauty, even the solitude; but I've had to give up a few amenities. It will be more comfortable to make your calls from the study. This way."

The house was quiet. No Miss Isher, that frumpy housekeeper, in sight. Rose pushed open the study door and stepped to one side to let him enter. Did she position her leg so that his thigh would fleetingly touch her? Was his imagination running away with him? Yes, that was just the problem of a narrow doorway. But had he been off the market so long that he was misreading signals?

"The house phone is there on the desk. Help yourself. We even have an old-fashioned phone book if you need one."

Ben removed his phone from his pocket. "I should have what I need in my contact list, but thanks. I appreciate your help." He put the creel on the nearby couch and moved to the desk.

"I need to run down to the barn. It's payday and I have a few people waiting for me. Make yourself at home. Help yourself to a water or soda." She pointed to a bar fridge tucked into the far corner next to a liquor cabinet. She walked toward the door, then turned, "I'm having a late dinner. Nothing fancy, just something Evangeline prepared before she took off for town. Probably a pasta dish and salad. I'd love to have you join me." The look was seductive—slightly open lips, lowered eye lids, just the hint of a smile.

"Thanks. Let's see how quickly I can get help out here."

Suddenly a single knock on the door interrupted any further discussion of dinner. Rose opened the door and a man poked his head in. "*Vamos. Apurate.*"

"Ah, I'm being summoned. No one has patience when they are waiting for money. I should be back in half an hour." With a smile, she was gone, pulling the study door closed behind her.

Ben knew he didn't have time to waste, but what did he expect to find in the study? First, he needed to check in with Red Bull and arrange to meet and fix the SUV. Could he be certain that the phone was clear, not tapped? They'd decided ahead of time that if he used a house phone, they would keep it simple, actually let the call go to voicemail—Ben needed a mechanic, could Red Bull help? He'd mention dinner and suggest Red Bull pick him up in an hour and a half. Then, he could give exact directions as to how to reach the SUV. Nothing else. Nothing to arouse suspicion.

Quickly Ben did a cursory inspection of the room for cameras. But he didn't see anything suspect. Maybe the judge wasn't being careful—didn't feel the need to be. The ranch was pretty isolated. He picked up the desk phone, dialed Red Bull, and left the voicemail. Then, he quickly opened and shut the desk drawers. Extra paper, pens, a pamphlet on a new cattle supplement, several invoices for feed and veterinary supplies, a fence repair estimate—not one item that seemed out of place for a working ranch.

Might as well get something to drink. He walked to the bar fridge and chose a bottled sweet tea. And then he saw it. As he was standing back up from bending over the fridge, a stack of newspapers and two magazines on the edge of the bar caught his eye. On top was what looked like a notebook, maybe a ledger, or a journal. The cover was leather and the name across the lower edge was in gold script: Rose Marie Gonzales Aguilar.

Ben opened it. Several pages of poetry in Spanish, a recipe, a map in glossy color taken from a magazine showing several of the monuments around South Dakota, the photograph of a family posing at the border, a Welcome to the Estados Unidos banner stretched across the bridge.

Other photos tucked in between pages were of family members, or what appeared to be—fishing, riding horses by the ocean, in the mountains—just a personal collection of mementos including one that made him stop. It was a picture of a boy and a girl, probably in their late teens, the girl hanging onto the boy and pointing at the tat of Pancho Villa across his back. The girl was Rose. Was the male David Gonzales? If Rose's father's name was Gonzales, was David her brother? Ben snapped a couple photos of the pair, even zooming in capturing only their faces.

There didn't seem to be anything else of interest. He rifled through the pages one more time, and he had almost closed the journal when he saw it. The last page had been torn, with the top half of the page missing.

Ben couldn't have told why he knew, but he felt certain that if this page were to be compared to the half page used for Micki Sterling's suicide note, the pieces would match. He quickly picked up his phone and photographed the page and took another shot of the journal cover, carefully replacing it on the stack of reading material exactly as he had found it.

That photo was potentially dynamite. It could easily prove that Micki was here at the ranch—possibly killed here before someone drove the body in her car to her mother's house near Pierre. That is, if the writing was hers. Actually, even if it was forged, it certainly suggested that suicide was only a cover. And didn't it exonerate Red Bull? Remove him, at least, as the impetus for her wanting to kill herself in the first place?

He'd barely settled into the dark brown overstuffed chair next to the lone window in the room when Rose walked through the door.

"Oh good, I see you've helped yourself to something to drink. I'm starving. Let me put another plate out in the dining room and see what Evangeline has left us in the kitchen. C'mon, I'll show you the rest of the house."

The rest of the house looked like a picture from a magazine. Ben was impressed. He supposed his newly discovered grandmother was the designer of the brick motif behind the two, industrial sized, restaurant-issue stoves and walk-in freezer refrigerator combinations. This kitchen could feed a pretty hefty sized crew. The flooring was Talavera tile—something Ben hadn't seen outside New Mexico. Cabinetry pulls were more south of the border ceramics; this time with a definite Old Mexico theme. Benches, an island, bar stools, and a viga enhanced ceiling were all hewn of chunky pieces of natural wood.

"I love this kitchen." Rose was putting a dish in the microwave. "Looks like we have lobster ravioli and Caesar salads. Sound okay? Oh, and I found some garlic bread just ready to pop in the oven."

"Sounds great." And it did. Ben was starving.

"Are you a wine drinker?"

"I'm fine with water."

Finally, everything was on the table. Rose indicated the chair opposite the one she was scooting out from the table, sat, shook out her napkin, helped herself to the ravioli, and passed the bowl to Ben.

"I heard on the radio this morning that the Spearfish sheriff lost his only child to suicide." She didn't make eye contact, but poured dressing on the salad and began tossing it before placing two helpings on plates in front of her.

Was this a fishing expedition to find out how Micki's death was being handled? Well, he could play along. "It's been tough. Were you aware that his former wife died, possibly as the result of a hunting mishap? Just last week, in fact. Coming so soon after that, his daughter's death has been a shock for Sheriff Sterling."

"Did they say anything about a note being found? I heard there was one, but I don't think the contents have been released—at least, nothing was reported—but why would a young woman take her life? I hope the note will give her father some closure."

"I haven't heard anything about a note. I think she was distraught over her mother's death. And I heard that her ex-husband died just last month."

"Her ex?"

"I don't think they were married long. He was a paid protester. He came here to join the group rallying against the pipeline. I've forgotten his name but his death was an accident."

"How was that?"

"Poor guy had diabetes and reacted to an insulin dose."

"Tragic. It's all just a tragedy. I wonder if Sheriff Sterling will stay in Spearfish?"

"It would be difficult to imagine him anywhere else. This is his home."

"I suppose you're right. The judge has always spoken highly of him."

"When did you say the judge will be back?"

"Day after tomorrow. His trips are seldom more than three or four days in duration. The life of a circuit judge is a little demanding. More garlic bread? I left it in a warm oven."

"No, thanks, I'm fine. Everything's delicious." And it was. Ben was amazed. The ravioli was swimming in a creamy sauce full of chunks of lobster with just a hint of vermouth. This did not come out of a package.

"You know, the judge shared with me who you are." Rose waited for his reaction but Ben wasn't biting. He simply nodded. "I can't imagine what it must be like to find a father after all these years. I feel so conflicted. It wasn't right of him or of Frannie."

Ben tried not to flinch as Rose placed her hand lightly on his arm.

"I wish I could make it up to you, prove that the judge is really a loving man. I meant to offer earlier that if your mechanic or friend isn't able to fix your car, or isn't able to pick you up, you can certainly spend the night here."

Her hand didn't move. It was still anchored just below his elbow, one finger lightly massaging the surrounding skin. "I'd love to get to know you better." The huskiness in her voice hadn't been there before. "In fact, the judge himself suggested we have you to dinner. He's sorry about how dismissive he was when you were here a few days ago."

All Ben could think of was the line from the poem— *Won't you come into my parlour, said the spider to the fly. The Spider and the Fly* was one of his first reading adventures as a child. He'd found the discarded library book in the trash and its contents were a lot racier than the *Adventures of Dick and Jane* until his grandmother took the book of poetry away. Seems like it was something only girls read.

"Thank you for offering. I appreciate that." He dislodged her hand by reaching for his glass of water. They continued to eat, this time in silence. Finally finished, he folded his napkin and placed it on the table before he stood. "I'm not sure who's picking me up, I should probably wait on the porch."

Before he could take a step toward the door, she came around to his side of the table and threw her arms around his neck. "I have a perfectly delightful idea for dessert," she whispered then pulled his head downward to meet her mouth. But he put his hands on her waist and stepped back, pushing her ever so slightly out of reach.

"Rose, I can't do this. I don't think this is a good idea for either one of us."

"We would be good together. I'm never wrong. I believe that you've been sent to me. You need to give us a chance." She took a step forward but he deftly turned toward the door, putting several steps of distance between them before addressing her again.

"I have a wife and two sons whom I love very much. I have a demanding job miles away from here, a career that is just taking off—I like where I am in life. I will not sacrifice any of that for something that would not be fair to you or to my family. I value honesty and live my life honoring that trait. I will not be a part of duplicity. I'm flattered by your interest but that is all."

Rose dropped her arms to her sides and shrugged. "If that's truly what you want."

Ben nodded. And then he heard the front door chimes. Saved. Had anything so simple ever sounded so good?

Chapter 35

Pine Ridge Reservation, Ben's Temporary Office

"Good work, pal." Red Bull was looking at the pictures Ben had taken. "It's getting late but I want to email these to Sergeant Cummings. Should I include Mac?"

"I guess I would. It's his daughter and it might change his view of what happened—get you off the hook maybe."

"That's only going to disappoint him. Mac needs someone to blame. He's never going to accept that Micki and I had a pretty good thing going. He might be her father but I have a vested interest in finding her killer."

"I wish we could find out if David Gonzales was Rose's brother."

"By the way, does she always dress that way? I mean she's hot but hooker heels and a dress that looked like she painted it on? Odd way to dress for an evening at the ranch. When she opened the front door, I couldn't believe my eyes."

"I thought so, too." Ben didn't offer to share what amounted to a come-on at dinner. Had the dress been for his benefit? Even the false eyelashes? Maybe, his driver had called ahead and said he was bringing Ben to the house. Or maybe he should just not flatter himself. That could be the 'uniform' for ranch wear.

"I doubt we'll hear back from Sergeant Cummings or even Mac before morning. Why don't we meet at Mac's office at nine? I'm not sure what the next step is—guess I'll leave it up to Spearfish law enforcement. But what you've found gives Mac new people of interest. He, or Sergeant Cummings, at least, needs to be doing some interrogation."

Red Bull took off and Ben locked the office and walked home. He wished he could prove Rose's connection to David Gonzales. If he remembered correctly, the coroner had said that a family member, a sister to be exact, had showed up to claim the body and have it shipped to Mexico. He could show his picture of the teenaged Rose to the coroner. It was dated, maybe ten years old, but he'd be able to recognize her. He wasn't sure what that would prove, but it would open another avenue of investigation.

But first he needed to check in with Julie. He hoped there would be positive news about Nathan's adoption. He was anxious to share some good news with both Nathan and Zac.

And there was!

"I just heard this afternoon. The paperwork is in order and has been forwarded to be recorded. Tribal records will add the name Pecos to Nathan Yazzi. He's going to be thrilled. Congratulations, Ben—once again you're a new dad. But that's not the biggest news. Are you sitting down?"

"Yeah." What news was bigger than becoming a dad?

"I got the DNA findings back from the lab. Ben, the judge is *not* your father." Julie paused for that to sink in. "The pen was a goldmine of markers. There was an almost fully intact print on the pen's cartridge that belonged to the judge; thank God, his prints are on file so a comparison could be made. Now, we know for certain that the source had been in his possession. But your DNA and the DNA from the pen weren't compatible. You two are simply not related."

"I honestly believe that my mother thought she was telling the truth. But she was ill at the time—knew her time was limited—and it's possible she chose a rich boyfriend simply because he would have the money to take care of me. DNA wasn't even on the horizon thirty-odd years ago. I owe the judge an apology, or at least an explanation, and need to return his pen."

"It's in the mail. You should have it this week. In some ways, I'm relieved. I think the money would have been more than a burden. It would have been an entirely different thing if the judge had received you with open arms, but he didn't. And it was obvious that he expected you to try to get his money. He was even dismissive over giving Zac money for college. I didn't hear you give one example of him having any humanitarian virtues. No, I'm thankful it's turned out this way."

"You know, I have to agree. I'm beginning to think he's not a very nice person, just someone else completely motivated by profit. The lithium mining that will impact the Pine Ridge Reservation is another example of his disregard for the wellbeing of the people in this state. I hope it will get resolved in the reservation's favor."

"What do you think is going to happen? What's a best-case scenario?"

"That the mining will be stopped—at least where it impacts Pine Ridge water rights."

"Didn't you involve the BIA biggies in Washington?"

"Yes, I expect it to turn into a contentious court case, and quickly."

"All the more reason why it's good news you won't be involved in any way—at least not as a possible recipient of Udahl money. I believe both boys are more than bright enough to earn scholarships. They'll be fine without a handout."

"I know you're right. I admit to feeling relieved."

Ben sat at the dining room table after Julie hung up. Once again, he realized how difficult it was to be separated and vowed not to be apart again—at least not for a long time. But the news of the DNA test results was shocking. He'd convinced himself of the relationship his mother had presented. He hadn't even known that he wanted a father until he almost had one. But it took an element of drama out of his life. He wasn't going to miss that.

Finally, he was able to shut his mind down long enough to feel sleepy. He had a feeling that tomorrow was going to be an interesting day.

Chapter 36

Ben was up at six. His mind was still playing and replaying his conversation with Julie. Just one big loop. He had somehow been re-orphaned, if there was such a thing.

But he needed to get back to business. He wanted to drop by Coroner Tully's lab before meeting Red Bull at Sheriff Sterling's office. A quick call and Jake Tully said he could offer fresh coffee and a chocolate doughnut if he wanted to come now. Ben wasn't sure about sweets in the morning, he was pretty much an eggs and hash browns with a side of bacon kind of guy, but the coffee sounded good. He looked again at the close-up of Rose Aguilar. Even as a teen she was gorgeous. But what an interesting life—from somewhere in Mexico to South Dakota? There was a story there somewhere. He was glad he wasn't a part of it.

Jake Tully met him at the door to his lab. Rumpled clothing made it look as though he'd spent the night there.

"Boy, an offer of coffee got you here in no time. Take this, I'll let you doctor your own." He handed Ben a cup. "It might be a bit strong—there's a choice of milk or half and half over there, plus sugar—the real stuff and the fake." He pointed to a cart parked next to the counter holding a coffee machine. "My wife, God rest her soul, always said this stuff could put hair on a billiard ball."

Ben smiled, said no to a proffered doughnut, opened two creamers and then a third. The aroma of coffee was pleasant compared to the normal scent of preservatives like formalin that pervaded most coroners' labs. Even the ever-present odor of Clorox was minimal.

"First of all, I need to ring up Mac Sterling and offer my condolences. I can't believe he lost his former wife and only child in less than a week. I know they were somewhat estranged, but still, any time you outlive your child, it's a shocker."

"I agree. I don't think it's been easy for him. In fact, that's why I'm here. There are a lot of unanswered questions. I remember you saying that a family member claimed the body of David Gonzales—a sister?"

"Yes, in fact, she was his fraternal twin. A beautiful woman, about twenty-eight, and completely distraught by her brother's death."

"Is this the young woman? The picture would have been taken about ten years ago."

Ben showed him the picture on his phone.

"Yes. That's her. She was pretty as a teenager, too. She

was the one who suggested the death might have been the result of an insulin overdose. Apparently, her brother had struggled with ill health since childhood. The Pancho Villa tattoo was just one more thing that helped him be accepted as one of the boys. She thought he had probably taken part in a Sun Dance maybe as a dare—again trying to fit into a macho world, that sort of thing."

"Odd. According to Red Bull, there hadn't been any Sun Dance ceremonies recently. Did she tell you she lived near here?"

"No. She flew in to claim the body. I remember briefly discussing crossing the border once myself at El Paso."

"This young woman has been living at Judge Udahl's ranch for the last few years. She's an administrative assistant and manages the ranch in the judge's absence."

"That can't be. Let me see the picture again." Ben handed his phone back.

"Someone's lying. This is the woman who claimed David Gonzales's body. I'd stake my reputation on it."

"Did you say she had it shipped back to Mexico?"

"Originally, that was the plan, at least that's what she said over the phone; but before she left here, she made arrangements for the body to be sent for cremation in Pierre."

"Any suggestion about other family?"

"Their mother had passed. She mentioned that something like her son's death would have been too much for her mother. There were lots of tears. The young woman was obviously very upset."

"I think I know the answer to this before I ask, but did she tell you that David Gonzales was, in fact, David Gonzales, PhD, a geologist?"

"No. If anything, she seemed to play up the gang aspect of the tattoo—indicated that he ran with a dangerous crowd."

"I'll let Sheriff Mac know that we've talked. I'm sure he'll want to question you, too. There are just too many pieces to the puzzle that are missing."

Ben thanked the coroner, rinsed his coffee cup in the lab sink, and took off for Mac's office. There was so much that simply made no sense. And those with the answers were dead. All but Rose Marie Gonzales Aguilar.

* * *

Ben pulled up to the curb in front of the Sheriff's office and parked next to Red Bull, who was just getting out of his truck.

"Anything new?" Red Bull asked as the two of them walked through the downstairs door.

"Had an interesting conversation with Coroner Tully. Rose Aguilar is the fraternal twin of David Gonzales, among other things. But you'll hear all this upstairs."

The office was a little crowded. He and Red Bull stood at the back; Sergeant Cummings, a deputy, Mac Sterling, and Sally Haines either stood or sat on the edge of desks. Everyone was watching Cummings who had already spread out the original suicide note on a work table next to Mac's desk. He was just about ready to slip the printer copy of the page Ben had photographed underneath so that the two edges would be parallel.

"And look at that." Cummings stood back as Mac leaned in. "A perfect match. No denying this is the bottom half of the page used for the suicide note. Tell us again where you found it, Dr. Pecos."

Ben reiterated what he had found on his visit to the ranch, including the journal with family pictures and this bottom half of a page. He then shared what Coroner Tully had remembered from his meeting with David Gonzales's twin and handed around his phone containing the photo of the smiling teens.

"Damn." This from Red Bull seemed to speak for everyone. "I think we need to pay Miss Rose a visit. Shall we caravan? Meet here in one hour and go to the ranch as a group? That should give Mac a chance to get a search warrant via e-mail from the county court. Remember, we're working with a judge here. We have to be certain that we follow protocol.

Questions?"

Ben thought Mac looked ticked that Red Bull was taking over but he didn't say anything, just nodded, then told Sally to put in the order for a warrant. Red Bull suggested coffee, and everyone but Mac and Sally trooped downstairs.

* * *

Mac got up and shut the office door, returned to his desk, checked his contact list and dialed.

There was one person who could possibly shed some light on what he'd just heard, someone who might have known about the twin sister ... or anything else that might be important. Jeffery answered on the first ring. Thanks to a pandemic, the tattoo business must be slow if maybe non-existent.

"Mac, just the man I was going to call today. I'm stunned by Micki's death. I want to offer my condolences.

I can't believe that it came to that. I thought she'd moved on."

"Thank you, Jeffery. I appreciate that. The last couple days have been one hell of a ride. First Debbie, then Micki. And none of it makes sense. I guess that's why I'm calling. I want someone to tell me why Micki would take her own life. You guys were close once. You knew her."

The silence lasted so long, Mac was afraid Jeffery was going to hang up. What had Mac learned in school? Interrogation was an art and required patience. When you put a question out there, wait for an answer. Learn to live with silence if you felt the person was struggling with what to say. Under no circumstances should you interrupt the cycle of first the question, then, watch the perp and wait for an answer.

Mac heard Jeffery exhale. "I guess it can't hurt to tell you now. Micki's marriage to David was a mess. I came in handy as a sounding board. We'd remained friends and she didn't have anyone else to talk to—certainly, not her mother. Debbie tried her damnedest to drive them apart. She was relentless in badmouthing him around town, railing on about how he was beneath Micki—for no reason other than he was Mexican. She wouldn't allow him into her house. She hated him so much she risked alienating her daughter just to drive him away. They ran off to marry just to not have to face Debbie. She was the one who started the rumor that he was using Micki to stay in the US, and that he was a for-profit protester. I know for a fact that he was educated in the States and a green card was not an inducement. But I think finally Micki believed her, thought she was nothing more than a means to an end for David, and it didn't involve love."

"Debbie was always over the top crazy about foreigners entering this country." Mac shrugged, then decided to share one of his own problem areas with his ex-wife. "We live in South Dakota, but she was sending money to a group who promised to build a wall."

"I can believe that. Well, all shit hit the fan when Micki turned up pregnant."

"Huh? When was this?"

"About three months before they broke up. Debbie wanted Micki to get an abortion but David, being a devout Catholic, went ballistic. Finally, Micki realizing that the marriage wasn't going to survive, baby or no baby, relented. I loaned her the money and she took a long weekend to a clinic outside Sturgis. Debbie was elated; David never got over it. Micki was the pawn between the two. I felt sorry for her."

"Was she distraught enough to take her own life?"

"No. In the last six months she had moved on. Even the death of her mother wouldn't have pushed her over the edge. Debbie was controlling, always had been, their relationship was messy. Sometimes only children get the brunt of it all. I was relieved when Micki started going out with Red Bull. I think he added a sense of stability to her life. They had only been together a month or so, but it had promise. I think he valued her opinion, treated her as an adult with the ability to make her own decisions. But Red Bull was pretty much the last straw for Debbie."

"One last question—did Micki know David's sister? Or maybe I should ask, do you know his sister?"

"Ah, the *puta*. She made life hell for Micki and David. That one's evil, maybe manipulative is a better word. Steer clear if you can."

Mac thanked him, said he'd been really helpful and appreciated his candor. He hung up after promising to let Jeffery know of any new developments. Then he leaned back in his desk chair to let it all sink in.

What a mix of feelings.

Was he relieved to know that Micki hadn't killed herself? Because nothing pointed to that. He'd be interested in knowing if Red Bull had even known about the baby. And Red Bull killing David Gonzales? Not likely. He and Micki weren't even a couple until recently. When David's body was first discovered and Mac had called Red Bull to the scene, he hadn't indicated he even knew the guy. And Mac believed him.

So, that left some pretty weighty questions hanging out there—who would have wanted Micki dead? Who would have wanted Debbie dead? Because he couldn't buy into the 'hunter making a mistake' scenario and hadn't his pal Rudy at the gas station proved that there had been a case of mistaken identity? Someone thought Debbie was her daughter? Then there was the implication of Red Bull's involvement—who would want him taking the rap for a murder?

Unless you were part of a reservation that was about to be plundered for money. And if David Gonzales's death wasn't accidental, how would that be known now? An urn of ashes seldom gave up secrets.

Sally interrupted his thoughts by handing him the emailed search warrant. Ready. Mac picked up the keys to the cruiser and went downstairs.

Chapter 37

Yes, it was a caravan but they voted for no sirens, no lights, and Ben was pleased. Better to not announce their visit until they had to. And what did they really have that was incriminating? Other than two scraps of paper that once had been one?

The judge would still be out of town, according to Rose's information. And that was probably a good thing. It would be easier to work with Rose and the housekeeper, Evangeline Isher. There wasn't a lot they could do if Mac Sterling hadn't gotten the search warrant. Still, it would be easier to serve without interference by the judge.

Ben could only hope the journal would still be on the edge of the bar. Of course, he was not looking forward to seeing Rose again—but, at least, he'd be in a crowd. He smiled. There had been a time when he wouldn't have needed protection from a drop-dead gorgeous woman. But that was before marriage and fatherhood. Interesting how times could change so quickly, and he wouldn't have it any other way.

* * *

"So, what do you think we'll find?" Red Bull had pulled his pickup in behind Sergeant Cummings' cruiser as they turned onto the highway. Mac and Sally Haines rode in Mac's Jeep, the third in line. A small convoy of law enforcement, Ben thought. He hoped it wasn't going to be a wasted trip. At least it was a united front of local expertise.

"I'm hoping we'll find concrete evidence of Micki Sterling having been there. But being able to confiscate the original journal with the torn page would be a start. I just don't trust the judge. My guess is he's smart enough to legally wiggle out of anything."

"The judge—your father, you mean."

"Actually, he's not." Ben reiterated Julie's information. "I don't know whether I'm sad or relieved."

"I guess I'd be pissed the way old lady Udahl handled things, but overall, I'd be relieved. At least you didn't realize you'd been refused help by a bigot until you were old enough to handle the information."

"You're right, that's a positive." Ben laughed. "How's that saying go? Thank God for small favors?"

They rode in silence before Red Bull added, "My worry is what the judge was doing in secret. Desecrating sacred indigenous land in a way that could be unimaginably problematic for the tribe and others living close by. The lithium mining project is not going to win much favor from locals or the reservation. I received notification that BIA was putting in a cease-and-desist order representing Pine Ridge. It should freeze all work—at least stop any excavation in that area until a new survey can be completed and tests done. Water is the biggest concern. It wouldn't take much to upset what's already a precarious balance between irrigation needs versus personal use requirements."

The battle was going to be fought in court. Ben smiled. Nathan's grandmother was right. Times had changed and it all depended on paper arrows now.

"The judge won't be too pleased."

"Luckily, I don't think there's anything he can do."

"If we're really lucky, he's still out of town and won't be there today."

"So, we'll be dealing with Rose what's-her-name?"

"Gonzales Aguilar—should make things easier."

Ben hoped he was telling the truth. He wasn't sure he was ready to meet Rose again so soon after escaping her clutches. And what would her reaction be to a search warrant? When they turned in the long driveway leading up to the ranch house, he was struck by a lack of activity. Even the last time he visited in the evening, there were vehicles parked all over.

Today, there was exactly one car, a Lexus sedan with a Washington state plate, a rental, probably. No other cars, no trucks parked in front of any of the three garages. No vehicles to the side of the house. And the front door was wide open; two men and Evangeline Isher were on the porch.

Cummings and Mac parked side by side, but before either could get out of their vehicle, Ms. Isher ran toward them screaming.

"They're gone. Everybody's gone. What am I going to do?" With that, she sank to the ground, sobbing, and covering her face with her hands.

Mac reached her first and helped her stand. By now seven people were standing around her in a semi-circle. The two men who apparently belonged to the Lexus stayed on the porch.

"Who's gone?" Cummings stepped forward.

"Everyone. Rose, all the workers ... and the judge. I called the courthouse to have him come home quickly and they said he had taken a two-week leave. That's a lie. I know that's a lie. I just know something terrible has happened to him." More crying and Mac produced a perfectly folded white handkerchief from a jacket pocket.

Red Bull walked up to the two men still standing on the porch. "And you are?"

"My apologies. We should have introduced ourselves earlier, but I'm totally in the dark as to what is happening here. I'm Anthony Tanner, CEO of Technology Forward. This is my lawyer, Ralph Sanders. We're here to inspect and sign off on the sale of a lithium mine. TF is a company of fifteen investors always looking to fatten our portfolio. We invest all over the world in start-ups or high-return tech projects with an eye to the future. I'm tooting my own horn, but we have an impeccable reputation. Judge Rex Udahl contacted us some months back, saying his project might be of interest to our group."

"He was selling the lithium mine?" Red Bull asked the question that everyone was thinking.

"Yes. I understand it's very near a working mine? He's shared the assayer's results. We have photos of equipment in place. I know the judge travels, but his wife was kind enough to set up this visit. She has a group ready to take us to the mine site this morning."

"Wait. What wife?" This from Ben.

"Ms. Rose Udahl. She has been handling the paperwork. I understand she is the judge's assistant, as well as his wife."

Ben noticed no one said anything but the looks of incredulity were noteworthy.

Even Ms. Isher had stopped crying, but then she took a step toward Mr. Tanner. "That is absolute bullshit. Excuse my French. The judge is *not* a married man and *not* to Ms. Aguilar."

She wasn't trying to disguise the anger in her voice. It didn't sound like the two of them got along. Ben could see how the two women might not be close.

"Ralph, show Ms. Isher the consent document."

The lawyer immediately began to rummage through his briefcase before handing a folder to the CEO. "Here we go. The agreed upon sale price is five hundred million. In order to establish our place in line—we understand there were three investors vying for the privilege of buying Pine Meadows Lithium Mining Corp—we wired the required two and a half million guarantee money, day before yesterday. Here's the receipt. The transaction was handled by Spearfish Community Bank and Trust. The signatures on this document are of the Judge Rex Udahl and his assistant Rose Aguilar Udahl." He handed the document to Ms. Isher. "She is listed as his wife."

"Forged. This document is a forgery." Ms. Isher was so angry she was shaking. "I cannot believe that woman. This is criminal." She abruptly handed the consent form back.

"Well, I believe we need to talk to the woman who calls herself Mrs. Udahl."

"And that's what I'm trying to tell you. She's not here. No one is here. Not one of her so-called workers from south of the border, and not the judge. Gone. They are all gone."

Chapter 38

Judge Udahl's Ranch

Finally, the group quieted and Ms. Isher invited everyone to follow her inside to the study.

Mac had handed her the warrant and offered to explain any wording that she might not be familiar with, but she declined.

The room had been stripped of electronics, wires coming up out of the floor with nothing attached. The fifty-four-inch TV was face down on the floor, apparently pushed off of its stand and discarded. Desk drawers had been haphazardly pulled out; papers scattered. The door to the bar fridge was wide open showing empty shelves. The room had been ransacked, and it looked like a last-minute haphazard grab and run, not a well-planned exit.

Artwork had been left. Several Raku pottery pots were still on a sideboard. Obviously someone decided it was too risky to travel with breakables. Two oils on the wall opposite the desk were likewise abandoned. Whoever left the premises was traveling light.

"Any idea where Ms. Aguilar might have gone?" Sergeant Cummings stood in the middle of the room, letting it all sink in. "Or when she might have left?"

"Yesterday was my day off—well, it wasn't my regular day off but Rose insisted that she needed me here on Friday and I needed to trade days. She never explained; she just gave orders. And whatever suited her was always all right with the judge. She wasn't his wife, but she had a way with him."

"Did she ever sign documents—either for the judge or in place of him?" Red Bull asked.

"All the time. She was the estate's administrator. She took over for the judge's mother before she died. She had Power of Attorney."

Mac had excused himself and stepped out of the room and into the hallway with his cell phone in hand. Ben watched as he seemed to be placing a call.

Ben turned his attention back to the room and continued looking through several stacks of newspapers and magazines. He didn't realize so much had been written about modern ranching, and it looked like the judge had a subscription to every monthly magazine available on the subject. A person could learn about cattle nutrition, grass/hay vitamin content, saving orphan calves, among other timely subjects, if Ben could believe the titles listed on their covers. But no journal. Under the circumstances, that was no surprise. Even a good-sized wall safe was hanging open.

"Everybody, let me have your attention." Mac walked to the front of the room. "I called a good friend at Spearfish Bank and Trust. Two and a half million was deposited into the judge's account two days ago. Yesterday, following instructions brought into the bank by Ms. Aguilar, the entire sum plus a cushion of fourteen thousand usually kept on hand for emergencies, was transferred to a bank in El Paso, Texas—the El Paso Del Norte. The request was signed by both Judge Rex Udahl and Rose Aguilar and it was notarized. Apparently, this was nothing new. The judge often bought and sold cattle in Texas; he worked closely with a Charolais breeder from McAllen. So, two and a half million raised no flags. He'd spent some ten million improving his herd over the last five years."

"I don't have to tell you that the two and a half million from Technology Forward is long gone." Cummings turned to face the group. "It's south of the border by now. I think the problem facing us at the moment is where can we find the judge? At this time I don't think we can rule out foul play."

This was met by a sharp intake of breath and a cry by Ms. Isher.

"I'd like for us to split up. My guys can take a look-see at the maintenance facility and check the two barns closest to the house. Dr. Pecos and Officer Red Bull could start on the house itself—of special concern should be Ms. Aguilar's living quarters. Sheriff Sterling and I will take this study and the judge's quarters. I'll get a box or two of latex gloves from the car."

He turned to Mr. Tanner and Mr. Sanders. "I need to ask the two of you to wait in your car or return to Spearfish—I'm assuming you have hotel reservations?"

"This is awkward, to say the least. We were invited to stay here at the ranch, but we can go ahead and book something in town. We need to plan our next steps but everything rests on whether the judge is available to make all this right. Here's my card. Please keep us in the loop."

* * *

Ben walked to the door of Rose's room. Actually, he'd call it more of a suite. She certainly hadn't wanted for anything, but now the place was in chaos. Two walls were devoted to closets and with doors wide open and half their contents on the floor, just sifting through what was left was going to be slow going. Ben pulled on bright blue gloves from the box that had been left on the corner of the desk in the study.

He walked to the first closet. What a mess. It was difficult to know where or even how to start looking—especially since he had no idea what to look for.

For starters, the clothing that spilled out onto the bedroom floor wasn't cheap. Ben was no expert on haute couture but names like Chanel and Dior were pretty widely known. Handbags, scarves, hats were all jumbled together. And at the back of the nearest closet stood an open safe with a couple jewel encrusted bracelets still inside. Every place he looked was evidence of haste.

Could she have overlooked something? Probably. It would be so helpful to know what he was looking for. He took out his phone and photographed the closets' contents, then the contents of the safe. Just to be thorough, he ran a hand around the inside of the safe, the back, the top, and sides. Nothing.

He backed up to stand in the center of the room and did a three-sixty turn. The one thing that stood out was the nightstand, a single two-drawer wooden cabinet painted white with apricot highlights. It wasn't open. That seemed odd when every other receptacle in the room containing any personal item had been emptied. Could it have been overlooked?

Red Bull was working on the bathroom and adjacent walk-in closet so, he might as well take a look at the nightstand. First, Ben checked the bed. A California King with box springs and a memory foam top layer making all one unit—negated anything being under the mattress. But Ben slid the mattress off the bed frame to check the floor anyway. Nothing. He even flipped over a small area rug beside the bed. Nothing.

He sat on the edge of the bed and opened the top drawer of the nightstand. Kleenex, a full box, and several sheets that appeared to have makeup on them wadded and tossed to the side. Four pens, a pencil, an eraser, an empty plastic water glass. The belt from a dress or top of some sort. An eight-year-old phone book and a phone, Apple series, not new. Ben took pictures before taking the phone out of the drawer and slipping it into a plastic bag.

Ben moved on to the bottom drawer. Scraps of paper, a jumble of some with lines, some plain, but all filled with the alphabet. But it wasn't exactly the alphabet in order. It was a page of single letters like M's and S's, both upper case and lower, and nearly every other letter of the alphabet practiced over and over like someone was trying to perfect a style of handwriting.

But then, wasn't that exactly what was happening here? Someone *was* practicing another person's style of penmanship in order to duplicate that style. Because interspersed with the practice sheets were two grocery lists, a letter contesting an electric bill, several hand-written lesson plans, and a sealed and stamped envelope addressed to Sheriff Mac Sterling from a Micki Sterling Gonzales, Pierre, South Dakota.

It wasn't much of a stretch of the imagination to know where these samples had come from. It would have been an easy thing for David to hand over his wife's writing or simply for his sister to help herself, maybe during a visit with her sister-in-law.

Then Ben did something that he wasn't quite sure why but he felt was right—he slipped the sealed and stamped envelope into his jacket pocket. It just struck him that maybe it was private; it didn't need the eyes of an examiner going over it. The family's problems didn't need to be broadcast any more than they had been. Most families stumbled now and then and after the recent deaths that Mac was grappling with, this could possibly add to that injury or help in some way. It seemed important to find out.

Ben sat back on the bed. He hadn't found the journal but this might be twice as good. He took pictures and then gathered all the loose pages and put them into a plastic bag.

"Find anything?" Red Bull walked out of the bathroom.

"I just might have." Ben showed him the alphabet practice sheets. "I haven't looked through the tablets yet."

"Even a few words matching Micki's note would be enough to point a finger at someone else doing the writing. That's a find."

"You guys have a minute?" Cummings stood in the doorway. "I don't want to make this a long day for everyone, but I found some interesting things out back."

Red Bull and Ben followed him around the house to the maintenance barn. "For starters, I'm pretty certain that fragments of this rope will match the rope used in Miss Sterling's hanging. I've also found several strips of adhesive tape in the first aid kit. A miniscule patch of adhesive, like that found on this tape, was lifted from the victim's cheek. The lab also has reported scratches on the inside of the passenger side of her car—matching fiber found underneath her fingernails. And these tire tracks in the soft dirt here? I'll bet a perfect match for the Mustang's booties, most likely nineteen-inch rims. The lady had some pricey rubber on her car. All this leads me to believe that she was subdued here and taken to her mother's house to be murdered."

Mac looked faint but steadied himself by grasping the edge of a work bench. "We let her down." This directed at Red Bull. "But why? Why kill her?"

"I think it could be any number of things. She didn't get along with Rose. I think Rose blamed her for David's death. They had separated and he was distraught, then the abortion ... I think that sealed the deal. They were more than just at odds; there was some real hatred." Red Bull paused as a deputy walked in from outside.

"Anybody got an idea of what these are? Found them among garbage in the big dumpster out back. Dried blood on all of it." One of Sergeant Cummings' deputies held out two slender pieces of bone and a small cylindrical bone.

Red Bull stepped forward and took them looking at each carefully. "They've been used in a Sun Dance. The small piece of bone is actually a whistle made out of an eagle's wing. Dancers carry them. Looks like David

Gonzales might have died here and the death was made to look like the result of an Indian ceremony, in an attempt to incriminate me."

"But what would that have gained them?" Ben was at a loss.

"I honestly think it was done to derail the lithium project. Just a smoke screen that might have bought them some time if the reservation had no chief law enforcement official and no one was reporting what was going on up by Spearfish Creek."

"I think we've got enough stuff here to keep the lab busy. I've put in a couple calls but looks like our girl made it to Chihuahua which gives us a new set of problems. I'm bringing over our search team with cadaver dogs. If the judge is somewhere out here on the ranch, we'll find him."

"Everything seemed so rushed. It looks like at one point, Rose had ideas about closing the five hundred million dollar deal herself. Instead, she settled for two and a half million—that's a big difference," Ben said.

"My guess is that you're showing up as a possible long-lost son expedited things. You were just another in line to inherit and throw a monkey wrench in the lithium deal. I think she was forced to do something. And two and a half million is far better than nothing. Grab the money and run while you can. Smart," Mac added.

Chapter 39

Pine Ridge Reservation

Red Bull dropped Ben off at his car in Spearfish. The afternoon had dragged on and it had gotten late. Nothing new was found at the ranch, unless finding the judge's car locked in a garage stall next to the house was going to yield something.

According to Ms. Isher, all of the judge's luggage was still in his closet—packed and never used. It appeared he hadn't left the ranch. Sergeant Cummings had his crew getting ready to take the Lincoln into the lab in town; a tow truck was on the way.

Mac had taken the time to take Ms. Isher home. She was still too shaken to drive. Cummings was leaving two deputies overnight to guard the premises, with two more deputies to arrive by eight the next morning with four cadaver dogs. It was all winding down and Ben had mixed feelings.

Had his showing up asking for tuition money for Zac really hastened Rose's plan? Rose couldn't have been pleased that a relative had turned up, a son who would have first rights to an inheritance. And his own life—would he have been in danger if he had stayed the other night? Rose had tried hard enough to get that to happen. It would have been an opportunity to get rid of the one obstacle that stood in the way of a possible five-hundred-million-dollar payoff. Would it have been tempting to kill him?

Lucky for him fight turned into flight. A two and a half million-dollar payday already in the bank was obviously a lot more lucrative than possible jail time for fraud—and maybe more for murder.

It was beginning to look like Rose was the mastermind. Was claiming marital status just a ruse? It was a smart move and might have qualified her to collect the five-hundred million. But now the question was, would she ever be caught? Was the extradition treaty with Mexico all that solid?

Since 1978 it had been used in instances of drug deals and the incarceration of notorious dealers. El Chapo came to mind. But would Rose have even stayed in Mexico? Wasn't Central America a much safer bet to get away and not be returned? And could the murder of Micki Sterling even be irrefutably linked to her? And the fate of the judge was still unknown. Too many what-ifs.

When he'd first heard about David Gonzales and a Pancho Villa tat, hadn't there been rumors about a gang belonging to a south-of-the-border cartel? A dangerous group of mercenaries living on the judge's ranch? It appeared that the judge had brought David Gonzales on board because of his credentials—or at the insistence of his twin? Did Rose find out that David had contacted his old professor? And had put himself in position to double-cross his twin? That and a possible five hundred million dollars probably got him killed. Rose knew how to make his death appear health related. There would probably be a number of questions that would never be answered. Loose ends. He hated not having complete closure.

But Ben was feeling a real need to get his life back to normal. No drama would be a relief. He needed to spend some time with Nathan before he left and make certain the plans for Nathan to fly to Seattle the first week in January were firmly in place.

Ben still liked the idea of Nathan staying in South Dakota for six weeks before going back to school. At least he wouldn't worry about him. In addition to being vaccinated, Ben could not think of a safer place than Nathan's being with other boys, out-of-doors, getting the experience of a lifetime.

The proof of Nathan's having taken part in a Sun Dance was healing nicely. Nathan wore the scars like a badge. And maybe they were. Ben knew without a doubt that they would earn him points with the macho kids in his class at school. He was looking forward to telling Nathan that the adoption request had been accepted by the Navajo Nation and would be final by the time he returned to school in Bellingham. He'd let Nathan tell Zac the good news.

Ben had asked Red Bull to ask the senior guide at Nathan's camp to let him have dinner off 'campus' that evening. This would probably be their last time together and called for a cheese-crust pizza with sausage and black olives.

Food that wasn't forced onto a stick and held in a fire—though Ben admitted that Nathan's description of shish kabobs with prairie chicken and beef chunks had made Ben believe he'd really missed out on some great food. Even the evening that offered appetizers of chunk snake meat had sounded good. Well, maybe not quite but it seemed to be a hit with Nathan, even though Ben refused to believe that it really did taste "just like chicken."

True to his word Red Bull was standing beside Nathan at the edge of camp. Ben pulled the SUV up, and walked toward them.

"Hello, *son*. Have you outgrown hugs?" Ben was grinning. It was the first time he'd used that word and it felt right.

"*Dad?* Are you kidding? Is it Dad? For real?"

"It is. Completely legal by the end of the next month."

"Congratulations, to both of you." Red Bull stood back as Nathan grabbed Ben around the waist and held on. "I think you two better get going if you don't want to stand in line. Lots of tourists will be wanting to eat pizza tonight."

* * *

Nathan called Zac from the restaurant. Ben heard the whooping and hollering three feet away from the phone in Nathan's hand. Zac was ecstatic. Ben could tell gaining a brother meant the world to him. He understood; he'd always wanted siblings himself. Even Raven got on the phone to congratulate Ben and Nathan.

Ben told Raven he'd email Nathan's travel itinerary but he'd already snagged plane tickets for December 26. There shouldn't be any hiccups. She'd have two boys on her hands until January 15 when school opened again.

Nathan interrupted to ask Zac if he should bring his snowboard, then followed up with his story of having participated in a Sun Dance and promising to tell Zac everything. Thankfully, the pizza came and Zac had to put his questions on hold. A couple last words to Raven about sending money for clothes, and Ben put the phone back in his pocket.

"This is great," Nathan mumbled around a mouthful of pizza.

"The food or your new family?"

"Both, but especially my new family."

"I'm glad I won out over pizza, but I'd have to admit this stuff is pretty good." Ben grinned. "Any misgivings about staying at camp until you go back to school?"

"No, I want to. The camp has been great. I've been asked to come back next summer and be the counselor in charge of horses. If the pandemic's over, it'll be held in July and August. Maybe I could bring Zac."

"Sounds like a plan."

Dinner was a success, if not just a little bittersweet for Ben. It would be awhile before seeing the boys again. As soon as he and Julie established residency in Florida, they would have the boys out for an extended stay. And in the meantime, they were only a plane flight away. In fact, he didn't want to get anyone's hopes up before he talked with Julie, but a Christmas visit in about six weeks might be perfect. They could fly to Seattle, celebrate Nathan's joining the family, maybe tour the school in Bellingham, spend time with Zac—it would be a great ending to a crazy year.

Chapter 40

Pine Ridge Reservation

By the end of next week, Ben would be in New Mexico. He was pleased that the Pine Ridge rehabilitation program was in good shape, with the two eager young graduate students in charge and two more to join them in the spring. By then the planned expansion of the Pine Ridge Community Center would be complete—another set of bathrooms, a partial kitchen, and an enlarged conference room. The village was not only supportive of the program, but had offered help in meeting the physical goals of adding space, buying and installing appliances, updating the electric, and extending the plumbing to meet the existing sewer line. A government grant through IHS had made things move quickly. The area was not only adequate, it was inviting. A dedication was being planned for over the holidays.

When the text came in, Ben wasn't surprised. Packed, but never used luggage, his car locked in a garage; it was difficult for Ben to think that the judge would be found alive. So, Sergeant Cummings' description of a shallow grave some mile and a half from the ranch house was no surprise. A bullet in the back. There was a planned celebration of life in the judge's honor at the Court House in Deadwood, Lawrence County, day after tomorrow. RSVP if he could attend.

* * *

The gathering in the rotunda of the Court House was somber. Several told stories of how the judge had encouraged their careers. A quartet of musicians from the high school played a medley of classical pieces, supposedly the judge's favorites according to his administrative assistant. He was to be cremated with his remains added to the mausoleum in Pierre's Riverside Cemetery, that thirty-five acres of well-maintained final resting places which included Frances Udahl's burial site. The group broke up after a prayer, some wiping away tears, others hugging and saying goodbye.

Ben and Red Bull walked out of the building together and were just getting into Red Bull's pick up when Mac waved for them to wait.

"I've got some unfinished business here." Mac pulled out his billfold and handed Red Bull a check. "That's the three thousand for Debbie's cremation. I appreciate you helping Micki out."

Red Bull took the check, then held out his hand. "No hard feelings?"

"None. I realize now that I wasn't fair to you, and I didn't give my daughter enough credit for recognizing a good man when she met one."

"One last thing." Ben reached into his pocket and pulled out the unmailed letter. "I found this at the judge's ranch. Obviously, I didn't open it; I felt there was enough evidence without something this personal being added to the pile." He handed the envelope to Mac.

"I appreciate that." Mac paused for a moment, then tore open the flap and pulled out a single, small sheet of paper. The message was short. Mac read it, folded the letter, handed it to Ben, and didn't try to stop the tears. Ben looked up questioningly.

"Go ahead, read it. Nothing secret."

Ben smoothed the paper and read, "When you get this note, call me. I have information that you need to know. I love you, Mac. I'm sorry I don't show it sometimes." Michelle, aka Micki, followed by a grinning emoji and dated the day before she was most likely murdered.

"A cry for help that I never heard. But this note means the world. I'm glad you saved it for me. I'll be taking some time off. I'm going to take Debbie's remains to North Carolina to rest with her parents. When they release Micki's body, I'll keep her here in South Dakota—it's the only home she's ever really known. And maybe I'll rethink retirement, take it early; I wouldn't mind sleeping in every once in a while. You guys take care. And Doc? Why don't you think about visiting us again? Next time I won't put you in jail."

Ben laughed. "Promise?" He shook Mac's hand. "Just leave me some fish in Spearfish Creek and I'll be back."

Ben and Red Bull watched Mac get into his Jeep and after one last wave, pull out of the parking lot.

"Hey, it's been a crazy few weeks but I hope I see you again."

"You can always visit me in Florida." Ben was grinning.

"Oh yeah, fat chance—you've got alligators down there." Both men laughed.

+ + +

Thank you for taking the time to read *Paper Arrows* If you enjoyed it, please consider telling your friends or posting a short review. Word of mouth is an author's best friend and is much appreciated. Thank you,

Susan Slater

What's next up from Susan Slater?

Susan brings us the next in her exciting Dan Mahoney mystery series, with *Widow's Walk*.

A St Augustine ship's captain has retired to run a tourist attraction—a fleet of four schooners that take water tours along the Intracoastal and Atlantic. The business is insured with Dan's company—United Life and Casualty. The story opens when the owner's wife falls to her death from the widow's walk tower on their home. Come to find out the Captain has insured her for two million. Is he the killer? He's having money problems. But then one of his schooners catches fire and sinks —another million in insurance from Dan's company.

Now, a finger is directly pointed at the Captain—only Dan believes he's innocent. Could a rival tour company be involved? Or the Captain's new wife, twenty years his junior, who married him one month after he buried his wife of thirty years? The suspects abound, as always, in this highly anticipated new book from award-winning author Susan Slater, coming in spring of 2022.

Ben Pecos returns …

Ben and Julie have settled in Florida, where Ben is now the HR consultant for troubled employees at a casino on the Seminole reservation at the edge of sawgrass country. Between an Indian Elvis impersonator, drugged out band members, dealers setting up con-games, someone pilfering the till, and tourists who end up missing, Ben has his hands full and gets sucked into a plot that puts his life in danger. His sons, Zac and Nathan, visit and, of course, get into trouble. Watch for *Quicksand*, coming in the fall of 2022.

And outside the mystery genre, Susan Slater has two new titles coming in late 2021!

0 to 60 is a contemporary romance which finds Shelly Sinclair rebuilding her life after her husband of thirty-five years dumps her for a much younger woman. At sixty, Shelly is finding a new home, dealing with her elderly parents, starting a new career, and dating for the first time in decades. A sexy, zany, and poignant story that captured Hollywood attention and was optioned for a movie.

The Caddis Man is a sweeping family saga that spans fifty years and half a world, from the wide Kansas farmlands to the missionary settlements in the Congo, through the events of two world wars and the Great Depression. This is historical fiction at its finest, and a great choice for book clubs.

Books by Susan Slater

The Ben Pecos Mystery Series
The Pumpkin Seed Massacre
Yellow Lies
Thunderbird
Fire Dancer
Under A Mulberry Moon
The Thaw
Ghost Dust
Paper Arrows
A Way to the Manger (a Christmas novella)

The Dan Mahoney Mystery Series
Flash Flood
Rollover
Hair of the Dog
Epiphany

Standalone Novels
0-60 – contemporary romance
The Caddis Man – historical fiction
Five O'Clock Shadow – mystery-thriller

+ + +

Get another Susan Slater book FREE—click here to find out how!
Visit Susan's website at susansslater.com where you can sign up for her free mystery newsletter and a chance to win some very cool stuff.
Contact Susan: susan@susansslater.com
Follow Susan on Facebook

www.ingramcontent.com/pod-product-compliance
Lightning Source LLC
Chambersburg PA
CBHW020605110726
47899CB00002B/386

* 9 7 8 1 6 4 9 1 4 0 6 6 1 *